THE URGE TO KILL

THE URGE TO KILL

A DI Matt Barnes Thriller

- 9 –

by

MICHAEL KERR

ISBN 979-8864432020

A powerful urge is a force or
continuing undeniable impulse that
drives a person to carry out an
activity or achieve a goal, be it for
good or evil merit.

PROLOGUE

DAWN had broken on a bitterly cold March morning, and through the clinging fog appeared a sprawling line of figures, moving slowly and wraithlike, heads down as they searched an area that was a part of ancient woodlands on a hillside crisscrossed by a profusion of nature trails and meadows. The men and women were working a section of Oxleas Wood in Eltham, south of the river, walking the grid, as this type of search was often referred to.

Officer Reg Kirkwood came to a stream that was narrow enough for him to stride across, but he stopped at its edge, to stare down in sudden shock at the sight of the body of the young woman that they were searching for, but that he had not personally expected to discover. The corpse was laid on its back, and the wide-open blue eyes appeared to be staring up at him. The face was bereft of expression, unmindful of the cold water that flowed over it, filling the gaping mouth. Reg noted that there was a small, perfectly round hole almost in the centre of the woman's forehead. After taking several deep breaths and regaining a degree of composure, he radioed his find in, to then stay next to the scene until the team leader and other officers arrived.

Natalie Swift had been found less than forty-eight hours after being reported missing by her partner, Greg Davis. The couple lived in a first-floor flat on Falconwood Avenue, just a couple of minutes' walk from the large wooded area where Natalie jogged every weekday morning, to relish the peace and solitude which she thought of as being the lull before the storm, prior to having to travel to Hackney where she was an aide to a Tory MP, carrying out various duties which in the main facilitated the day-to-day working life of the backbench politician.

Natalie was now dead, beyond any further consternations in life; robbed of a future at the age of twenty-six by a killer who had struck almost three months previously, not too far east, in Peckham.

CHAPTER ONE

IT was eight thirty a.m., two days after Natalie Swift's body had been found when Detective Chief Superintendent Julia Stone received details of two murders, both deemed to have been committed by the same perpetrator, and so passed to the elite Serious Crimes Unit which Julia headed up; its main function being to investigate serial killings in the Metropolitan area of London.

Julia read through the two files that had been handed to her by an officer of the Homicide and Major Crime Command, which was within the Met's Frontline Policing directorate, and sipped Earl Grey tea – alleged to have been the late Queen's favourite hot beverage – as she studied the details.

Detective Chief Inspector Matt Barnes was in his office, drinking black coffee and catching up with paperwork, which he found displeasing but appreciated that it was a necessary part of his job, when Julia entered through the open door and took a seat at the other side of his desk.

Matt saw that his boss was holding two manila folders, and immediately reasoned that the documents inside them would relate to suspected serial murders.

"Looks like you've got something for us to get our teeth into," Matt said, placing his almost empty mug down on the only spot that was not covered by reports and overtime sheets.

"Two homicides of young women that appear, beyond any reasonable doubt, to have been murdered by the same unknown subject," Julia said as she handed the folders to him. "Give them the once over and tell me what your first impression is."

Matt took the time to get up and refill his mug, before sitting back down and opening the first of the two folders, to withdraw the file and give the contents his full attention. The first victim, Brenda Cummings, had been a twenty-year old blonde who had lived in a council semi in Peckham with her parents and a younger brother. She had worked locally as a shelf stacker for a supermarket, and had been shot to death in Peckham Rye Park and Common, back in December, having been murdered in broad daylight in a shrub-covered area adjacent to the public toilets, just a short walk from the Japanese garden; a popular area of the Victorian park and common which had formal gardens, woodland, a lake, sports areas and a scenic cafe.

The deceased had met a friend, Gillian Crowe, and had left her sitting on a bench next to an ornamental pond while she visited the loo. Gillian had stated that she had become engrossed with checking her mail and scrolling through Facebook, and that it was more than fifteen minutes before she began to wonder what was keeping Brenda. After first checking the toilets, she had looked both ways along the narrow path that fronted them, to see what appeared to be a trainer laying on the ground less than fifty feet away. Running to it, Gillian recognised the solitary pink and white Nike to be Brenda's, and although fearful, she had called out her friend's name and left the path, parting bushes, to almost immediately be confronted by the sight of Brenda sitting on a bed of rotting leaves in a small clearing. Her back was up against the trunk of a mature oak tree, her head hung forward, and her hands resting palms up on the ground. Going to her, Gillian noticed blood on the front of Brenda's blouse, and crouched down next to her, to gently raise her head, only to realise immediately that Brenda was obviously dead. Running back to where other people were present, Gillian phoned the emergency services.

Matt read the crime scene, autopsy and forensic reports appertaining to the murder, studied the photos of the corpse, and also a business card sized colour picture of a clown's face, which had been removed from a small cellophane packet which had been found in a pocket of the deceased woman's jeans. On the back of the picture, which was on copy paper, was a message handwritten in upper case: **BEHIND THE PAINTED SMILE OF THIS CLOWN DWELLS A SAD, BAD, PROBABLY SLIGHTLY MAD AND SOLITARY MAN.**

Placing the paperwork back in the folder, Matt removed the contents of the second one, to initially look for and find another small picture of a clown's face, to turn it over and read: **I DO WHAT I DO BECAUSE I CAN, AND BECAUSE I AM UNABLE TO SUPPRESS THE DARK URGES THAT GOVERN ME.** The sealed transparent sachet that had held the picture had been recovered from a pocket of the woman's jog pants.

"We've got a full-blown psycho game player out there," Matt said, before he read through the initial reports that accompanied the second picture.

"I know," Julia said. "And to date we have no trace evidence whatsoever. The press have been notified of the details from an inside source; no doubt some copper that gets well paid to spill his or her guts to them. The connection hit the headlines this morning, and they've already tagged him the Killer Clown."

"That's not very original. There was an American serial killer by the name of John Wayne Gacy who got to be called the Killer Clown. He sexually assaulted and murdered at least thirty-three young men and boys. He had also regularly performed at children's hospitals and charitable events as Pogo the Clown, or Patches the Clown. He was executed by way of lethal injection back in nineteen eighty-four."

"I read about the case Matt, years ago. Gacy was a very complex individual, but stupid to have placed most of the bodies in the crawl space of his house."

"He let what he'd done get to him, and confessed to the crimes."

"Let's hope that *our* current killer clown is behind bars before he murders as many as Gacy did."

"I'll drink to that," Matt said, and had a mouthful of coffee. "The strange thing about these murders are that apart from the gunshots to the stomachs and heads of the victims, there were no other injuries, or evidence of sexual assault."

"What does that signify?" Julia said.

"Perhaps they were both targeted, but for no reason we know of as yet."

"Hard to believe that the first victim was taken out by a hitman. She was a shelf stacker in a supermarket."

"Could be he just gets off on killing. We'll talk to family, friends and work colleagues of the first victim, even though they will have been interviewed. As usual we'll start at the beginning and work the case as if it had just broken."

"Fine. Keep me up to speed, because the ghouls on the top floor will be bending my ear for updates until we have something to keep them at arms' length."

When Julia had left, after asking him how Beth was, Matt read through the files again before heading for the squad room, which was next door to his office, to let the team members on duty know that they had a new serial case to investigate.

Detective Inspector Pete Deakin and DCs Errol Chambers, Kelly Day and Jeff Sewell were completing paperwork pertaining to a cold case that they'd been working for weeks, and had solved. The murders of a couple and their six-year-old son in the house where they lived in Finchley had been committed over fifteen years ago, and the investigation had gone cold. Only now, and with fresh eyes, had the team discovered that a man originally suspected of the killings was the perpetrator. Eric Coyle, now a self-employed plumber aged fifty-two, had been reinterviewed by Pete and Errol, and gave the same statement, almost word for word, that he had given back in the day, along with an alibi that could not at the time be disproved. It had been Errol that noticed the gold dress ring that Coyle was wearing on the third finger of his left hand. There was a raised crest of a lion's head on it, and they knew from details given by relatives of the murdered family that a ring fitting the description of one stolen from the house had belonged to the murdered man.

Arrested on suspicion of murder, Coyle had broken down after just two days of intense interrogation, admitting to having panicked and stabbed the family to death, due to the young boy screaming and waking his parents, as he was committing burglary.

Eric Coyle had liked the ring, kept it, but had not worn it for several years, until he believed that he was home free and beyond being a suspect in the unsolved case.

"Great work with the cold case, guys," Matt said as he handed the folders to Pete. "Now we can get back to our principal means of earning a crust."

"What sordid case have you got for us, boss?" Pete said, smiling as he took what he knew would contain details of murders committed by a serial killer.

CHAPTER TWO

IT was all hands to the wheel. With the full team on duty and fully briefed, Pete delegated specific lines of inquiry to each of them. Their best hope for a quick result was if some aspect of the two victims' lives had intersected at some point in time, which could be a connection that would hopefully lead them to someone that they had both known. Pete and Matt doubted that it would be that easy. The young women appeared, at face value, to have nothing in common. The chances of a supermarket worker and an MPs assistant being members of the same gym, or having been educated at the same school, or having the same group of friends was a stretch, not a probability, but not beyond being a possibility that needed to be investigated.

Time really was of the essence. Matt and the team were convinced that the killer would definitely strike again, and would continue to murder young women until he was apprehended. Experience told them that serial murderers did not have an off switch. Each crime that they committed gave them an increased sense of power, and a reinforced belief that they were too smart to ever be caught.

"Both of the victims had been shot twice," Pete said, addressing the assembled detectives. "Once in the stomach and once in the head."

"Perhaps one of them was the target and the other just a distraction," Jeff said.

"We need to check and see if any other women have been murdered in the same way," DS Marci Clark said as she began to fix crime scene photos and the two pics of clown faces to a whiteboard with Blu Tack, before using a non-permanent marker to pen details beneath the images.

"Hopefully we'll find a connection between them," Pete said. "They could have been friends on some social media platform."

"I'll drive out to the crime scenes to get a feel for the surroundings that the perpetrator chose to operate in," Matt said. "I need to get away from paperwork and my claustrophobic office for a while."

"I'll come with you," Pete said, "while the team go through everything we've got and hopefully come up with a lead."

Matt drove the pool Mondeo out to Oxleas Wood in Eltham, South London, to where the second victim, Natalie Swift, had been discovered by a police search team, while Pete went through a copy of the file appertaining to the murder. Entering the car park off Crown Woods Lane, Matt pulled in to a space close to the on-site café.

"Let's grab a coffee before we hike out to where she was found," Matt said.

"Are you buying?"

"Yeah, as long as they don't charge Starbucks or Costa prices. I like my java black, hot and inexpensive."

Sitting at a Formica-topped table next to a picture window that had a view of a trail that led into the mature trees that flanked it, they discussed the case.

"Run through the details again," Matt said.

"Natalie Swift was twenty-six, lived in a flat nearby with her partner, Greg Davis, and worked in the city for a well-heeled back bench member of parliament. She used to go jogging every weekday morning at daybreak, before returning home to have a shower before catching a tube to work," Pete said as he flipped through the pages. "Her partner reported her missing, and after first checking with family members and friends, a missing person report was initiated and a search was organised. Her body was found in a stream, and due to the MO and the picture of the clown, the homicide team knew that they had a serial on the loose, and passed the parcel to us, so to speak."

"That means we're starting in on this second killing with a blank sheet. Right?"

Pete nodded. "Correct," he said. "They just did the groundwork by arranging for CSIs and a pathologist to attend and do their thing. What we have is initial scene of crime reports and pics to work with, but nothing from forensics yet. The first murder was investigated fully as being what was thought to be a one-off, though, so we have interviews with the parents, brother, friends and workmates of the victim."

"But there were no leads," Matt said as he finished his coffee and pushed his chair back, ready to walk out to the crime scene that was clearly marked on a photocopy of the immediate area.

Just twenty feet away from the point in the stream where the second body had been discovered, they could make out a square patch of flattened grass that they knew signified the spot at which the incident tent had been erected. Walking off the bark-covered trail, down an incline, Matt and Pete approached the narrow and shallow stream in which the body of Natalie Swift had been unceremoniously dumped. There was a dense stand of trees nearby, where Matt believed the killer would have been lying in wait, ready to rush out and attack Natalie as she had jogged past.

"I can see the cogs turning," Pete said. "What comes to mind?"

"That he was waiting for her. It was early, and yet he was here, ready to take her out when she came by."

"Do you believe that he knew her?"

"Not necessarily. He could have stalked her, known her routine, and decided that this was the perfect place to do the deed. Everyone has habits and routines, and one of hers was to run here on weekday mornings, probably taking the same route."

"What about the first murder?"

"That could have been carried out on the spur of the moment. He would have no way of knowing that Brenda Cummings would go to the public toilets in Peckham Rye Park & Common. He saw an opportunity and took it. Her friend only found her trainer on the path because it had come off. Perhaps she had bent down to fasten a loose lace, or took it off to shake grit or a small stone out of it. We'll never know."

"We know that the shooter is a risk taker," Pete said. "It was almost lunchtime, and she had gone to the park with a friend."

They walked back to the café, and Matt asked the teenage girl behind the counter if the manager was in.

"Yeah," Marti Hudson said. "He's in the office out back. Who shall I say wants to see him?"

Pete withdrew his wallet and opened it to disclose his warrant card.

Marti turned, went out through a door behind her, and came back less than thirty seconds later, followed by a skinny, middle-aged guy wearing a long-sleeved check shirt and baggy blue jeans. He wore his thinning hair in a thin ponytail, and walked with a pronounced limp.

"I've already talked to the police," Barry Palmer said as he took a long look at Pete's ID. "Is this to do with the jogger that got topped the other day?"

"You've got a security camera on the back wall facing the entrance." Matt said, ignoring the man's question, having taken an instant dislike to him. "Are there any others?"

"No, just the one, and it's been bust for a couple of months."

"Did you know the murdered woman?" Pete said.

"No. She didn't use the caff. But I've seen her run past dozens of times. Makes me wish my leg wasn't crocked, and that I could get some decent exercise."

"Accident?" Pete said, not caring, just being inquisitive.

"A bullet from a sniper in Afghanistan that blew my kneecap out. I was lucky I guess, because the guy standing next to me caught one in the neck and didn't survive."

"What next?" Pete said as he and Matt returned to the car.

"Natalie lived close by with her partner. Let's see if he's at home and has anything interesting to tell us."

Greg Davis eventually opened the door of the first floor flat on Falconwood Avenue in Eltham, after Pete had rung the bell three times. He was red-eyed and unshaven, and to Matt's way of thinking, the young man's grief was palpable and appeared to be genuine. Although being a person of interest at this stage of the investigation, Matt was convinced that he was no more than a victim of circumstance, overwhelmed by his loss.

"Who are you?" Greg said.

"Police," Pete said, once more holding out his open wallet to display his warrant card.

"Have you caught the bastard that murdered my Natalie?"

"No, sir. We're in charge of the case, though, and you may be able to help us with our inquiries."

"In what way?" Greg said, standing aside to let them in. "She went out jogging and never came back."

"You'll know all her regular contacts, and will have her laptop," Matt said. "Someone was aware of her routine and was probably waiting for her in the park."

"It had to have been a stranger that did it," Greg said. "Natalie didn't have any enemies."

"You could be right, sir, but we need to interview everyone that she knew," Pete said. "Where were you at the time when it happened?"

"Why, am I a suspect?"

"We need alibis from you and every person that knew her," Matt said. "The supposedly nearest and dearest to a victim are in many cases the perpetrator."

"I was here. Natalie gave me a peck on the cheek, told me that she loved me, and took off. I had a shower, made coffee and waited for her to come back."

"Did she have anything with her?"

"She carried a small bottle of water, house keys and her mobile phone in a bum bag."

"Did she ever mention that she'd had an altercation with anyone, or believed that she had been followed?" Pete said.

"No."

Armed with Natalie's laptop, plus a couple of dozen names, addresses and phone numbers, Matt and Pete left the grieving man, who was apparently totally devastated; at the beginning of a journey through the pain of loss that would in all probability stay with him permanently, to burn in his memory for the rest of his life.

That was it. Pete decided that when they got back to the Yard, he would send Kelly and Errol to interview Natalie's parents. Everyone that Natalie had known would be approached, to be subsequently dismissed from their inquiries or be red flagged. There was currently no forensic evidence from either of the murder scenes. Open spaces such as parks and commons were frequented by a great many people, and so there was an abundance of trace that could not be linked to an individual. Perhaps fibres from the second scene would prove to be a match to some retrieved from the first, although that would only tell them what they already knew, that the same perpetrator was responsible for both of the crimes.

"Do you think that the pictures of Ronald are relevant?" Pete said as they crossed Westminster Bridge and drove the short distance along Victoria Embankment to New Scotland Yard.

"Ronald?"

"Yeah, Ronald McDonald, the clown character that was used as the symbol of the burger chain. They dumped him a few years back."

"I didn't realise he'd gone. Why did they get rid of him?"

"A bunch of snowflakes claimed that a clown mascot targeting children for fast food is unethical, and a lot of doctors and other health professionals agreed and said he should be retired, and so he eventually was."

"Hasn't stopped kids or adults eating at Macs. And as for the pics, I think they're just part of the killer's game playing. He'll have been aware that the media would pick up on it, and will be well chuffed that they've tagged him the Killer Clown. There were no latent prints on the pictures or the packets that they had been placed in, and no footprints or other trace. We're still waiting for feedback relating to the second shooting, but I doubt that much will be forthcoming, apart from confirmation that the bullets retrieved from both of the bodies were fired by the same gun, which will be no surprise."

"It'll be solid proof that the same perpetrator carried out both killings, though," Pete said. "We know that each gun barrel is unique and produces individual markings, in addition to a bullets groove impressions as it passes through, so an examiner can determine whether a given bullet was fired from a particular firearm."

"Even the calibre of the gun can be identified, but not the make or model. Without a suspect we're still at square one," Matt said as, after parking the pool Mondeo, they made their way into the building and took a lift up to the floor where the staff canteen was located, to continue discussing what little they knew over cups of coffee.

"The bullets from the first murder were fired from a nine-millimetre handgun," Pete said as they sat at a table overlooking the Thames. "I'd bet my shirt on the slugs from the second victim being a match. Neither of the women had been physically assaulted, just gunned down in cold blood."

"I've got the feeling that this case is going to be a bitch to solve," Matt said. "Two disparate females shot dead, with no obvious motive. It could be just some wacko started up who floats his boat by killing for the sheer hell of it."

"Perhaps, but I think the first kill was to set up the second."

"Why?"

"Just a gut feeling that Jeff is right and the killer's prime target was Natalie Swift, and that he or she wanted it to look like random slayings. The clown head pics could be no more than a distraction to make it look like the work of an unhinged serial killer."

"Which leads you to what conclusion?"

"That someone had a reason to want Natalie dead."

"You think someone took out a contract on her, and that whoever did wanted it to appear the work of a psycho?"

"Yeah, so that there would be no way he would ever be suspected of being involved."

"Could be," Matt said, "But I believe that it's the work of a thrill killer. If your take *is* right, then hopefully that'll be the end of it, because professional hitmen only kill for money and are usually impossible to run down."

"If I am right, there's someone out there who had a motive to have Natalie murdered, which means we aren't looking for a serial killer, but for whoever hired the shooter."

"For now, all we have are options to consider, Pete. We need to go through the first victim's computer. With any luck something or someone will link the two women."

"I would think that Brenda Cummings laptop would have been checked out and then returned to the family home. I'll get two of the team to get it, and to interview her parents."

CHAPTER THREE

SITTING on the sofa in the lounge, he watched a violent movie called The Equalizer, which starred Denzel Washington as a former special service commando who faked his own death in the hope of living out a quiet life. Instead, he comes out of self-imposed retirement to save a female sex worker, and finds his desire for justice reawakened after coming face-to-face with members of a brutal Russian gang. When the movie ended, and all the bad guys had been taken care of, he thumbed the remote to turn the TV off, went through to the kitchen, made a chicken and cheese sandwich, poured himself a large Scotch on the rocks and reflected on the, to date, two young women that he had shot dead. Executing them had been the most exciting acts he had ever carried out in his life, and the motivation to kill was for the most part due to his becoming the owner, unexpectedly, of a silenced handgun several months previously. Closing his eyes, he relived the events of the late November evening which had changed his life and set the demon within him free.

At ten p.m. on that fateful evening he took the lift up to the third floor of a multi-storey car park which was just a couple of minutes' walk from Tuco's Mexican restaurant on Old Brompton Road, where he had enjoyed a fully loaded Tuco burger with a side order of refried beans and a glass of Corona beer. As he thumbed the remote to unlock his car, a voice from behind him said, "Hey, honkey, hold it right there." Turning, he was faced by a slim young black guy wearing a hoody fleece and jeans, pointing a silenced gun at him.

"What I want you to do is take out your wallet, phone and wristwatch and place them on the ground in front of you, along with your car keys, and then back off. Do anything stupid and I'll fucking shoot you."

"There are CCTV cameras," he said to the punk who was attempting to rob him at gunpoint.

"I know. One on every floor, fixed to the wall above the lift doors. And the one that could tape me is now broken, so just do what I told you to, now."

He was scared, but in some surprising way invigorated by the threat to his life. "Okay," he said as he withdrew his wallet and phone and bent down to place them on the concrete in front of him. Timing was everything in life. As the would-be mugger lowered the gun slightly, obviously convinced that he was in total control of the situation, he hurled the remote with several keys attached to it at the man's face, and darted forward to shoulder him in the chest with enough force to knock the skinny guy down on to his back.

Jerking his head back in reaction to being hit on the cheek by the bunch of keys, Frankie Dawson pulled the trigger of the gun. The bullet went wide and high, to hit a pillar and ricochet through the windscreen of a 4x4 that was parked in a slot on the other side of the aisle. An almost simultaneous blow to Frankie's chest knocked him off balance, for him to fall and strike the back of his head on the solid concrete with enough force to stun him. He had dropped the gun, and when able to gather his thoughts and push himself up into a sitting position, he was faced by the guy he had planned on robbing, now pointing the pistol at him, and smiling.

The silenced semiautomatic gun felt comfortable in his hand, and gave him an overwhelming sense of power and control. He had the almost irresistible urge to shoot the wide-eyed piece of shit in the face, but loosened his finger on the trigger.

"I took your wallet out of your pocket while you were dazed," he said. "I'm a little surprised to find that you have a driving licence. It appears that your name is Francis Dawson, and that you live at an address in Bethnal Green."

"What are you going to do, call the filth?" Frankie said.

"No. What I *should* do is shoot you dead, but I'll just keep the pistol and your wallet," he said, stepping forward and whipping the steel silencer of the gun across the young man's temple with enough force to render him unconscious, before retrieving his wallet and phone, then climbing into his car and driving away from the scene.

Opening his eyes, after reliving the bygone late-night confrontation with the mugger, he poured another Scotch and decided that he would at some point visit Francis Dawson, due in the main to his needing more ammunition for the gun, which only had five bullets remaining in the magazine. He would then blow the fucker away, and leave his calling card of the clown's face to baffle the coppers, who were obviously pulling out all the stops in an attempt to identify, locate, and apprehend him.

Time for bed. He had a busy day coming up, so finished his drink and called it a night. He would drift off to sleep with the thoughts of the two women he had already murdered up front and centre in his mind. The most satisfying aspect of shooting them had been the look of abject terror in their eyes as he had grinned at them, asked a few obscure questions, and then told them that they were about to die. The first bitch had exited the park toilets in Peckham Rye Park and turned right along a pathway, instead of the short route back to where he had seen her sitting on a bench with another woman. Had she retraced her steps, then she would in all probability still be alive. He had just walked up to her, showed her the gun and told her to make her way through bushes at the side of the path, and she had obeyed him, answered the questions he asked her, and gone to her death like a lamb to the slaughter, to make a high-pitched whining sound and fall to her knees as the first slug hit her just above the groin, dropping her to the ground. He had stared into her large bovine eyes, hesitating for several seconds before delivering the kill shot to her forehead, which drove her backwards, where she came to rest in a sitting position against a tree trunk.

His second victim was a jogger he had stalked for the best part of two weeks, and when he had appeared in front of her, she had just stood fixed in place with a surprised look on her face, which quickly turned to one of dread as he pointed the gun at her. He asked her the same set of questions that he had asked the first woman, before shooting her in the pubis. Looking around in all directions to satisfy himself that there was no one in sight, he had then shot her in the head, and she had fallen back and sideways, to roll down a grassy incline into a narrow stream. After recovering both the spent shells, he had left the scene, to make his way back to where he had parked his car. His choice of killing was, to his way of thinking a no contact sport, because he had no intention of leaving any trace evidence at the scenes of his crimes.

CHAPTER FOUR

IT was late when Matt arrived home at the cottage in Woodford Wells. As he parked behind Beth's Audi, he could see that the lounge and hall lights were still on, despite the fact that he had phoned Beth earlier and told her not to wait up because he would be working late.

"Had a busy day?" Beth said, opening the front door after having heard the tyres of his Vectra on the gravel-covered drive, causing the security light to illuminate the front of the cottage, allowing her to see that it was him.

"No busier than usual, sweetheart," he said as they embraced. "Just no obvious reason for the two murders that we're investigating."

"Let me fix you a drink, and then bring me up to speed on what you *do* have."

"We have nothing but hunches, and they don't lead us in any particular direction, yet."

Beth poured them both large JDs with a splash of ginger ale and ice cubes, while Matt went upstairs to have a quick shower, before donning his dressing gown and moccasin-style slippers and returning to the kitchen, where Beth was sitting at the table in the nook.

"Cheers," Matt said, taking a large swig of the bourbon, after they had clinked their glasses together. The frustration of the investigation began to melt away like the ice in his drink. Being at home with Beth was a buffer to all consternation; a foil to the pressure of his work.

"What hunches do you have?" Beth said, having been given details about the new case when it broke. Matt valued her interest and input, due to her having previously been a criminal psychologist, before changing direction to now work at Morning Star, which was a rehab facility near Uxbridge for psychologically fragile children with a variety of mental health issues.

"Several," Matt said. "To date we have no trace evidence from either of the scenes apart from bullets retrieved from the bodies. We received CCTV footage this afternoon that had been taken by a camera fixed to the wall above the toilet block in Peckham Rye Park, and it showed the first victim, Brenda Cummings, enter and then leave the small building a couple of minutes later. Within seconds a guy appeared, hands in the pockets of his fleece and wearing a baseball cap. He kept his head lowered and turned away from the camera, which is reason to believe that in all probability he followed her and did the deed."

"Was he wearing anything that could be easily identified?"

"No, the cap had no decal on it, the fleece was dark, and he wore jeans and trainers. All generic. Nothing out of the ordinary."

"I take it he wasn't picked up by any other camera."

"Correct. And both killings were little more than executions. Neither of the women had been physically assaulted or robbed, just shot to death."

"What do you make of the images of the clown faces that were left at the scenes?" Beth said as she took the now empty glasses through to the utility room to refill, still within earshot.

"That they're no more than a ploy to divert our attention. He wants us to believe that there's some significance, but I don't buy it," Matt said as Beth returned and placed the drinks on ceramic coasters.

"What do you think is his motive?"

"I think that he's nothing more than a thrill killer. Some guys get their kicks out of playing golf, gambling, doing drugs or any of a thousand things that make them feel good. Pete and Jeff believe that the second victim, Natalie Swift, was targeted, and if that's true, it means that we're not looking for a serial killer, we're looking for someone that had reason to have her murdered."

"What do other members of the team think?"

"The majority think that they were random killings."

"If they *are* thrill kills, they can be premeditated *or* random, motivated by the sheer excitement of anticipating the acts. While there have been attempts to categorize multiple murderers, identifying the crimes as being a type of hedonistic need to kill, the actual details of events frequently overlap category definitions, making attempts at such distinctions problematic. Those identified as thrill killers are typically males aged under forty, and the common denominator among those who commit the crimes is that they usually feel inadequate and are motivated by a need to exert power over others. They frequently make their victims suffer. Sadism is fairly common. The killer might torture, degrade or rape his victim. And they often have an ideal victim type, who have certain similar physical characteristics."

Matt gave what Beth had said a lot of thought as he sipped his drink, and ruled out some of the details as not fitting his take on the perpetrator being a thrill killer.

"You're frowning, Barnes," Beth said. "Why?"

"You've seen the files and photos. The first victim was overweight and plain looking, with long straight blonde hair. The second was tall, slim and attractive, with short dark hair. Plus, neither of them had been tortured or raped. The killer had just shot them and left the scenes."

"He could be just starting up, being ultra-carful, wary of close physical contact; satisfying himself with the fear he will have instilled in the women before shooting them. If he is driven to kill, then I daresay he'll become more emboldened, raise his game and do more than just pull a trigger."

"And if it was a contract killing?"

"Then there will be no more murders carried out using the same MO, or images of clowns' faces left to muddy the water, if one of the victims was in fact targeted. I would think that if it was a paid hit, then Natalie Swift would be the woman perceived to know something that was believed to be a threat to someone."

"You know all the details, Beth. What's your call on the motive?"

"At this point in time it's hard to say, but I have the bad feeling that you do have an active thrill killer at large, who will no doubt kill again."

"Let's have one more for the road and talk about what kind of day you've had," Matt said, standing up and taking the glasses to replenish with large measures of Jack Daniels. "I need to give my brain a break from the case for a few hours."

Beth was tired and ready for bed, but knew that Matt needed to clear his mind of the case for a while, and so told him that Sylvia Mitchell, the clinical director at Morning Star, intended to celebrate her sixtieth birthday the following month at the facility, to include the staff and children, to make it a special occasion for all.

"Sounds like a no booze affair with soft drinks, finger food, cupcakes and games like pin the tail on the donkey and musical chairs," Matt said. "Am I invited?"

"Of course, but I'll fully expect you to find some excuse that prevents you from attending."

"You know me so well."

"It wouldn't hurt to show your face."

"I could do that, then get a phone call after half an hour or so and have to leave on police business."

"That would be better than nothing."

It was one-thirty a.m. when they called it a night and went to bed. Just talking to Beth for a while and drinking the bourbon had relaxed Matt and dulled the intensity of his thoughts on the current case that the team was investigating.

CHAPTER FIVE

PETE had phoned Jeffrey Sanderson, who had been Natalie Swift's employer, on his home number in Purley, after being told by an aide at his office in Hackney that he had taken a few days off, due to there being no imminent business that would require his presence in the House of Commons. Sanderson had expected to be contacted, and duly arranged to be interviewed at his home at three p.m.

DC Kelly Day drove the pool Astra out to Purley, while Pete read through his notes on the MP for the third time and decided that Natalie's employer could have feasibly had a motive to want her out of the way, permanently.

Kelly was impressed by the large detached Georgian house, as she drove through open wrought iron gates and parked on the gravel-covered drive in front of it.

"You think that this guy could be the killer, boss?" Kelly said before they got out of the car.

"No," Pete said. "He'll probably come across as being squeaky clean, but he's a politician, so I'll take whatever he says with a pinch of salt. He'll most likely have concrete alibis, but that doesn't mean that he didn't pay someone to commit murder."

"Without a motive, there's not a lot we can do."

"We can ruffle his feathers, and then keep digging for a reason that he would have thought that having Natalie murdered was the only answer."

"Do you reckon that Natalie knew something that would have ruined his career, or put him in prison?"

"He could be as innocent as the day is long, but until we know that for certain he's a viable suspect to my way of thinking, as are any other people with links to Natalie."

Walking up three steps to a black gloss painted door that appeared identical to the one in Downing Street, minus the number ten, Kelly thumbed the porcelain bell push.

The door was opened after no more than fifteen seconds to reveal a tall, slim woman with dark shoulder-length hair and even features.

She was wearing a cream, long sleeved blouse, navy-blue slacks and bright red slingback court shoes. Kelly pegged her as being in her mid-forties.

"How can I help you?" Frances Sanderson said, looking at both of them in turn.

"I'm Detective Inspector Deakin, and my colleague is Detective Constable Day," Pete said as he offered his warrant card to the woman, who took it from him and studied the image of him and the details, before handing it back. "I arranged for us to interview Mr Sanderson."

"You'd best come in, then," Frances said, standing aside to let them enter, before closing the door and beckoning them to follow her along a long hallway which had several doors to either side of it. Stopping at one which was partly open, Frances pushed it back and said, "The police are here to see you, Jeffrey," indicating that they should enter, before walking away from the room without entering it or saying another word to Pete and Kelly.

"How can I help you, officers?" Jeffrey said, closing a laptop on his desk as he stood up from a swivel chair to approach and greet them by holding out his hand, first to Kelly and then to Pete, who both grudgingly shook it.

On sight, Pete had taken an instant dislike to the tall politician, who he knew to be fifty years old, and had his thinning grey hair lacquered to his scalp. He wore high-end casual clothing and black leather loafers.

"We're interviewing everyone that knew Natalie Swift, to hopefully be given information that will assist us with the investigation, and also eliminate people as suspects."

"Are you implying that I'm a suspect?"

"I'm inferring that she was murdered by either someone that she knew, or by a total stranger, and so until we can account for the whereabouts of everyone that had links to her at the time of her murder, then yes, we'll need to know where you were on two pertinent times and dates."

"On the date that Natalie went missing I was here at home until eight a.m., my wife can confirm that. I then drove to my office in Hackney, where my two other employees, Mark Knowles and Cara Allen were already working."

"And where were you up until approximately three p.m. on the seventh of December last year?"

Walking back to his desk, Jeffrey took a large leather-bound diary from a drawer and leafed through it to the date, to nod as he studied an entry and said, "I was at a meeting in the House of Commons from ten a.m. till noon, and then, accompanied by three other MPs, we relocated to The Strangers' Bar, which is one of several drinking holes in the Palace of Westminster. I can give you the names of the members that I was with."

"Fine, we'll take details before we leave. Do you have any idea why anyone would target Natalie?"

"No. She was a lovely, intelligent young woman, and I am appalled that some maniac has taken her life."

"Did she ever mention that she felt at risk from anyone, or believed that she was being stalked, or seemed to act differently from usual, as if she had something on her mind?" Kelly said.

"No. The day before she went missing, Natalie appeared to be relaxed, without a care in the world. I doubt that she knew anyone that wished her any harm."

With details of the MPs that Sanderson had told them he had been drinking with on the date of Natalie's murder, Kelly drove Pete to the man's office in Hackney to interview his other two employees, who were expecting the visit due to having received a phone call from their boss.

For the second time that day Pete presented his warrant card for inspection, and asked Mark Knowles and Cara Allen if there was somewhere that they could interview them individually to discuss the death of their colleague.

Mark led the two detectives to a small room that was for the most part used by Sanderson to hold surgeries and give people an opportunity to meet him and discuss matters of concern to them. He usually met with constituents once a week and advertised the dates locally or online. On occasion he would take up an issue on a constituent's behalf.

"Would you like a cup of tea or coffee?" Cara said before Mark ushered them into the room.

"Coffee black, please," Pete said. Kelly declined.

Mark sat behind an Ikea desk and waited for the two detectives to ask their questions.

"How did you get on with Natalie?" Pete said as he sat on the edge of a straight-backed wooden chair that reminded him of the ones from his primary school days; hard and uncomfortable, probably a ploy to dissuade people from getting settled and taking up too much of Jeffrey Sanderson's time.

"She was a terrific person," Mark said. "I find it almost impossible to believe that Natalie is no longer with us. She was a colleague and a friend, and I keep thinking that she'll just walk through the door, large as life with a smile on her face."

"Do you have any knowledge of anyone that would wish her harm?"

"No."

After interviewing both Mark and Cara and being furnished with details of where they were at the time that Natalie went missing, Pete and Kelly left the office and drove back to the Yard.

"Nothing gave me the feeling that Sanderson or either of his employees were persons of interest," Kelly said as she drove into the city.

"Nor me," Pete said. "If their alibis hold up, then all we'll have done is eliminated them as suspects."

"We need to find someone that had a motive to shoot Natalie and Brenda."

"If we don't, then we're looking for a needle in a haystack; two stranger on stranger murders committed by some sicko who'll no doubt kill again."

"If one of them was targeted by someone, then we'll dig him out of the woodwork," Kelly said.

"True, but my money is on it being a serial killer with no connection to either of them."

"Which will make it a long hard slog to find the stone he's hiding under."

Pete shrugged. "He'll escalate, make a mistake, or be seen and hopefully identified by a member of the public. We'll take him down, eventually."

"After more young women are murdered."

"Yes, unfortunately. All we can do is work the case and hope that he fucks up."

"Have you dismissed the idea of Natalie Swift being shot because of something she knew?"

"No, it's still something to run with, but I don't really buy it."

Only Matt and Jeff were in the squad room. The other detectives were visiting the homes of contacts of the two victims, hoping to get a lead on someone that held a grudge against them or, hopefully to come face to face with a person of real interest that they could consider to be a worthwhile suspect. Every member of the team were carrying their firearms, due to the fact that they were now actively engaged in searching for a perpetrator who was obviously armed and highly dangerous.

"Anything?" Matt said as Pete made his way across to the main feature of the room, which was an old coffeemaker on a small table in the corner, to fill a mug with the caffeine laden liquid that kept many cops going through long shifts.

Kelly went to her desk, to write up the details of the meetings with the MP and his employees, listing the date and the times and content of the interviews, which she had written down in her pocket notebook.

"Nada," Pete said to Matt. "The MP and his two remaining employees don't look good for it. We'll check out their alibis, but I think it'll be a dead-end."

"And I've got nothing from either of the victims' laptops", Jeff said. "There are no common denominators that link the two women. Neither of them had any online trolls, and I've been through their emails, social media platforms and private messages, but can't find anything to follow up on."

"Could be an ex-boyfriend of Natalie or Brenda," Kelly said. "Some scrote that was given the elbow by one of them and couldn't take rejection. The clown pics could be no more than a ruse to have us believe that a serial killer has started up."

"As of now, all we have are theories," Matt said. "Hopefully someone that the team are currently out interviewing will be able to give us the name of some guy who had reason to wish one of the victims harm, but I won't hold my breath. Although I'm pretty sure now that we do have a thrill killer out there, and that he'll definitely kill again."

CHAPTER SIX

APRIL seventeenth, one a.m., and Sonny Mason was sitting in his ground floor flat in Bethnal Green, hunched over a grease-stained glass-topped coffee table and snorting a line of coke through a rolled up twenty-pound note. A CD was playing on his music centre; Jimi Hendrix singing 'Machine Gun' which featured the now long dead singer's guitar-dominated hard and psychedelic rock sound. Sonny found it almost impossible to believe that Hendrix had only been twenty-seven years old when he had aspirated on his own vomit and died of asphyxia while intoxicated with barbiturates, over fifty years ago. *Christ*, Sonny thought, he hadn't been born until ninety-four, which was twenty-odd years after Jimi had passed. Sitting back, high on the coke, he let the music do the talking and drifted off to sleep, only to be woken by someone knocking loudly on his door.

He had parked up on Old Ford Road and walked to the address he had for Francis Dawson on Cyprus Street, to climb the four steps up to the front door of the three-story Victorian terrace house, pulling on a pair of flesh-coloured medical grade latex gloves that fitted like a second skin. The door was closed but not locked, probably due to the amount of footfall that passed through it day and night. Knocking at the door of the first flat he came to, from behind which the sound of music emanated, he waited a few seconds and then knocked again, harder and for longer.

Sonny opened the door to be faced by a white guy wearing a baseball cap, a thick fleece, jeans and trainers.

"Yeah?" Sonny said. "What do you want?"

"I'm looking for Francis," he said. "Which flat does he live in?"

"I don't know any Francis."

He took the leather wallet that he had confiscated from the would-be mugger from his pocket, opened it and withdrew the photocard driving licence, to hold it out for the young man to see.

"That's my cousin, Frankie. Nobody calls him Francis. How come you've got his wallet?"

"I found it and was passing nearby, so thought I'd return it to him."

"He used to live in flat four on the first floor, but he took off back in December."

"Where does he live now?"

"Just give me the wallet and I'll get it to him."

Without any hesitation, he drove the heel of his left hand into the centre of Dawson's cousin's chest, causing him to reel backwards and fall down on his arse. Closing the door, he pulled the silenced semiautomatic pistol from the waistband of his jeans to point at the man, who stared up at him with a startled look on his pockmarked face.

"What's your name?" he said.

"Sonny…Sonny Mason."

"Okay, Sonny Boy. Do you own a gun?"

Sonny shook his head. He no longer felt stoned. The sight of the pistol being aimed at him gave him complete clarity of thought.

"Where's your mobile phone?"

"On the coffee table."

"Move an inch and I'll put a bullet in your head, Sonny," he said as he went to the table, to sit down on the chair in front of it, pick up the smartphone and scroll through the contact list to find the name Frankie.

"Give me his address, now, and I'll be on my way."

Sonny told the armed man his cousin's current address, which was in a first-floor flat only three streets away. He knew without any doubt whatsoever that the guy intended to shoot him, and then make his way to Frankie's flat and kill him.

"What do you want with him?" Sonny said.

"He attempted to mug me back in November, and I got the better of him and relieved him of this gun and wallet. That would have been an end to it, but I need ammunition, and I'm sure he can provide me with some."

Sonny made his move, dived forward and used both hands to tip the coffee table up on to its side, for it to collide with the shooter's legs as he snatched off a shot. The bullet did no more than pass harmlessly through Sonny's mass of dreadlocks, to lodge in the wall behind him.

Withdrawing a lock knife from a pocket of his cargo pants, Sonny released the blade and lunged at the man who had just attempted to shoot him. He lashed out over the edge of the table and heard a grunt of pain as the honed blade sliced through the fleece to cut the forearm of his attacker's gun hand.

Kicking the table back, he pulled the trigger again and was relieved to see Sonny blown backwards, to hit the floor with a blossoming patch of blood on the front of his grubby grey tee shirt. Grey and red were a good combo, he thought as he stood up, took careful aim at the Rasta's forehead, but paused to relish the look of fear in the young guy's eyes, and the stream of blood escaping from his open mouth to run down his chin, before squeezing the trigger again and to take great pleasure in seeing life almost instantly converted to death as the bullet penetrated Sonny's brain.

Pocketing the knife, which would no doubt have traces of his blood on it, he left the flat, to arrive less than ten minutes later outside the house where Frankie Dawson lived, having left the car where he had parked it on Old Ford Road. The front door was locked, and so he made his way down the street to an alley that gave access to the rear of the terrace houses, which he had counted to be sure to break into the right house. A rotting timber gate was easily forced open, and the yard behind it led to a back door which was in no better condition, where one well-placed kick proved enough to splinter the wood around the lock. The noise it made didn't bother him. The loud music that he could hear emanating from several of the flats would have masked the sound, although he waited for a couple of minutes to be certain that his entry had not been heard.

In the low-lit hallway he could see the front door and the underside of a stairwell. Reaching the stairs, he was about to climb them when a door opened on the first floor, and above the sound of music he heard a voice say, *'Okay, Frankie, I'll see you tomorrow, bro.'*

Backing up, he hid in shadow under the stairs with his gun drawn, listened to footsteps descending them, and heard someone walk to the front door to open it and leave, closing it behind him.

Moving quickly, gun drawn, he climbed up to the first floor and knocked at the door of flat five.

"What've you forgotten, Clyde?" Frankie said as he opened the door, to take a couple of steps back at the sight of a white guy holding a silenced pistol that was pointed unwaveringly at his chest.

"Remember me, Frankie?" he said as he entered the flat and used the heel of his shoe to shut the door behind him, not taking his eyes or the gun off Dawson for a second.

"No, should I?"

"Maybe not. It was quite dark in the car park where you attempted to mug me back in November."

"That didn't happen, man. This is a case of mistaken identity."

With his left hand, he withdrew Frankie's wallet from a pocket, tossed it to him and said: "After I'd put you out for the count, I took your wallet, along with this gun."

"What do you want, honky, an apology?"

"No. I want to give you a chance to redeem yourself and survive this meeting, so back off a few feet and don't do anything that you wouldn't live to regret."

"How'd you find me?" Frankie said as he took a couple of steps back into the middle of the room.

"I went to the address on your driving licence and had a word with your cousin, Sonny. He told me where you lived before I shot him."

"You killed Sonny?"

"Yeah, he made a move on me, so I blew him away."

Frankie wanted to react, to attack the guy, disarm him and beat him to death with the gun, but the space between them suddenly seemed to be as long as a basketball court, and he didn't want to die, so just gritted his teeth and hoped that he would get a better chance to turn the situation around.

"Sit on the floor with both of your hands palm down on the carpet, and be aware that I know you'll have got hold of another gun, which at a guess will be stashed somewhere within easy reach."

"Like I said before," Frankie said, "what the fuck do you want from me?"

"Ammunition. There's only a couple of rounds left in this magazine, so I need more bullets."

"I can't help you. I don't have—"

"Bullshit, Frankie. Tell me where you keep it, or I'll shoot you in the balls. I have no reason to kill you, so give up the gun and ammo."

"My gun's in the bedroom under the left side of the bed, and there's a full spare mag under there with it."

"Music to my ears. Get up, put your hands behind your neck, fingers linked, and let's go and get them."

Frankie did as he was bid, entered the bedroom and knelt next to a small table that had nothing on its top but a cheap lamp and an ashtray.

He used the silencer to strike the kneeling man behind the right ear with enough force to put out his lights, then with a couple of plastic ties, secured the unconscious mugger's wrists and ankles and hauled him away from the bed, before reaching underneath it to find a pistol, magazine and a silencer nestled on top of a thick layer of dust. There were no other bullets, though.

It was ten minutes later when Frankie came to, groaning at the fierce headache he was suffering from, grimacing and shivering as he realised that he was now in his bathroom, sitting in the tub, which was two thirds full of ice-cold water, and his wrists were tied together, as were his ankles.

"You're nothing but a dumbfuck nigger junkie," he said from where he was sitting on the lid of the toilet seat, still holding the gun he had originally taken from Frankie. The other Glock pistol, which he had found to be fully loaded, was in a pocket of his fleece with the mag and silencer. "You should have pissed off out of The Smoke. You would've been safer finding a hole to hide in up in Brum, Manchester, Leeds, Newcastle, or even Jockland. Problem is, you've got a herd mentality, and so you stayed in the area, and told your cousin where you were living."

"I didn't reckon that we would ever see each other again, but thought it would be wise to change address, just in case you held a grudge."

"I don't hold grudges, Frankie. I've got the gun and spare mag, now all I need is your stash of spare bullets. And don't deny having any, because if I have to spin your flat to find them it will piss me off, bigtime."

Maybe it was the chilling look in the man's eyes that convinced Frankie to tell him that there was a box of ammo in the cupboard under the kitchen sink, in the cavity beneath its raised chipboard floor, which was not screwed down.

"I'll go and get them. Just relax and think good thoughts."

Frankie wasn't about to relax, or think of anything but getting out of the shit situation he was in. He got to his knees, leaned over the side of the bath and used his feet to propel him up and over, to land on the floor. Fear gave him the stimulus to climb to his feet and hop through into the living room to the door that opened onto the hallway. Turning around, he fumbled with numb fingers to grasp the doorknob, and was about to turn it when the intruder appeared, pointed the gun at him and said, "Move away from the door and sit down, Frankie. Do it now."

Frankie obeyed, hopped over to the nearest easy chair, and sat down, shivering violently with both cold and fear in equal parts.

"You've got what you came for, so are we done?" Frankie said as the guy transferred the gun, silencer, spare mag and the box of bullets he had acquired into a plastic supermarket bag that had been crumpled up on a counter in the kitchen.

"Almost. I just need to tie up one loose end before I leave," he said as he removed his silenced pistol from where he had placed it in the waistband of his jeans, to aim it at Frankie's head.

"You said you had no reason to kill me," Frankie said with a pleading, quavering edge to his voice.

"I lied. You've seen my face, and know that I shot your cousin, so I need to be sure that you don't talk to the police."

"I swear to God I won't tell anyone what happened."

"Perhaps you wouldn't, but better safe than sorry, eh?"

Frankie pissed himself, although was unaware of doing so as he bowed his head and began to cry.

CHAPTER SEVEN

A full week slipped by before the team got news that did no more than confuse them. The killer had struck again, twice, but had left no images of clowns' faces, and the victims were not females.

"This is a spanner in the works," Pete said as he read the files from Ballistics pertaining to the murders of two young black men found dead in flats just several streets apart in Bethnal Green. "They got a match of bullets to those recovered at the two scenes south of the river."

"Could be that the gun has changed hands," Jeff Sewell said.

Pete shrugged, unconvinced that the killer they sought would give or sell the murder weapon to someone else.

"Do we have all the relevant reports that will have been raised by the detectives that originally ran with the case?" Marci said.

Pete nodded. "Yeah. DCI John Stott of one of the Major Investigation Teams was given the case, so all the preliminary groundwork has been done. Once the bullet match was verified, Stott redirected all he had to the SCU. The only blood that techies found at the scenes came from the victims, although there were numerous latent prints that we can follow up on."

"It's a break," Kelly said. "We can get a match to anyone that becomes a suspect. Maybe we'll get lucky."

"Prints alone won't put someone in a dock," Jeff said.

"No witnesses?" Matt said, standing up from the chair he had been sitting on, holding a mug of coffee in his hand.

"From the files, each and every tenant living in the flats at both addresses have been interviewed, and none of them had any information," Pete said. "Neighbours were also doorstepped without any success."

"We need to talk to everyone again," Matt said.

"It's a close-knit community with an abundance of ethnic minorities. I think that Errol and Tam would have more luck than us whiteys. We, the police, aren't popular to start with, so we need every advantage we can get."

"Sounds good to me," Matt said.

"I'll run off copies of the reports we have for everyone to study," Kelly said.

"And when you've done that, I'll get everything written up on the whiteboards," Marci said.

It was one-thirty p.m. when Matt and Pete sauntered up to the bar in the Kenton Court Hotel on Tottenham Court Road. Most of the customers that had called in for lunch had finished up and left, and only a few were still sitting at tables, talking and drinking.

"Haven't seen you two reprobates for a couple of weeks," Ron Quinn said. "I thought that you'd found a new watering hole to spend your ill-gotten gains."

"Hell, no, Ron," Matt said. "This is the go-to pub for us, where we enjoy being badmouthed by a big Cornish lummox landlord."

"This is a hotel, not a pub, and as I've told you more than once, I'm not a lord, and I don't own much more land than the car park out back. Also, time is money, so what are you drinking?"

They both ordered pints of best bitter.

"The love of my life is out back in the kitchen, would you like her to rustle you up something to eat?" Ron said.

"One of your grilled steak and onion sandwiches would hit the spot," Matt said.

Pete licked his lips. "Make that two."

"At a guess, your squad are working the Killer Clown case," Ron said half an hour later, having served them the sandwiches that his partner, Anne, had cooked, and left them to eat in peace.

"Good guess," Matt said. "But we can't give you any juicy details. If we did, we'd have to kill you."

Ron smiled. He'd known Matt and Pete for quite a few years now, and counted both of them as good friends.

"Time to saddle up and get back to the ranch, pilgrim," Matt said in a voice that was at best a third-rate impression of John Wayne. "And say hi to Anne for us when she finishes up in the kitchen, and tell her that the sarnies were ace."

"Anne had popped out to have her hair done. It was my chief cook and bottlewasher, Tommy Clark, who made the sandwiches."

"Let Tommy know that they were delicious."

"I'll do that. He'll appreciate the praise."

"Do you have any ideas re the case?" Matt said as Pete drove them back to the Yard.

"Nothing springs to mind. We usually know what type of killer we're looking for, but this nutjob is a one-off. There's no obvious reason why he murdered the two women, because he didn't rob or sexually assault them, and now it would appear he's gunned down two guys in the East End."

"The bullets retrieved from all four shootings are a match, and I very much doubt that our unknown subject sold the gun on, gave it away, or had it stolen, so we've got nothing."

"I think it's the same guy, Matt, and that he's lost the plot, if he ever had one, and has now gone full tonto, killing people purely for the thrill of it, simply because he can."

"The two young black guys, Frankie Dawson and Sonny Mason were cousins, so there's a link. We just need to find out what it is."

Jasmin Walker – whose family, friends and even her workmates at the local Mac's called Jaz – was scared, and had been since the guy who'd lived in flat five on the first floor had been murdered. She didn't feel safe, and had the urge to go back to live with her mother in the high-rise tower block in Stratford where she lived, but didn't want to lose the independence she currently enjoyed.

It was the end of her shift, and as she left work and began the ten-minute walk back to the house on Griffin Street, she looked forward to frying the raw beef patties that she had wrapped in serviettes and placed in her shoulder bag, considering them to be a perk of the job, when two men approached her in the car park.

"Miss Walker?" Errol said, holding out his warrant card for her to see. "We'd like to have a word with you."

"If it's about the guy that was murdered, then I've already been interviewed," Jaz said as she walked away from the two detectives.

"Not by us," Tam said as he and Errol trotted after her. "Our unit is investigating the case now, and so we need to talk again to everyone concerned."

"I don't know anything that could help you. The first I knew about it was when half a dozen cop cars pulled up in the street, and a bunch of you lot entered the house."

"We still need to run through it with you again, Miss," Errol said. "Bear with us, because we need to find whoever murdered the young guy as quickly as possible, because he wasn't the only victim that evening."

Jaz knew that they would not take no for an answer, and they had a much better attitude than the white detective that had initially and brusquely bombarded her with questions and treated her as if she was a suspect. She was not a fan of the police. Being young and black in London had its disadvantages. Her brother, George, who was three years older than her, had been a victim of stop and search numerous times. You had to be a person of colour to appreciate that institutional racism was still a big problem. The two men in front of her were not white, though, and she was tempted to tell them details that she *had* kept to herself.

"I'm headed home on foot," Jaz said after making the decision to talk. "Meet me there and I'll answer your questions."

Errol parked the pool Mondeo outside the house, and he and Tam waited until the young woman appeared and walked towards them before exiting the car to meet her.

"You want a cup of coffee?" Jaz said when the two detectives were seated side by side on cheap pinewood chairs in front of a matching table in the small kitchen of her flat.

"Please," Errol said. "Black, no sugar."

"Have you got tea, Miss Walker?" Tam said.

"I got teabags. And call me Jaz. No one calls me Miss Walker."

They made small talk until Jaz set the drinks down and sat opposite them.

"Did you see or hear anything out of the ordinary on the night that the guy in flat five was murdered?" Errol said after taking a compact voice recorder from a side pocket of his jacket, to place on the tabletop and press the record button.

Jaz reached out, picked up the recorder, switched it off and said, "I'm not about to have anything I say on tape. And I have no intention of repeating what I tell you. This is a one-off event."

"Okay, Jaz," Errol said as he slipped the recorder back into his pocket to, unbeknown to Jaz, switch it back on. "What information have you got for us?"

"That I'd been on a girls' night out on the evening that Frankie was killed. It was after two a.m. when I arrived home in a cab. As I walked up the steps, the door opened and a white guy appeared. He stared at me, but didn't smile, say a word or make any attempt to stand aside and let me pass. He was menacing, and if a couple that lived in one of the flats hadn't showed up, then I have the feeling that he would have harmed me, but I could be wrong."

"Had you ever seen him before?" Tam said.

"No."

"Can you describe him to us?"

"He was under six foot tall, maybe five-ten, and had what you'd probably call even features. It was his eyes that caught my attention, though, they were very dark brown, almost black, and lacked any kind of emotion."

"What about his hair?" Errol said.

"He was wearing a baseball cap. What I could see of it was short and maybe mid-brown. It was quite dark, so I don't really know. He was unshaven, like so many guys are these days."

"What age would you put him at?"

"He looked to be in his thirties."

"Any visible scars or tats?"

Jaz shook her head.

"Okay, what was he wearing?"

"The baseball cap, which could have been black or navy-blue, a fleece the same colour and blue jeans. And he was wearing white trainers."

"Anything else about him come to mind?" Errol said.

"No. He just seemed to be a little weird. The kind of flaky type that you wouldn't want to be around, or come face to face with on a dark night, like I did."

"That was really helpful, Jaz," Errol said. "Between you and us, the guy could well be a serial killer, and we need to identify, locate, and take him off the street. We need for you to assist us by describing him to a police artist."

Jaz pushed her chair back, jumped to her feet and said, "No way. I've given you a description of a total stranger to me, and that's as far as I intend going with this."

"I don't want to alarm you unduly, Jaz," Tam said. "But you need to realise that the perpetrator may view you as being a risk to him. You saw the guy, and so he knows that you could identify him."

Jaz had thought the same thing, but had decided that she was being paranoid, up until now. Truth was, the killer did know where she lived and could come back and murder her if and whenever he chose to.

"Do you seriously think that I'm really in danger?" she said.

"Possibly," Tam said, and Errol nodded in agreement.

"I don't need this shit," Jaz said. "I'll have to move out."

"Probably for the best," Errol said. "You won't be able to feel absolutely safe until he's detained, and that's why it's vitally important that you describe him to the police artist, to help not only other potential victims, but to protect yourself from being in harm's way."

"Okay, I'll do it, but I want one of you two to be present."

"No problem. Do you have somewhere to go?"

"When?"

"Now. Best if you pack some essentials, and we'll drive you to wherever you intend on staying for the time being."

"My mum lives in a high-rise in Stratford. I'll phone her and tell her to expect me."

"Which flat do the couple that turned up at what could have been a very fortunate time, live in?" Tam said.

"Flat three on the ground floor. Their names are Desmond and Shirley Ashton."

Tam knocked on the door of number three while Errol stayed with Jaz, but the couple were obviously out. He and Errol would do a call back.

Fate sometimes has an unfathomable way of working for or against anyone. He had made the decision to follow the young woman – who had seen him leave the terrace house on Griffin Street in Bethnal Green – and kill her. When he had initially come face to face with her at the front door of the house, he had decided to pull her inside, close the door and put a bullet in her head, but a couple had appeared, and the woman said, 'Hi, Jaz, how're you doin' girl?', and so he had left. Now, he tailed her as she walked the short distance to a McDonald's restaurant, where she was obviously an employee, due to her not leaving the burger joint for approximately eight hours. When she eventually emerged from the front door, she was approached by two guys in suits, and one of them showed her his ID. They were obviously detectives, and spoke with her for a few minutes before returning to their car, to drive in the direction of Griffin Street, as she walked back, to presumably meet them there.

No problem. He would watch and wait, and then, when the cops had left, he would take care of business.

CHAPTER EIGHT

AFTER dropping Jaz off at the main entrance of the high-rise in Stratford and telling her that they would contact her on her mobile phone when they'd jacked-up a meet with the police artist, Errol also recommended that she call in sick until they deemed it safe for her to return to her place of work.

Tam and Errol drove back to the Yard. Matt, Pete, and Kelly were in the squad room checking copies of CCTV from the area in Bethnal Green where the two young black men had been murdered, without any success. The neighbourhood was not CCTV friendly, and the small amount of footage from the few undamaged cameras available was of no help to them.

"Any luck?" Matt said to Tam, as Errol headed for the coffeepot, drawn to it by the aroma it gave off.

Tam grinned at Matt, Pete and Kelly. "Bingo," he said. "A young woman by the name of Jasmin Walker lives in a flat on the first floor of the house on Griffin Street and may have come face-to-face with the killer. She gave us a description of him and reluctantly agreed to a meet with a police artist."

"If it *was* the killer, then she may be in danger."

"That's what we thought. She packed a bag and we drove her to her mother's place in Stratford," Errol said as he wandered across the room with a large mugful of steaming java in hand. "A couple came back from a late night out as she stood in the doorway of the house, facing the suspect. With any luck they will also be able to give us a description of him. They weren't in when we interviewed Jasmin, who prefers to be called Jaz, but we have their names and flat number so we'll get to them asap."

"I'll give Dick Curtis a bell," Pete said. "He's the best police artist in town."

"He lives out at Greenford in a bungalow now, just a stone's throw from the River Brent," Matt said. "Perhaps it would be the perfect place for him to meet with the girl and work his magic."

"Yeah," Pete said. "A private house would probably be better than an interview room here."

He'd waited, parked over sixty yards away between a panel van and a beaten-up old Ford Fiesta, after seeing the woman and the two coppers enter the house where he had shot Frankie Dawson in the forehead, which had been an act which he'd decided was a public service; taking a scumbag off the streets to save countless people being victims of the no-good jive-arse mugger. It was forty-five minutes later that the threesome left the house, to climb in the unmarked police car and drive off. Tailing them, keeping other vehicles between his and their cars, he watched from a distance as the Mondeo parked outside the main entrance to the first tower of Kingsley Hamlets – which comprised four high-rise blocks in Stratford – for the young woman, Jaz, to get out with a large holdall and enter the building. He guessed that the coppers had advised her to move out for her own safety. He drove home, wondering how to find out what the bitch's surname was, and which flat she was staying at. She had, without doubt, given the two plods a description of him. She was a threat to his continued freedom, and so was now living on borrowed time. As for the couple who had unknowingly saved her life on the night he had shot Dawson, by appearing at the bottom of the steps to the house at an extremely inappropriate moment, he was not concerned, having instantly lowered his head to cover his features with the bill of the baseball cap he'd been wearing, and immediately leave the scene.

Dick Curtis was putting the finishing touches to an oil painting featuring several elderly men playing dominoes in the local pub. Albert Hicks, the owner of the Crooked Billet on Ruislip Road, had commissioned a painting of his most regular customers, who were also his friends, and intended to hang it behind the bar.

Tall and looking almost unhealthily thin, Dick's greying hair was long, tied back in a ponytail, and his short beard was salt and pepper in colour. Having received a phone call from DI Pete Deakin, he had agreed to a visit to his bungalow by two officers accompanied by a young woman who was believed to have come face to face with a killer, and Pete wanted him to develop a sketch from her description of him.

It was ten-fifty a.m. on a bright morning in late April when DCs Errol Chambers and Kelly Day turned up at Dick's door and introduced him to Jaz. Both Kelly and Errol accepted the offer of tea and coffee respectively. Jaz asked if he had Diet Coke as an alternative, which he had a bottle of in the fridge.

"I suggest that you two go out on the patio and sit in the sun while I get to work with Jaz," Dick said, not needing the two detectives looking over his shoulder while he attempted to create a likeness of the unknown murderer from whatever details Jaz could give him.

"How come you do this kind of work?" Jaz said to Dick as he led her through to what he thought of as being his studio-come-office, where he spent the majority of his waking hours.

"Hard to believe, looking at me now, but I used to be a copper, and my hobby was art. Working up likenesses of people just became something I could do, so I still help out when I can."

Jaz couldn't envisage Dick Curtis as having ever been a copper. He looked like a relic of the hippie days, with dried daubs of paint on his check shirt and well-worn jeans. At a guess, he drank Scotch, smoked weed on occasion, and listened to prehistoric heavy metal bands like Led Zeppelin, Black Sabbath and the like.

"Take a seat," Dick said as he settled at one side of a wooden desk, to make room on the top by moving sheaves of drawings, a large ceramic mug full of pencils and brushes and his laptop to one side. All that remained in front of him was an A4-sized pad of high-quality cartridge paper, and several pencils.

Sitting opposite the artist on a rail back chair, Jaz waited as Dick initially drew a large elliptical shape – like an egg – on a page of the pad.

As a police sketch artist, or forensic or composite artist as they were often dubbed, Dick took this aspect of artwork very seriously. His sketches were in many instances used by the police to release to the public as an aid to identify and apprehend criminals.

"I'm led to believe that you got a good look of the man who was leaving the house you live at as you were about to enter it," Dick said.

"Yes, but only for a few seconds."

"What was your first impression of him?"

"That he was white, and that his eyes brought those of a great white shark to mind. They were dark, like pools of ink, without any trace of emotion."

Dick drew a faint line across the 'egg', a third down it, to pencil in two eyes of regular shape and distance apart. "Was there anything else you thought was unusual about his face, Jasmin?"

"Everyone calls me Jaz, apart from my grandmother, who doesn't like nicknames. And no, I don't recall anything else that stood out. He had what you'd probably call regular features."

"Will you do me a favour, Jaz? Close your eyes and put yourself back on the doorstep that night. See his face again and freeze it like a photograph."

Jaz took another sip of the Coke, to then set it down with a trembling hand and close her eyes to relive the fleeting moments that she had been in close proximity to the man that the police said was a killer. Swallowing hard as the guy's features became a three-dimensional image, Jaz studied it carefully, finding the process chilling, even though the mind picture was no more than a memory that she had conjured up at the artist's request.

Dick watched the anxious young woman. Her eyes were tightly closed, she was chewing her bottom lip, and employing both hands to hold the edge of the table in a death grip, but he said nothing because she had obviously succeeded in recalling the alleged murderer's face.

As if a hypnotist had clicked his fingers to break a trance she had been under, Jaz loosened her grip on the table, opened her eyes and gasped as she broke free from what had been a frightening experience.

"Are you okay?" Dick said.

"I guess so."

"I realise that it must have been an ordeal to relive a terrifying confrontation like that. Thank you for doing it. Will you describe him for me?"

Jaz said nothing, and Dick took that to be assent.

"Let's start with the shape of his face, was it wide, narrow, long, square, or oval?"

"Squarish, I guess."

"Were his cheekbones prominent?"

"Not really. But he did have stubble on his face."

Dick lightly pencilled in the details to his work in progress and said, "That just leaves his hair, nose and mouth."

"He was wearing a navy-blue or black baseball cap, but what I could see of his hair was dark brown and short. His nose was straight and narrow, and his mouth appeared to be thin-lipped. He didn't say anything, so I didn't see his teeth."

Dick drew as he talked. "Did you notice any tattoos, scars, or whether he wore an earring?"

"Not that I can recall."

"Okay, Jaz," Dick said as he turned the pad around and placed it in front of her. "How is this shaping up?"

Jaz studied the rough sketch and could see a strong likeness to the man she had been describing. "His eyes were much darker and a little wider apart," she said. "And his nose was a fraction longer, and his chin was a little firmer."

Taking the pad back, Dick began to adjust the likeness, only to stop as Jaz stood up and said, "I need a pee and a cigarette."

"The loo is second on the left in the hall, and you can smoke in here, because I do. We'll have a short break from this, and then hopefully refine it until you're happy that it's a dead ringer for the suspect."

Jaz re-entered the room a couple of minutes later, to gasp and take a step backwards when Dick held up the drawing to show how he was progressing with the changes he had made. "That looks very much like him," she whispered. "I think you've nailed it."

"Rate it out of ten," Dick said.

"Definitely nine. What will happen now?"

"I'll make a photocopy of it, take a pic with my phone, and give DI Chambers the original. At a guess, this guy's face will be on all the TV news channels this evening, asking Joe Public to pick up their mobiles if they recognise the individual, and to also warn them not to approach him, due to the likelihood of him being armed."

"I'm not going to feel safe for a second while he's on the loose," Jaz said as she lit a cigarette.

"That's understandable. You'll just have to keep a low profile for the time being. Hopefully he'll be identified from the sketch, if it's as near the mark as you believe it to be."

Dick walked out of the bungalow behind Jaz, to hand a sturdy envelope containing the pencil drawing of the unknown subject to Errol.

"Thanks, Dick," Errol said as he withdrew the sheet of cartridge paper from the envelope and studied the image of the suspect, before passing it to Kelly.

"This could be a case breaker," Kelly said as she studied the sketch of the man who was now their prime suspect.

CHAPTER NINE

IT was six-thirty p.m. when Matt got home from the city. It was still daylight, and would be until after eight. Parking his Vectra next to Beth's Audi on the wide gravelled drive, he let himself into the cottage.

Beth had been in the kitchen, sitting in the nook and working her laptop, with a cup of freshly brewed Twinings tea next to it on a ceramic coaster. Matt had phoned to tell her that he was on his way, and so she met him in the hall for the customary hug and kiss that they always greeted each other with. Neither of them took their relationship for granted, knowing from past experience that life was a fragile state of being that could end any second of every day that dawned.

"You're becoming a part-timer, Barnes. This is early for you."

"I'm just taking a couple of hours break, and then going back to the mill, now that we have a lead."

"The Killer Clown case?"

"Yeah, bullets retrieved from the two young black dudes that were shot to death in Bethnal Green came from the same handgun used to murder the women south of the river."

"Is that your *lead*?"

"We also have what we think is a description of the killer. A woman came face-to-face with him as he left one of the scenes in east London, and described him to Dick Curtis, the police artist we use. The woman said that the resulting sketch of him was bang on. It'll be all over the news by now. Julia will be facing the press and TV cameras as we speak, so we'll expect a shitload of phone calls from the public, all convinced that they know the killer's identity."

"Do you want a cup of coffee?" Beth said as she led the way back into the kitchen to switch on both the coffeemaker and the TV.

"I thought you'd never ask," Matt said, smiling, feeling that the break the squad had got could lead them to the shooter.

After less than fifteen minutes, the sketch of the suspect filled the screen, and the talking head on the BBC Freeview news channel stated that the police wished to interview the man in connection with murders committed in Bethnal Green, and that if anyone recognised him, then they should phone the telephone number that appeared on the banner at the bottom of the screen. This was followed by a live broadcast from outside New Scotland Yard where, alongside Pete Deakin, Julia Stone was holding court, facing the cameras and warning the public that the person of interest that they sought was believed to be armed and highly dangerous, and under no circumstances should be approached.

"What other details can you disclose, Detective Chief Superintendent?" Ken Brooks of the Daily Mirror enquired.

"Nothing as yet," Julia said. "Apart from the fact that the same handgun was used to carry out both murders."

"Do you have a motive for the crimes?" Linda Dennison from Channel 4 News said.

"Not at this time. Nothing appears to have been stolen from either of the locations. Money and drugs were discovered by officers, which points to the murders not being undertaken for material gain."

Derek Pybus from The Guardian said, "The initial reports of these shootings stated that the two victims were cousins. Do you have any reason to believe that this was a gang related crime against these men?"

"We are considering all possibilities," Julia said. "At this moment in time it is essential that we identify the man pictured in the police artist's sketch. Some people will recognise him, and I urge them to call the number that will now be displayed at regular intervals on all news channels."

That was it. Julia thanked the gathered media ghouls, and she and Pete turned tail and beat a hasty retreat back into the inner sanctum of the Yard, having faced the cameras and microphones to feed them no more than was necessary.

"That was brief," Beth said. "I note that Julia didn't inform them that you know for a fact that the same firearm was used previously to shoot the two young women."

"It was the same gun, but we don't know that it was used on all four victims by the same perpetrator."

"All your eggs seem to be in one basket, hoping that somebody recognises the suspect from the drawing and picks up the phone."

"Correct."

"What about the woman who described the shooter, is she in danger from him?"

"I doubt it. She's moved back into a flat with her mother, told nobody, and now that the likeness of him is being aired, there would be no point in him attempting to find and kill her. He will be a little paranoid now, and will most likely believe that she is in the Witness Protection Programme, or being guarded twenty-four-seven."

"Sounds as if supposition is all you've really got at the moment. You and I both know that homicidal sociopaths are totally unpredictable."

"What do *you* think he'll do, Beth?"

"If the man she saw up close *is* the killer, I believe that he will consider her to be a continued threat that he cannot afford to ignore. If the sketch of him is recognisable to someone that knows him, then he will expect, at some point in time, to be interviewed. To then be identified in the flesh by the woman would put him under a spotlight and cause him to lose his anonymity, plus his freedom to continue murdering people. I'm almost certain that he will make a point of finding and silencing her."

"Perhaps putting her in a safe house is the way to go."

"I think so. Do you want something to eat before you go back to work?"

"Just a sandwich and another mug of coffee, please. Then I'll have a quick shower and get back to the Yard."

By the time Matt entered the squad room, the team had the details of more than forty members of the public who had already phoned the assigned number after seeing the picture of the suspect on TV.

"What's the plan?" Matt said to Pete.

"To prioritise and start doorstepping and interviewing those that live south of the river and also in the East End. We'll need uniforms seconded to deal with the rest, because the phone keeps ringing. Apparently there are a lot of guys who fit the description that Jasmin Walker gave to Dick Curtis."

Matt agreed. "I think that Miss Walker should be stashed somewhere safe for the time being. If the guy she saw *is* the killer, then he will have seen his likeness and know that she described him to us."

"It's a little late in the day for him to make a play against her."

"If I were in his shoes, I wouldn't want someone out there who could point me out in an identification parade, would you?"

Pete shook his head. "You'd think that he would have taken care of her at the scene, as well as the couple that probably turned up at just the right moment in time to unwittingly save her life."

"With hindsight, he'll probably wish that he had done, if the guy *was* the shooter."

"The couple, Desmond and Shirley Ashton have now been interviewed. They both said that they didn't see his face, because he was wearing a baseball cap and lowered his head as they appeared behind Miss Walker. They said he took off without a backward glance. All they could confirm was his approximate height, and that he was wearing a dark fleece and jeans. Plus, no one else at the address admitted to having seen or heard anything untoward."

Pete walked over to where Marci was pushing red plastic headed pins into a large map of Greater London, which was Blu-Tacked to a cork board on the wall next to the whiteboards.

"We have locations of six households south of the river, and seven in the East End," Marci said.

"Let's do our homework, look up the addresses on Google maps, and do a background check on the names we have," Pete said.

Within less than thirty minutes the team had all available information on the occupants of the addresses. One of the names was that of Dennis Austin, a guy that had done time for committing actual bodily harm (ABH) during an altercation at a pub in Peckham.

"Let's go and talk to people who at this moment in time are potential suspects," Matt said. "And bear in mind that if one of them *is* the killer, he will be armed and won't hesitate to shoot his way out of trouble. If you think one of them is good for it, back off and let him think that he's in the clear. We can pick him up on our terms."

"We'll work in pairs," Pete said. "Errol with me, Marci with Tam, and Matt with Jeff. You can hold the fort, Kelly. We'll call you if anything breaks."

Kelly couldn't conceal her expression of disappointment. She felt as if she was being left out in the cold. To her, it would have been fairer to draw straws or toss coins to decide who got left behind to man the phones.

"South or east first?" Matt said to Pete.

"South, because I think it's the area the killer lives in."

Leaving the Yard in three unmarked pool cars, they drove south of the river and headed to the addresses they had decided to call at first.

Pete had not asked Matt whether or not he had wanted to be an active member of the late evening's outing to carry out interviews. Matt liked to be in the thick of every investigation, and would have probably, no, definitely pulled rank if he had not been made to feel fully inclusive. He was a detective chief inspector now, but was ill at ease being a desk jockey, taking a back seat and not being at the sharp end of every case.

Pete and Errol pulled up outside a semidetached house in Thornton Heath, to walk up a short concrete path. Pete knocked at the door and took a step backwards; an intuitive action to keep out of arms reach. No answer. He knocked again, louder, and after twenty seconds a female voice said, "Yeah, who is it?"

"Police," Errol said. "We need to have a word with Tony Draper."

"About what? It's late and Tony is in bed."

"It's important," Errol said. "Please open the door."

"Tony," Jackie Draper shouted. "There are bloody coppers at the door. Get your arse down here and deal with them."

Pete and Errol smiled at each other as they waited for a couple of minutes, to then kill their expressions of amusement as the door was unlocked and opened by a guy wearing a grubby tee shirt and crumpled shorts. Disconcertingly, he was holding a walking stick.

Pete held up his warrant card and said, "Are you Tony Draper?"

"Yeah. Why the fuck are you knocking on my door at this time of night?"

"Ask us in and we'll tell you."

"No way," Tony said. "I've got a clear conscience."

Errol withdrew a photocopy of the sketch that Dick Curtis had drawn from Jasmin Walker's description and held it out for Draper to take and look at.

"Recognise him?" Errol said.

"No. Should I?" Tony said as he took an unsteady step backwards, leaning on the cane, to study the image in the well-lit hallway.

"Notice the similarity it has to you?"

"What do you think, Jackie?" Tony said, holding the sheet up by finger and thumb for her to see.

"Could be your brother, if you had one. He's a cruel-looking bastard, though, whoever he is. I saw this on TV earlier and could see a slight likeness, but seeing as how they're looking for a killer, I knew it wasn't you."

"Do we get to come in and ask you a few questions, Mr Draper, or would you rather accompany us to the local police station and talk to us in a more formal setting?" Pete said.

Tony scowled and gestured for them to enter, and as they followed him into a small living room, leaving Jackie to close the front door, both Pete and Errol doubted that they were in the presence of the serial killer they sought. He was at most five-foot-eight tall and had a pronounced limp, which caused him to rely heavily on the cane.

"Had an accident?" Pete said as the guy eased himself down in an armchair and indicated that they should sit on the settee.

"I've been on a waiting list for a fucking hip replacement for eighteen months now, taking painkillers and wondering if the NHS will ever get around to fixing me up. Feel free to check it out."

"We still need for you to tell us your whereabouts on specific dates and times," Errol said.

"He hasn't been further than the back garden for the best part of six months," Jackie said from behind them. "Who gave you his name and address?"

"Members of the general public that have seen the news item and believe that they recognise the suspected killer have been phoning since it was released," Pete said. "As for who put you in the frame, that's confidential."

After going through the motions with Tony Draper, and making notes, Pete and Errol left the house and made their way to the second address they had, certain that Draper was not the Killer Clown.

In Peckham, Marci and Tam were at a small thirties-built bungalow on Consort Road, which was a short walk away from Peckham High Street. The owner of the bungalow was Dennis Austin, and they were both on red alert as Tam knocked at the door, aware that Austin had done time for ABH.

CHAPTER TEN

DENNIS had just topped up his third glass of Scotch with ginger ale and was about to add a few ice cubes when someone knocked at his front door. It was late and he wasn't expecting anyone, so felt wary. By the time the door was rapped again, louder this time, he had added ice to his drink and taken a swig. Curiosity got the better of him, and so he placed the glass down on a counter and made his way from the kitchen to see who was disturbing his evening.

"Dennis Austin?" Marci said, holding out her warrant card as the door was opened to reveal a broad-shouldered guy in his late-thirties, of medium height and with short dark hair combed back from his brow.

"Detectives," Dennis said after taking a close look at the ID. "What the fuck do you want at this time of night?"

"A word, sir," Marci said.

"About what?"

"Ask us inside and—"

"That isn't going to happen."

"Behave, Dennis," Tam said, producing a copy of the suspect's likeness and handing it to him. "Someone saw this on the telly, gave us a bell and said it looked a lot like you. You're just one of a great many guys that we need to have a word with."

"Who gave you lot my name?"

"That's confidential. Don't you watch the news?"

"No, it's all doom and gloom. I just record movies so that I can fast forward past the poxy commercials."

"Let's cut the small talk," Marci said. "Invite us in or we'll do this at the nearest police station."

Dennis took deep breaths, fisted his hands, but held his temper. The last thing he needed was a problem with the Old Bill. He jerked his head to the side, indicating that they could enter, and led them through to the kitchen. "Take a seat," he said, "and tell me why you're in my face."

"This is a murder inquiry," Tam said, ignoring the invitation to sit. "We need to know where you were on specific times and dates."

"What happens if I don't know?"

"Then you'll be viewed as a possible suspect."

"Because of a fucking drawing of some geezer that bears a slight resemblance to me?"

"Yes."

"This is police harassment, all because I had a punch-up in a pub. The muppet I hit reported it, and I was charged with ABH, and his mates fingered me for starting the fight."

"The record shows that you hit him with a chair, and then kicked him a couple of times in the head for good measure while he was flat out on the floor," Marci said. "You got sent down for nine months, to be released on licence last November."

"Whatever," Dennis said. "Tell me what dates you want alibis for."

"To begin with, the seventh of December last year, between midday and six p.m."

Dennis frowned, then walked over to a counter, picked up his glass of Scotch, gulped down almost half of it, wiped his mouth with the back of his hand and belched loudly, before taking a spiral notebook from the top of a biscuit barrel next to a wall-mounted phone and flipping through the pages, to visibly relax and even smile as he handed the notebook to Marci.

"Check the entry for December the seventh" Dennis said.

"It reads, Colin Penwright, Bromley, 7/12 at 9 a.m. Fill us in Mr Austin."

"It's where I was. I left here at about eight a.m. as I recall, and was at Colin's place in Bromley before nine, and didn't get home until after six p.m."

"Who exactly is Colin Penwright?"

"An old pal. He owns the CP Scaffolding Company on Nightingale Lane. I sometimes do work for him if he's short of staff."

"Are you a roofer?" Tam said.

"No, I'm a Jack of all fucking trades, due to having a prison record."

"Okay, tell us where you were on the morning of the twelfth of March."

"If there's no entry in that pad for it, then I've no idea. If I don't have any work to go to, I stay in bed till midmorning, and after a late breakfast I usually pop in the Prince of Peckham pub on the high street for an hour or two."

"Do you rent this bungalow?" Marci said as she made notes of what he had told them.

Dennis shook his head and said, "I couldn't afford to. This was my parents place, and it's bought and paid for."

"Are they around?"

"No. My dad died of prostate cancer five years ago, and my mam topped herself eighteen months later. She couldn't live without him and get past it, so got pissed, swallowed a shitload of sleeping pills and strung herself up from the rail of a bedroom wardrobe. Being an only child, I inherited the bungalow and a few quid."

"Sorry for your loss."

"You don't give a fuck about my loss, so if you're done asking me questions, you know where the door is."

"You have a bad attitude, Mr Austin," Tam said.

"It's more a case of me saying what I think without any sugar-coating, and I'm sure that both of you are thick-skinned enough to live with that."

Marci and Tam then asked Dennis where he was on the night that Sonny Mason and Frankie Dawson had been murdered, but he had no alibi and told them that at the time they were interested in, he would have been in bed. They left the bungalow without another word. They would check out the owner of the scaffolding company at Bromley in the morning, and also have a word with the manager or owner of the pub in Peckham.

As the other detectives were interviewing potential suspects, Matt and Jeff had parked behind a grey late model hybrid Jaguar F-PACE on the circle driveway of a large, detached mock Tudor house situated on a cul-de-sac in a residential area not far from Clapham Common.

"Nice gaff," Jeff said as the outside security light came on and lit the front garden of Laburnum House up like a football stadium. "Must be worth a fortune in this neck of the woods."

"Yeah, the guy is obviously well-heeled."

Three York stone steps led up to the solid oak front door, and Matt noted the security camera fixed to the brickwork above it, which was most likely linked to a live feed, so that whoever was ringing the bell could be identified.

Matt thumbed the bell twice before holding his open wallet aloft, for the houseowner to be able to see his warrant card, which was under clear Perspex in one of its pockets.

"Isn't it an unsociable time of night for you guys to be doing house calls?" Carl Gibson said as he opened the door. "I was about to go to bed."

"Time and tide wait for no man," Matt said. "I'm Detective Chief Inspector Barnes, and my colleague is Detective Constable Sewell. We'd appreciate a word with you, Mr Gibson."

"Let me take a calculated guess. This is probably concerning my slight facial likeness to the image being shown repeatedly on the news channels. I would imagine that someone who knows me has given up my name and address."

"Correct. May we come in and discuss it?"

"Of course, but don't you want to search me first, due to the warning given out that the killer you seek is most likely armed and dangerous?"

Matt gave the man a grim smile and said, "You're wearing a casual shirt and jeans, Mr Gibson, but if you really want to, feel free to give us a twirl and show us that you haven't got a handgun tucked in the back of your pants."

Carl turned three hundred and sixty degrees, grinned and then led them through to a spacious lounge with high-end furnishings and a mega-sized TV bracketed to the wall above an inglenook fireplace. "Take a seat, officers," he said. "While I go through to the kitchen and make us a cup of coffee."

"We don't have time to socialise," Matt said. "We have three dates that we need for you to tell us where you were at specific times on them."

"Shoot," Carl said. "Hopefully I'll be able to cover all bases and not be a person of interest to you, because I assure you that I'm not the kind of guy that considers murder as an acceptable pastime."

"Okay, Mr Gibson. If you can verify your precise location for one, or preferably all of them, then we'll be satisfied that you are not the person depicted in the mug shot that is being aired."

"Sounds good. Fire away."

One by one, Matt gave the times and dates on which Brenda Cummings, Natalie Swift, Sonny Mason and Frankie Dawson were shot to death, without naming the victims or giving the locations.

Carl shook his head and said, "None of those dates ring a bell. I could have been at the factory early on the first one, or having a round of golf on the second. As for the third, that was after midnight. I was most likely asleep in bed."

"That doesn't work for us, Mr Gibson. You need to concentrate and come up with something that we can check out," Matt said.

"My diaries," Carl said, and walked over to a desk in the corner of the room, to open a drawer and retrieve two dark green diaries from it. "One of these is last years, the other is current. Please repeat the dates for me."

Matt did, and Carl thumbed to the seventh of December in the first diary, to shake his head and toss it onto the desktop and open the second.

"Well?" Matt said. "Any luck?"

"Yes. I'd made a note to remind me that I was going to my girlfriend's flat at eight p.m. on the seventeenth of April," Carl said, "but have no entries for the other dates. I only make a note of meetings I need to attend, or anything else that I deem to be important."

"What time did you leave your girlfriend's?"

"I stayed the night at her flat."

"I'll need her name and address."

Carl gave them to Matt, who wrote them down in his notebook.

"You mentioned a factory," Jeff said.

"Yes, I own a factory on the Stone Trading Estate on Milkwood Road in Brixton; CG Aluminium Products."

"Making what?" Jeff said as he made notes.

"Food trays for the catering industry, pergolas, garden furniture and window frames, among other things. Why do you ask?"

"Just curious, sir. Every scrap of information could prove helpful. And the fact that you own a factory explains to me how you can afford a property like this in such a well-to-do area."

Matt handed Carl a business card. "Give me a call if you come up with something that will put you in the clear for the times on any of those other dates, sir," he said. "And be aware that we will be talking to all of your employees."

"About what?"

"One of them may have reason to remember if you were at the factory at times that we're interested in."

"Great," Carl said. "I really need for my workforce to know that I'm suspected of being a fucking killer."

"We'll be as discrete as possible."

It was two a.m. when the full team, with the exception of DCS Julia Stone, reconvened in the SCU squad room. They had nothing positive, just that two of the men interviewed could not furnish an alibi for the times on dates that the crimes had been committed.

"Anything of interest?" Pete said to Kelly, who had been feeling left out of the loop like a wallflower at a high school dance, sitting it out because none of the boys had taken an interest in her.

"No," she said. "Apart from the names and addresses of a shitload more guys that the public have phoned in, convinced that they could be the killer."

"It's all power to our elbows," Pete said. "We'll end up with a short list, and then narrow it down to one."

"You hope," Marci said.

"Yes, because hope is optimistic expectation of something that you know, given time, will come to pass."

"That's it for now, folks" Matt said. "We all need a little downtime, so go home, get some beauty sleep and then hurry back, because the hunt is on, and the sooner we apprehend this serial killer the better."

CHAPTER ELEVEN

BETH was in bed, dozing fitfully, unable to ever sleep soundly when Matt was working a live serial case. She could not relax until he was home, because she knew that he was capable of putting himself in the firing line, which was either a strength or weakness, perhaps both. He was totally committed to closing cases, and would do whatever necessary to capture a killer.

The buzz of her phone startled her, and she snatched it from the top of the bedside cabinet, relieved to see that the caller was Matt.

"Did I wake you up?" he said. "Or were you reading?"

"I was reflecting on the unsociable hours you work, Barnes. I was stupid enough to believe that when you got promoted, you'd spend most of your working days behind a desk."

"I'm a player, Beth, not what you would call good management material. I need to be involved, not on the side lines."

"I know. Where are you, now?"

"Heading home. I should be there in thirty minutes."

"Good. Coffee or Scotch?"

"Coffee with a drop of the hard stuff, please."

"Okay. See you soon."

When Matt got home, they didn't leave the kitchen, just sat at the table in the nook, Matt with his alcohol-laced coffee and Beth with a mug of milky tea. To Beth, Matt looked weary, and as per usual when working a case, his mental preoccupation with it was evident, although he attempted, unsuccessfully, to appear relaxed.

"How is it going?" Beth said. "Any useful leads?"

"Nothing to shout about. We already have a growing list of guys that fit the description, and don't have alibis for the dates we're interested in. Nothing substantial, though. A great many people can't remember what they had for lunch yesterday, let alone recall what they were doing at a specific time on most given dates."

"How many people have phoned in, believing that they recognise the face of the man the young woman described?"

"Approximately seventy and rising. Once they've all been interviewed, we should end up with a short list of hopefully not too many."

"Have you considered the possibility that the man seen at the address in Bethnal Green could have nothing to do with the murders?"

"Yeah, Beth, and dismissed it. He was a white guy in an almost exclusively black neighbourhood, so we're putting our shirts on him being good for it. Plus, currently we have no other leads to follow."

"There's no way that you can be certain about—"

"We're detectives," Matt said, more brusquely than intended, interrupting Beth. "We attempt to remove all uncertainty regarding circumstances of what is obviously murder. The goal is to absolve or charge individuals, which involves interviewing witnesses, collecting evidence, interrogating suspects and considering all related information. We have set rules of what we regard as warfare against the offenders we seek, and work cases until we get a result."

"I know that, but you become obsessed with the work and let it take you over, mind, body and soul. There's a bigger picture, with a lot more going on in life than what we do to earn money."

"I thought that you would know by now that what I do isn't about the pay. I have the need to stop serial killers, to save other potential victims from being murdered, and give the bereaved of those that have been a measure of closure. From what I see on the news, what's going on in life, the *big picture* as you call it, is: war, famine, disease, floods, poverty, climate change and all sorts of other disheartening shit that I have no way of changing for the better. I don't wear blinkers, Beth, but I'm a copper, not a politician or an activist. Truth is, I believe that human life on earth is on the slippery slope, and that we're all destined to becoming as extinct as any other species that has come and gone before us."

"That was heavy for you, Barnes. I reckon you should have a large glass of neat Scotch and lighten up."

"I reckon you're right. I just wanted you to know that I *do* think about what's going down, apart from whatever case I'm working. How was your day?"

"Fine, and Mr Fox turned up at dusk to sit at the front of the orchard and wait. He vanished when I put a couple of chicken breasts out for him, but was tucking in before I got back inside the cottage."

"We spend an arm and a leg on feeding the wildlife."

"You're a sucker for most creatures, great or small, as guilty as me when it comes to putting food out for them."

Later, when Matt had drained his glass, Beth asked if he wanted a refill.

"I'll pass," he said. "It'll be dawn soon, and like the old proverb says, 'time and tide wait for no man'."

"Just a thought," Beth said as they climbed the stairs. "Did you arrange for the girl that supposedly saw the killer to be put in the Witness Protection Programme?"

"No, she refused, but will be watched twenty-four-seven by officers of the UKPPS (UK Protected Persons Service), which is coordinated and supported by the National Crime Agency."

"For how long?"

"As long as it takes. The man she saw and described is hopefully the perpetrator. When we locate and arrest him, and he eventually stands trial, her testimony will go a long way towards putting him behind bars for the rest of his natural. She, Jasmin Walker, will then be able to get on with her life."

Four hours later, Matt was up, in the bathroom, shaving and showering. Beth had slipped on a robe, gone downstairs to the kitchen and switched on the coffeemaker, before deciding to fry bacon and eggs for their breakfast. Thumbing the TV remote, she was faced by a talking head; a blonde bimbo with big tits who was reading from a teleprompter, telling the viewers of global tragedy that was affecting so many people around the world. A jet had crashed in the Indian Ocean with no survivors, terrorists had blown-up a mosque in Paris, sending forty worshippers to the Promised Land and wounding a further ninety, and yet another teenager had been stabbed to death in London. Matt was right with his take on the news, which was mundane at best and soul-destroying at worst. Dipping in once a day to keep abreast of current affairs and events was definitely enough.

Forty-five minutes later they left the cottage in separate cars. Matt headed for the city, and Beth drove southwest to the Morning Star rehab facility in Uxbridge.

CHAPTER TWELVE

NINE days later. It was the fourth of May and he was now confident that the visit from the two homicide detectives would not lead to his being of any further interest to them, although the ongoing problem of the young woman he had come face to face with at the house in Bethnal Green was still unresolved. He would not feel truly safe until he had taken care of her, and so all his efforts were focused on endeavouring to discover which of the flats at Kingsley Hamlets in Stratford she was living in. Regular visits, to park within sight of the tower block that the police had dropped her off at, had eventually paid off, though. On three occasions he had noted a changeover of plainclothes guys whom he was convinced were detectives babysitting the woman. One of them could be coerced into giving up the flat number he needed. All he had to do now was follow the mid-grey Kia that the smaller of the two men drove, and pick his moment.

DC Alan Townsend was inside the tenth floor flat, drinking coffee and making small talk with Jaz Walker and her mother, when his phone rang. "Yeah, Bill?" he said to his colleague, more than happy to know that it was almost nine p.m., the end of his shift. He would soon be driving home to the semi in Walworth, where he had lived alone since his wife had left him over a year ago.

"I'm on my way up in the lift, Al. Anything exciting to report?" DC Bill Spencer said.

"No. I'm beginning to feel like one of the family, though. Cheryl and Jaz are really looking after me."

Ten minutes after the call, Alan was in his car and heading for home. A lot of the protection jobs he did were to say the least boring, but looking out for the two women was a pleasure, and he was almost positive that Jaz was in no danger from the unknown subject who may or may not have committed the murders in Bethnal Green.

Parking outside the attached garage of the house, which was now a soulless shell of the home it used to be, Alan let himself in, planning to microwave a meal for supper and watch the box for a couple of hours before hitting the sack.

As the door opened and Alan pocketed his keys, a kaleidoscope of bright colours filled his mind, then faded to black.

Easy-peasy, he thought, closing the door quickly as the detective fell forward, face down on the hall carpet. Turning the unconscious cop onto his back, he removed a handgun from the shoulder rig he wore, his wallet and smartphone from inside pockets of his jacket, keys from another, and a pair of handcuffs from a leather pouch attached to his belt, to hook one cuff around the pipe of a radiator and the other to the man's right wrist, to leave him there while he quickly searched the semi room by room, after first locking the front door. There was no one else in the house, and so he returned to the hall, ensuring that his prisoner was still insensible before unlocking the cuff he had attached to the radiator, to drag what was not, as yet, a truly dead weight through to the kitchen, where he secured the copper to yet another radiator before pulling down the blind at the window and switching on the overhead fluorescent tube.

Alan came to laid on the kitchen floor, next to the wall, suffering an intense throbbing pain that beat like a drum in his right temple. He felt dizzy, his vision was blurred, and he had no idea what had happened to him. It was as he attempted to climb to his feet that he realised his wrists were fastened behind his back to the radiator. Blinking rapidly to regain his focus, he was alarmed to see a figure sitting on a chair less than ten feet from him. The last thing he remembered was opening the front door, but nothing else. It was obvious that someone had struck him from behind, before dragging him through to the kitchen and securing him to the radiator.

"What the fuck do you want?" Alan said to the seated man. "Are you a burglar?"

The intruder raised a semiautomatic pistol that was fitted with a silencer, pointed it at his face, but said nothing.

"I'm a police officer," Alan said as his captor stood up, to walk across to one of the faux granite countertops and lift up Alan's open wallet to display the warrant card in an ID pocket.

"No, I'm not a burglar. It would be a blessing for you if I was. And I *know* that you're a cop, DC Alan Townsend; your warrant card reads that you're a UKPPS protection officer. You'll notice that I'm wearing latex gloves, a balaclava, and that I'm holding a silenced pistol that I used to hit you with. I intend to ask you a few questions, and if I believe the answers you give me, I will gag you and leave you here, alive. Only being honest with me will save your life. How does that sound?"

Alan did not reply, and his silence was rewarded by the intruder approaching him, to hit him across the face with the solid extension on the gun hard enough to fracture his cheekbone and elicit an outcry of pain through gritted teeth.

"There's always an easy way or a hard way, Al. I suggest that you screw your loaf and pick the former, to save you from suffering unnecessary pain and mutilation. You need to know that I'm the guy who shot and killed the two black morons, and prior to that, the young women south of the river, which subsequently got me tagged the Killer Clown by the media, due to pictures of clowns' faces that I left on the women's bodies."

"What guarantee do I have that you won't shoot me if I answer your questions?"

"I'd rather not murder a police officer, Al. That would be like sticking my head in a hornets' nest. A lot of unsolved homicides end up gathering dust as cold cases, but if the victim is a copper, then it stays live, and they keep working it until they get closure."

"What information do you think I've got that would be of any interest to you?"

"You're a member of a team protecting a young woman who is currently ensconced in Kingsley Hamlets, Stratford. She is known as Jaz. I want to know her full name, the flat number, and the names of anyone else at that address."

Alan thought it through. Bill Spencer would not open the door to anyone without being given proof of identity, and so to give this guy the details would not help him get to the girl.

"Time up, Al. Keep me waiting another three seconds and I'll cut one of your fucking ears off. Your call."

"Jaz is Jasmin Walker, and she is staying at her mother's flat, which is 109 on the tenth floor."

"How many cops are in the flat?"

"Just one."

"What's the procedure?"

"Four of us take it in turn to do eight-hour shifts, twenty-four seven, and check in by phone on the hour to our HQ."

"What else do I need to know?"

"Nothing," Alan said, wanting to tell the guy to go and fuck himself, but convinced that if he did, the crazy bastard *would* cut one of his ears off, and then keep maiming him until he was satisfied that there were no more details to be had.

"I don't believe you, Al. When you do the changeover, how does it work?"

"I make a call when I've parked outside, to tell whoever's on duty that I'm on my way up. When I get to the flat, I knock at the door twice, then a couple of seconds later I knock again, three times. That's it."

He searched the man's eyes and saw fear in them, and believed that he was telling the truth, because self-preservation was a powerful emotion; the basic instinct to protect oneself from harm in the face of danger.

"Okay, Al," he said, lifting the man's smartphone from the countertop and hunkering down next to him. "What's the name of the officer inside the flat?"

"Spencer. Bill Spencer."

Scrolling down the phone's contact list, he found the name and said, "I'm going to call Spencer, after I've told you what to say to him. Any problem with that?"

Alan shook his head, and the pain from the blows he had sustained flared up like hot coals, or nails being hammered into his temple and cheek. For a second or two he believed that he would throw up, but took deep breaths and swallowed hard.

After telling the pitiful-looking detective what to say, and then having him repeat it, twice, he told him to take a few more deep breaths and stay calm, then speed-dialled the number and held the phone a couple of inches from his captive's undamaged cheek.

"Yeah, Alan. What's the problem?" Bill said, standing up and walking out of the lounge and into the kitchen, to leave Jaz sitting on the settee watching a TV show.

"It may be nothing, Bill," Alan said. "But I think that I may have been followed from the flats. I caught sight of a dark-coloured Nissan several times in my rear-view mirror. When I got home and parked, it passed by with the lights off."

"What do you think, should I ring it in?"

THE URGE TO KILL

"Not yet. I'll head back to the flat now and see if I'm tailed again. I'm probably just being paranoid. I'll see you soon."

"You need to chill, Alan. This babysitting gig is getting to you."

"Better safe than sorry. Have some fresh coffee made, I could do with a caffeine fix."

He smiled behind the balaclava, switched off the phone and placed it back on the counter next to the wallet, bunch of keys and handgun.

"You did good, Al," he said. "You should've been an actor, not joined the filth. Just be aware that if you've lied to me, or omitted to tell me any details, I'll come back, blow both of your kneecaps off and gut shoot you."

"I've told you everything."

"Let's hope so, for your sake. Where will I find some duct tape?"

"I've got a reel of gorilla tape, second drawer down in the cabinet below the microwave."

After wrapping tape around Alan's head a couple of times, covering his mouth but not his nose, he placed the cold steel of the silencer's muzzle up against the copper's already swollen and bruised temple and said, "Are you ready to die?"

Alan felt as though his heart had frozen in his chest, and squeezed his eyelids tightly shut, unaware that he was pissing his pants.

"I'm only joshing, Al," he said. "You've caught me in a good mood this evening."

Driving back to the tower block in Stratford with the now sweat-soaked balaclava removed and laying limply on the passenger seat, he felt as though a great weight had been lifted from his shoulders. The only person that could identify him would soon be dead.

Back in the semi, Alan felt overcome with guilt; ashamed of not lying to the masked man who he knew would gain entry to the flat and in all probability murder Bill, Jaz, and Cheryl. He was a coward, and knew it. He had withheld one vital scrap of information, though, which with any luck would save at least one of their lives. As of now, he needed to free himself from the radiator within the next thirty minutes or so, to phone Bill back and warn him.

CHAPTER THIRTEEN

UNABLE to raise himself up or turn sideways, Alan grasped the bottom of the slimline, single panel radiator and attempted to pull it away from the wall. There was no movement. The cuffs were fastened around the pipe coming up through the tiled floor, and it was unyielding. After several tries he realised that he was not going to succeed in doing anything more than badly graze his wrists against the steel of the ratchet cuffs. He was furious, having read of many instances in which people had found almost superhuman strength when they or those that they loved were in mortal danger. Even though he was enraged and had the need to, he couldn't move the small, cheap radiator a fucking millimetre. If things went wrong for the killer when he reached the flat, and he survived, then he would most likely come back and carry out his threat. Alan was as helpless as a new-born baby, and knew it. He could not even shout for help, to hopefully be heard by his next-door neighbour, due to the tape that had been wrapped around his head to cover his mouth. But it was the only long shot chance of survival he had open to him. Slowly, tentatively, he endeavoured to open his mouth. Surely the power of his jaws would be enough to dislodge it. It took a long time. The tape gradually moved a fraction of an inch, and he was able to push saliva out from between his lips in the hope that it would weaken the adhesive. Eventually, his aching jaws won out, and the tape only clung to his bottom lip and chin, allowing him to shout for assistance at the top of his voice.

Brian Keaton was sitting in an armchair, dozing, with a David Baldacci paperback hanging loosely from his arthritic, swollen fingers. Brian was an eighty-three-year-old widower with only the company of his ageing Jack Russell terrier, Champ, giving him the will to get up each and every morning, to wash, dress and face another day, which had been almost impossible to contemplate after his wife, Betty, died. He was now just going through the motions, having lost the love of his life, whom he had been married to for almost fifty-nine years.

The loud sound of Champ barking from the hall woke him up, but he could hear nothing alarming.

"Quiet, Champ," Brian said. "Come back in here, now."

The barking continued, and so Brian took the book from where it had fallen into his lap, struggled to his feet and left the lounge, to see the dog sitting to attention with ears pricked up. Brian was a little deaf, but heard what he thought was someone shouting from next door, where he knew that a copper, Alan Townsend, lived alone. With his ear to the adjoining wall, he heard the words 'Help me' being repeated over and over again.

The front door to Alan's house was closed but not locked. Brian entered brandishing a brass poker, to follow the now hoarse shouting into the kitchen, a little afraid of what he would come face to face with.

Relief was Alan's chief emotion as his elderly neighbour appeared in the doorway, to stare down at him open-mouthed and wide-eyed.

"Thank Christ you heard me," Alan said. "I need for you to get my phone from the counter, Brian, bring up the contact list, find the name Bill S, make the call and hold the mobile next to my face."

"What happened?" Brian whispered, noting the blood on his neighbour's shirt collar, and the bruise on the side of his face.

"Just make the call," Alan said. "This is a life-or-death situation."

The phone rang but was not answered.

"End the call, scroll down the list to Mac, and ring it."

DI Bob McLeish was off duty, at home with his wife, Annie. They were sitting at the dining room table thumbing through travel brochures, intent on finding somewhere that they would both enjoy spending a couple of weeks at in summer. Annie was about to pour them a second glass of red wine when Bob's smartphone beeped.

"Yes, Alan. It's getting late, is everything okay?"

"The killer followed me home from the flat in Stratford, Mac. He coldcocked me and cuffed me to a fucking radiator. He's armed, and on his way back to Stratford now, and so Bill Spencer and the two women are in danger of being shot to death."

"I'll deal with it, and send a unit to your house. I'll get back to you asap."

All Alan could do was hope that it was not already too late. He didn't want to have to live the rest of his life with the deaths of three people eating at his conscience, with knowledge that he would be one hundred percent responsible for what happened to them.

"Are my keys on the counter, Brian?"

"Yes, with a wallet and a pistol."

"Take the keys and go out to the garage. On the left wall you'll find a pair of long-handled bolt cutters hanging from a bracket."

Brian did as he was bid, to return less than three minutes later with the tool and, following Alan's instructions, placed the short length of handcuff chain between the carbon-hardened steel jaws of the cutters, to then employ all his willpower and flagging strength, ignoring the fiery pain in his hands and fingers, to force the handles of the cutters together and exhale with relief as the powerful blades cleanly bit through one of the links as though it was butter.

"Thanks, you saved my life, Brian, probably literally," Alan said as he climbed a little unsteadily to his feet. "You'd best go back home now, lock the door and don't answer it to anyone but my colleagues when they arrive. At some point you'll be asked to give a statement as to what happened this evening."

After Brian had left, Alan called Bill's number once more, but there was no answer, and he feared the worst, knowing that if he had been able, his colleague and friend would have accepted the call.

Parking a few streets away from the tower block, he replaced the balaclava on his head, folded back on his brow to appear like a woollen beanie hat. He then raised the deep collar of the duffel jacket he was wearing and made his way to the twenty-four-storey high building, hands in his coat pockets and looking down in case a CCTV camera was functioning, which he doubted. Once inside, he took one of the two lifts up to the twelfth floor, to use the stairs and make his way down to the tenth and walk along the internal corridor to number 109. Standing to the side of the door, he took his gun from one side pocket of his jacket and the silencer from the other, which he screwed to the barrel of the gun. The powerful surge of adrenaline he experienced was stimulating. This was like living on a razor's edge, putting himself in the line of fire, knowing that the copper inside the flat would be armed. As he pulled the balaclava back down to cover his face, the thrill of what was about to go down heightened all his senses. It was showtime.

Inside the flat, DC Bill Spencer was waiting for Alan to phone him again when the door was knocked twice, followed by three more taps a couple of seconds later.

Getting up from the armchair he was sitting in, shaking his head as he tutted, mentally reviling Alan for obviously being so uptight at believing he had been followed home that he had broken protocol by not phoning before returning to the flat, Bill unlocked the door and began to open it, only to be knocked back with enough force to send him sprawling.

He closed the door behind him, using the heel of his shoe to kick it shut as he pointed the gun at the fallen man's chest. "Do not move an inch or I'll shoot you," he said. "Where's the girl?"

"In the bathroom," Bill said as he rapidly weighed up the chances he had of living through this predicament, even as he concluded that if he reached for the gun in his shoulder holster he would die where he lay.

"Where's the mother?"

"Spending some time with a friend who lives on the seventh floor."

"Okay, DC Bill Spencer, I want you to slowly remove your firearm using only a finger and thumb, and toss it under the settee. And then do the same with your mobile phone."

Bill did as he was asked, and said, "Have you harmed Alan?"

"I had to use a little physical force to persuade him to spill his guts and give me the information that I needed, but he's still in the land of the living, gagged, and cuffed to a kitchen radiator."

"I think that—"

"I don't give a fuck what you think. Sit up, take your handcuffs out and fasten your right wrist to your left ankle, nice and tight. Do it now, or suffer the consequences."

Removing the cuffs from the pouch fastened to his belt, Bill knew that if he followed the masked man's orders, he would be totally helpless and at risk of being murdered. He could not rely on the word of a killer who, for all he knew, had probably shot Alan dead.

It was a do or die situation. As he made as if to place one of the cuffs around his ankle, he threw the steel restraint full force at the intruder's face, frisbee fashion. It was a distraction technique to give him the few seconds he needed to gain his feet and make a bid to disarm the man. One of his mates, Stuart Schofield, a screw at Wandsworth nick, had said that on several occasions he had thrown his cap, clip-on tie or anything else to hand at a con's face, to give him the time to get the upper hand and diffuse what was a potentially violent set of circumstances.

The set of polished steel cuffs glinted under the ceiling light as they spun through the air, to miss him by less than an inch as the sudden, unexpected action caused him to lurch sideways to avoid being struck. He triggered the gun, but the bullet went high, missing its target, and by the time he was ready to fire again, the copper had made his move, sprung to his feet and grasped the wrist of his gun hand and brought a knee up into his balls, causing him to bend forward as agonising bolts of pain shot up into his stomach to immobilise him.

Bill twisted the man's wrist, but was initially unable to make him drop the weapon.

Somehow, ignoring the pain in his crotch and stomach, spurred on in the knowledge that if the copper managed to disarm him, then life as he knew it would be over, and he would most likely spend the rest of his days banged-up in a maximum-security prison. That thought gave him the strength to ignore the physical discomfort and retaliate by fisting his free hand, to bring it up with all the force he could muster into his adversary's abdomen.

Bill lost his grip on the man's wrist, the wind knocked out of him, and before he could renew his efforts to overcome the gunman, he was blown back and sideways as a bullet ripped through his left shoulder.

"You fucked up, Billy Boy," he said as he pulled the balaclava from his head and stuffed it in a pocket. "I came here to kill the girl, not you, but you had to try to be a hero."

Bill raised his right hand in supplication, as images of his wife and young son filled his mind, before a bullet drilled through his forehead, to enter his brain and rob him of all awareness.

He would have rather not shot the copper, but having been assaulted by him, he had allowed anger to cloud his thoughts, and reacted without thinking of the possible consequences. He needed to act fast now, kill the girl and put some distance between himself and Stratford.

The bathroom was across a passage that led into the lounge facing it. To the right was another door leading into the kitchen.

After taking a shower, Jaz had come out of the bathroom wearing a fluffy white towelling robe adorned with patches depicting

Paddington Bear, which reminded her of the TV sketch in which the late Queen had withdrawn a marmalade sandwich from her handbag. That was when Jaz heard male voices and then what could have been muted gunshots coming from the lounge.

It was him. He had found her she thought, recognising him through the partly open lounge door. There was no doubt in her mind that it was the man she had described to the police artist. How had he discovered where she was staying?

"I can see you, Jaz," he said. "Come in here, we need to talk."

It took less than a second to take in the whole picture. The police officer was laying on the carpet, face up and with blood on his face, and the man who had shot him was raising a gun to point at her. She knew that he did not want to talk to her about anything. He had come to kill her.

CHAPTER FOURTEEN

MARCI took a call from DCI Neil Anderson, a Protection Service officer.

"It would appear that one of our officers was followed home from the tower block where your witness is staying, and was physically coerced to give up the flat number." Neil said. "We have armed officers en route to the address. The witness fled into a makeshift panic room. She believes that the officer guarding her has been shot. Your squad was flagged for us to contact, should there be reason to."

"We'll be attending directly, sir," Marci said. "Thanks for contacting us."

Both Matt and Pete were off duty, but on call as always. Marci phoned Pete and brought him up to speed.

"Who have you got with you in the squad room?" Pete said.

"Errol, Jeff and Tam."

"Take Jeff and Errol with you and get over there, Tam can hold the fort," Pete said before giving Matt a bell and telling him what he knew.

"I'll meet you there," Matt said, hoping that responding officers would reach the high-rise in time to save the officer's life, but pessimistic, now wishing that he had pressed harder for her to voluntarily move into an official witness programme safe house.

"What's happened?" Beth said as Matt rapidly made ready to leave the cottage.

"An officer that had been relieved by another at the flat of Jasmin Walker's mother was apparently followed home, assaulted, and gave up the flat number. It is believed that the intruder has shot the officer who was guarding Jasmin."

"Is she okay?"

"Yeah. She phoned for help from the bathroom, which had been modified for her safety."

"How could he have known where she was staying?"

"The only logical probability is that he followed Tam and Errol when they drove Jasmin to the tower block. He obviously didn't know her surname, or which of the flats she was staying at, so spent time watching and waiting, to guess, rightly, that she was being guarded. Plainclothes officers that were changing shifts would stand out, and so he followed one of them and got lucky."

Matt left the cottage, to climb into his Vectra and speed off like a bat out of hell.

"I told you to come into the lounge," he said. "Do it, or I swear I'll shoot you."

Jaz froze at the sight of the gunman that she had last seen in the doorway of the house in Bethnal Green, but his voice broke the spell of combined shock and fear, and she stepped back quickly into the bathroom, slammed the door shut and shot the deadbolt across.

He smiled. The bitch could run, but she couldn't hide. Locking herself in the bathroom was just putting off the inevitable. Within less than sixty seconds she would be as dead as the dumb copper, suffering his trademark bullet to the groin, and then one to her head. She had been a consternation to him, but with patience and determination he had discovered her location and was now about to bring closure to the episode.

Knowing that the door would be locked, he kicked it hard, next to the handle, expecting it to fly open, but it did not give.

"Open the fucking door, or I'll shoot you through it." He said, aiming the gun at the centre of it.

Jaz was terrified, but felt reasonably safe. The police had arranged for a security firm to replace the hollow core wooden door with a steel-faced one, and they had also set rebar at points in the new steel frame, fixing the reinforcing bars through it at either side, into the walls. The bathroom now doubled as a panic room, with a mobile phone in the medicine cabinet to contact the number of the protection service headquarters.

With shaking hands, sitting cross-legged in a corner of the room, Jaz made the call, as the man who was intent on killing her fired a bullet at the door.

Surprise was his initial reaction as the now misshapen slug ricocheted off the impenetrable surface and whined passed him, less than an inch from his head.

"You can't get in, and I'm phoning the police," Jaz yelled.

Comprehension was instant. They, the police, had converted the bathroom into a fucking panic room. He had no option but to get away from the high-rise before they arrived.

"You'll never be safe," he shouted. "Giving my description to the police was the most stupid thing you've ever done in your pathetic life."

Taking the lift down to the ground floor, he left the building and unhurriedly strolled back to where he had parked his car, not wanting to attract any unwelcome attention. Common-sense dictated that any future attempt on the woman's life would be a perilous venture, because the police would undoubtedly transfer her to a far safer location. He would have to get past it and move on, because he doubted that he would be able to locate her again, to get a second chance to kill her.

Jaz had spoken to a detective inspector by the name of Paul Harvey and, with a shaky voice, relayed what had happened, and was told to stay where she was, and only open the door when he arrived and identified himself.

First responders at Kingsley Hamlets were Paul Harvey and three other protection officers, shortly followed by an ambulance and an armed response vehicle (ARV), crewed by authorised firearms officers who attended incidents believed to involve firearms or other high-risk situations.

By the time that Marci, Jeff and Errol arrived, the flat on the tenth floor was teeming with armed police, and Jaz was in the bedroom with her mother, who had returned from her friend Carmine's flat on the seventh floor. Paul and another officer were with them, keeping them out of the lounge, away from the corpse of the murdered officer.

"Neither of you will be able to stay here," Paul said to Cheryl and Jaz. "This flat is now a crime scene. For your own safety, Miss Walker, you will have to be placed in an official safe house, because what has just happened means that your life is at high risk from the man who has just shot and killed the officer."

"What about me?" Cheryl said. "I'm at risk as well, now. I need to be with Jaz."

"I'll see what I can arrange," Paul said.

"If my mum can't come with me, then I'm not going anywhere," Jaz said.

There was nothing that Marci and the others could do when they got to the flat. Errol, who knew Jaz, had a word with her, and she confirmed what they already knew, that it was the same man she had described to Dick Curtis.

When Matt and Pete turned up, they were issued with plastic overshoes, as was everyone entering the flat. DI Paul Harvey greeted them. He had known Matt for at least a decade, and after being introduced to Pete, he ran through the events as they viewed the body of the officer, which was still in situ, laying on the blood-soaked carpet, where it would remain until a Home Office pathologist arrived to carry out an examination of the corpse, and for CSIs to begin their work: documenting the scene, taking photographs, identifying and collecting forensic evidence and maintaining the proper chain of custody of that evidence.

"Police units are prowling the area, hoping to find the perpetrator," Paul said. "And uniformed officers are already doorstepping neighbours, in case he was seen entering or leaving the building or the flat. The dead officer's firearm and mobile phone are under the settee, and his handcuffs are on the floor on the carpet, several feet away from him. The piece of shit that did this put a bullet in Bill's left shoulder, and another in his head to finish him off."

Last to join the party was the pathologist, Dr Roshana Anwar who had, over the years, attended a great many murder scenes, including numerous of which Matt and his squad had investigated.

"Hi, Roz," Matt said, appraising the new slimline look of the 'slicer and dicer' who he hadn't seen for a while. "Have you gone part-time?"

"No, Barnes, I've just been spending a lot more time in the mortuary, and also always seem to have a shitload of bookwork to keep me in the office," Roz said as she quickly donned a lightweight Tyvek jumpsuit – which offered maximum protection against the incursion of many chemicals, blood and other fluids – along with latex gloves and plastic overshoes from the metal case which held all the equipment she needed to conduct an on scene examination of a cadaver.

"Are you still driving that rusty old custard-yellow Citroën?" Pete said.

"Yeah, it keeps passing the MOT, so why would I upgrade while it's roadworthy? I've got better things to do with my money."

"What we have here is a deceased police officer," Matt said, standing aside so that Roz could get a clear view of the body on the carpet. "He was shot in the left shoulder and forehead."

"Okay, give me some space to work in."

Matt and Pete went into the kitchen, where DI Paul Harvey had been cleared by the team leader of the crime scene investigators to make coffee.

"I'm arranging for Jasmin and her mother to be placed in a more secure witness protection setting, which will be a step up from attempting to ensure her safety here," Paul said as Pete took a couple of ceramic mugs from the second wall cabinet he looked in, to pour coffee in for both himself and Matt.

"I thought she had refused to be placed in a safe house," Matt said.

"That was before this evening. She knows that the officer was shot, and is now terrified and believes that the killer will make another attempt on her life."

"He will no doubt expect that she will be moved," Matt said. "There's a chance that he'll keep watch on the building until he sees WP officers arrive to transfer them to another location."

"That would be crazy. If he attempted to follow them, he'd be lifted. You used to be with witness protection, Matt, so you know the precautions and level of security they employ."

Matt knew that Paul was right, but bitter experience told him that there were no guarantees. Shit happened. It was folly to underestimate some homicidal maniac who was intent on carrying out an act to safeguard himself from the possibility of being detained, identified and imprisoned. Witnesses who were willing to testify against a murderer or big time gangster put themselves in the firing line. It went without saying that Jasmin Walker would now regret having admitted that she had seen the alleged shooter, and subsequently given his description to Dick Curtis. Assisting the police could feasibly bring someone out of the woodwork with extremely bad intentions.

CHAPTER FIFTEEN

IT was mid-May. He had been visited by two detectives from the SCU on the sixth and asked to tell them his movements on the evening of the fourth, and had furnished them with an alibi that appeared to satisfy them, which he knew, though false, would hold up when they checked it. He was on a list, which he imagined would be quite a long one, consisting of many similar looking individuals to him, whose names had been put forward by public-spirited people who didn't know when to mind their own fucking business. It was reasonable to assume that quite a few people of interest would not be able to come up with alibis for the dates in question, and so he had absolutely nothing to worry about. He had covered the evening that he had made his play to take out the young black woman in Stratford, and so would move on, because the urge to kill was growing, spreading through his being like a wild fire, demanding that he strike again to relieve the internal pressure and extinguish the flames for a while. He had no particular victim in mind. It would be exciting to just pick a female at random, to inflict a prolonged state of fear before employing a more hands-on method to take her life. Shooting people was fine, but 'a change was as good as a rest' was a proverb which, unlike many others, he agreed wholeheartedly with.

At eight-thirty p.m. on a warm Friday evening in late May, Beth and Matt entered the Green Dragon pub in the village of Abbots Langley, which was only a few minutes' drive from the cottage and very close to the Harry Potter Studio Tour in Leavesden.

Matt had booked a window table in the restaurant a couple of days earlier, and was looking forward to a steak meal with all the trimmings, and a couple of Scotches, due to Beth having offered to drive back home.

"We've never been on the Harry Potter tour," Beth said after a waitress had taken their order.

"You know I'm not a fan of that kind of thing," Matt said.

"I know. You'd rather watch violent crime movies."

"True. Most of them are over the top, but I can relate to the less outlandish ones."

The waitress returned with the drinks and told them that the meal wouldn't be long.

Matt sipped at the double measure of Glenfiddich single malt whisky, which had no mixer or ice added to dilute and ruin the mellow taste.

"Any progress with the ongoing case?" Beth said.

"Not since Norman Chandler, who is a senior ballistics officer, confirmed that the slugs recovered from the dead protection officer at the flat in Stratford were a match to the other murders."

"No other trace evidence?"

Matt shook his head. "All we do know for certain to date is that the guy who attempted to kill our witness is the one seen leaving the house in Bethnal Green after he'd murdered Frankie Dawson."

"Seems strange that he hasn't been picked up by any CCTV footage."

"He'll be well aware that technology could put him in close proximity to a scene where he has committed a murder. I don't think that he would use public transport or carry a mobile phone. Perhaps he drives to within what he considers is a safe distance from where he has decided to commit a crime."

"What's your next move?"

"To eat. The waitress is bearing down on us with our evening meal."

They stopped talking shop and enjoyed the food. After they had eaten and Matt had washed it down with another Scotch, Beth drove them home in her Audi, and within a few minutes they were in bed, naked, not having sex, but making love; there *was* a difference. It was a time when they truly became one, sharing the pleasure that was both physical *and* cerebral; an act that brought them as close as it is possible for two people to be.

Almost dawn on the last Friday of May, and he had settled in woods just ten or twelve feet from a paved trail that led from the A236 – the Croydon Road – to Seven Islands Pond, which was situated at Mitcham Common. The maroon Ford Cortina that he had driven to within half a mile of the location had been owned by his now deceased uncle, Arthur, and was old enough to be microchip-free, without any inbuilt technology to track its movements or the locations of where it had been. The false registration plates would not lead to his door, should they for any reason be caught on plate recognition cameras in the area of where he made his next kill. He had kept the vehicle because it was in such good condition, and garaged it in the lockup he rented for cash under an assumed name. The lockup was just a fifteen minute walk from his house.

He had selected his prey before his attempt to kill Jaz Walker had gone pear-shaped, and when the police had interviewed him again, he had an alibi that stood up to scrutiny. Time had gone by, and now he was back on track, all set to resume taking out what he regarded to be legitimate targets. The wait was part of the process; a time of anticipation. He unzipped the small green rucksack that he had brought with him, removed the pistol, checked that the magazine was fully loaded, and screwed the silencer to the end of the gun's threaded barrel. He then pulled on latex gloves and placed the balaclava on the top of his head, ready to pull down when he made his move. Just ten minutes later, he heard the distant slap of trainer soles on asphalt. His quarry was approaching fast, unknowingly racing headlong to meet her executioner, and then, should there be one, her maker. Looking through the leafy branches of a large evergreen bush, he could see her drawing closer, to wait until she was less than forty feet away from his position before making his move.

Up with the lark, to leave her husband, Terry, fast asleep at home, April Henderson left Reed Lodge, which was part of a large complex of flats on Windmill Road, to make her way into the adjacent common in Mitcham, South London; a four hundred and sixty acre tract of woodland, ponds and lakes in an idyllic setting.

April had her shoulder-length honey blonde hair worn in a ponytail, and carried her keys and smartphone in a bum bag that was attached to her waist by a nylon belt. She was slim, five foot ten inches tall and ultra-fit. Running was her main leisure activity, and she had completed ten marathons to date, and also did weight training and was a student of taekwondo, a Korean martial art which was a physical discipline and gave her both the confidence and the mental strength to cope with most problems that you needed fortitude to meet head on, deal with and get past in life. Marrying Terry three years ago on her twenty third birthday had been the best decision, to date, that she had ever made. They loved each other to bits, and the first floor apartment they lived in across the road from the common was both modern and spacious. Terry was a qualified chef, now the proud joint owner of a small but fashionable restaurant, Chic Cuisine, which was just a few minutes' drive from the Addington Golf Club, which he was now a member of and enjoyed a round when time allowed, usually one morning a week.

There was no warning of anything untoward. The trail ahead was clear, and April was running on automatic, wool-gathering as she headed towards Seven Islands Pond.

Pulling the balaclava down over his face, he stepped out onto the path, to point the pistol at the woman's chest.

April came to a juddering stop, shocked by the masked man's sudden appearance in front of her. There was a frozen moment in time that lasted no more than three seconds as, unmoving, they faced each other.

"If you attempt to run away or scream for help, I'll shoot you," he said. "Understand?"

"Yes," April said. "What do you want?"

"I want you to walk slowly off the path, into the trees. Do it now."

Rape, April thought. This bastard is going to rape me, or attempt to, and then probably shoot me. I'm in a truly life or death situation, and I have to keep calm and ensure that I walk away from this.

Walking behind her, keeping his distance as they moved through the undergrowth and trees, he picked his spot and told her to stop, turn around, remove the bum bag, drop it on the ground and then step away from it.

"If you make any sudden move, it will be your last," he said. "Just do exactly what I tell you to, and you'll get to survive."

After following his instructions, April stood with her arms hanging loosely at her sides, presenting no threat to the armed man.

"So far so good," he said. "What's your name?"

"April. What's yours?"

"If I told you, I'd have to kill you," he said with a crooked smile. "Are you single or married?"

"Married."

"To a man or a woman?"

"A man."

"Do you have any children?"

"Not yet," April said, and then stiffened her limbs, widened her eyes, parted her lips and stared intently over his right shoulder.

His reactions were almost instantaneous. Her sudden attention to something appearing behind them caused him to whip around to face whoever was there.

April did not hesitate. Her ploy had worked. Quick thinking gave her the chance she needed to defend herself, and she took it, leaping forward to turn sideways and deliver a powerful spinning kick to her assailant's head.

Even as he realised that he had been duped and turned back to confront her, he was struck a blow to his left temple which knocked him off his feet, dazing him and causing him to fall to the ground and lose his grip on the gun.

With only a split second to decide what to do next, April opted to run deeper into the trees to get away from the scene and from the man whom she fully believed had intended to kill her. Self-preservation took over. She could have approached him and attempted to deliver another kick that would fully rob him of consciousness, but he had climbed to his knees to face her, and so she could not have taken him by surprise a second time, and also did not know how physically capable he was. To underestimate someone like him could prove to be folly, and maybe even fatal. It was only after she had run at full pelt through the wood for perhaps twenty seconds that the loss of her bum bag came to mind. The shock of being faced by the gunman, and the impulse to flee had triggered her actions. Nothing else had come to mind. *Shit! It did now. Her phone was in the bag she had dropped, along with her house keys.* There was no way she could contact the emergency services to summon the police, and going back to where she had been confronted was out of the question. By now the man would have most likely picked up the gun and her bag, and would hopefully be beating a hasty retreat from the area. Or would he be attempting to follow her? She had no way of knowing, and so initially just kept running with no intention of stopping until she reached home, but almost immediately had second thoughts. If he was on her tail and caught sight of her, he could shoot her in the back, which felt as though there was a large gun range target pinned to it. Stopping next to a thicket of mature rhododendrons, she knelt down and rolled underneath the flower-laden branches into the gloomy space beneath them, intending to stay hidden until she thought it was safe to leave.

Using his right hand, he snatched up the pistol from the carpet of dead leaves and brittle twigs that covered the ground, and with his left he grasped the strap of his rucksack and looped it over his head before setting off in pursuit of the bitch who had got the better of him by kicking him so hard in the side of the head that not only did his face hurt, but his neck ached with what he thought was whiplash from the force of the blow. When he caught up with her, she would suffer a great deal of pain before he killed her.

Keeping as still as a statue, April waited, in no hurry to crawl out from the dark, dank sanctuary of the shrubbery that was shielding her from sight. Within no more than forty-five seconds, she heard the crunch of dead leaves and other detritus, and looking out from the safety of what she thought of as an animal's murky lair into the band of light below the drooping mass of leaf laden branches, she saw the lower half of his jean clad legs above the grey and white trainers he was wearing. There was nothing she could do but remain silent, unmoving, and hope that he did not find her.

He was wasting valuable time. There was no sight nor sound of her. She had either kept running or hidden, and so every second that passed gave him less time to quit the area before she raised the alarm. He turned and attempted to hurriedly retrace his steps to where she had dropped the bum bag, but lost his bearings in the trees, to come to the path further along from the spot where he had accosted her.

Fuck it! He needed to get to his car and head back to the lockup. Everything seemed to be going to shit of late. Mitcham Common and roads around it would be swarming with cops as soon as she reached home and called 999. He couldn't afford to run, though, that would attract attention. All he dare do was walk briskly and hope that she had found a hiding place in the wood and would stay there for a while, afraid to come out, not knowing that he had given up his search for her.

To April it seemed a small eternity before the motionless figure, standing so close to where she was concealed from his view, turned and walked away. That he had vanished from sight did not encourage her to crawl out into the daylight, though. Perhaps he was waiting nearby and thought – rightly – that she had gone to ground under the rhododendrons. Having been kicked so hard in the head just a few minutes ago, he would perhaps be far too wary to enter what could turn out be as dangerous as a lion's den. His eyes would have to adjust to the darkness, which would put him in danger. Slowly, tentatively, April reached out and grasped a tennis ball-sized piece of rock and made ready to strike him with it if he decided to check out her hidey-hole. The passage of time became fluid. Waiting for what may have been no more than fifteen minutes or over an hour, she slowly moved forward on her belly, using elbows and feet to propel her to the edge of the green curtain of leaves, to look left and right, still cautious, not wholly convinced that he had gone.

CHAPTER SIXTEEN

PETE and Jeff arrived at the flat on Windmill Road in Mitcham just a couple of hours after the incident had taken place. Due to the fact that a guy armed with a handgun and wearing a balaclava had confronted a female jogger was enough for DCI John Stott, the leader of the attending MIT – Major Investigation Team – to contact the SCU, after he had interviewed the woman and was almost certain that the man who had confronted her was in all probability the perpetrator tagged The Killer Clown.

Pete and Jeff met John Stott outside the complex of flats, eager to be given details.

"The actual victim in this case is the guy who approached a young woman by the name of April Henderson," John said. "She was jogging on a trail through the Common when he came out from hiding and pointed a gun at her. He began to ask her questions, and she suddenly stared over his shoulder, pointedly, as if someone had appeared behind him. He took the bait, turned to see who was there, and she high-kicked him in the side of the head with enough force to knock him down. She then ran off through the trees and hid under some bushes. The shooter had picked on an athlete who is also into martial arts."

"Did she give you a description of him?" Pete said.

"She told me he was maybe five-ten, and that he was wearing a balaclava, navy fleece, blue jeans, scuffed trainers and latex gloves. All she could see of him were his eyes, and said that they were dark brown. That's it. She stayed undercover for quite a while before daring to leave her hiding place and run home, so he had plenty of time to get away, although we still have units patrolling the area."

"Didn't she have a mobile?" Jeff said.

"It was in a bum bag along with her house keys, and he'd told her to take it off and drop it, once he'd ordered her off the trail and into the trees. Accompanied by a female officer, I drove her to the Common, and she showed us the spot where she had dropped the bag, and it was still there with her phone and keys inside it. Nothing had been taken."

"She was bloody lucky," Pete said.

"I think she had the presence of mind, plus the confidence and ability to distract him and deal with the situation. If one of the suspects you have from the image put out on the TV has a bruise on the left side of his face, then it could be a slam dunk."

"Does she live alone?" Jeff said.

John shook his head. "No, she's married. Her husband is with her in the flat. His name is Terry."

"We'll have a word with her, seeing as we're here."

"Fine. I told her that your squad was involved, due to this case now being a joint investigation, following the murder of the officer at the high rise in Stratford, so we'll be sharing everything we get. We have a forensic team on the way to the Common to search for any trace evidence, although the only contact between them was her foot to his face, so I doubt they'll turn anything worthwhile up, unless he bled."

Pete and Jeff went up to the first floor flat, displayed their ID to the man who answered the door, and were invited inside.

"Would you like a cup of coffee?" April asked when they had settled in easy chairs in the lounge.

"That would be good," Pete said.

Jeff shook his head. "Thanks, but no, I'm fine."

"I'll make it," Terry said, heading out of the bright and airy lounge into the kitchen. "How do you like it?"

"Straight from the pot, strong and black," Pete said, and to his wife, "Detective Chief Inspector Stott relayed to us what you'd told him, Mrs Henderson."

"Call me April. No need to be so formal."

"Okay, April. Is there anything additional you can tell us that you didn't think of until now, however insignificant it may seem to be?"

April closed her eyes to relive the confrontation with the man that she knew without any doubt had intended to shoot her. After a few seconds she said, "He had a small rucksack hanging from his left shoulder by a strap. It was olive-green and appeared to be made of nylon."

"Will you please run through everything that happened from when he first confronted you?" Pete said, taking a small Sony digital voice recorder from a pocket of his bomber jacket. "And I'd like to record it, if you don't mind. It will save my colleague from having to write it all down in his notebook."

"No problem," April said. "But I don't think I'll be able to add anything to what I told the other detective."

Terry appeared, to place a mug of coffee in front of Pete on a coaster atop the low hardwood table.

It was half an hour later when Pete and Jeff left the flat and headed back to base.

"Anything worthwhile?" Matt said when they entered the squad room.

Pete took the voice recorder from his jacket, handed it to Matt and said, "Two things that we can add to the mix. The guy asked the woman, April Henderson, some questions at gunpoint, and he was carrying a rucksack. Everything she could tell us is on the recorder."

Matt listened to the interview, twice. There was seemingly nothing to further the investigation. The perpetrator's height and build fitted the description of the guy who'd attempted to kill Jasmin Walker at the tower block and shot the detective who'd been guarding her. There had been no trace evidence, other than confirmation that the bullets recovered from the dead officer were a match to those from the four previous murders they were investigating. Due to the fact that no shots had been fired during the latest incident on Mitcham Common, all they could hope for was that there had been some transfer between the two individuals, but he didn't hold out much hope, because even if the kick to the shooter's head had broken the skin, the balaclava would have most likely absorbed any resulting blood from seeping through it.

Arriving home at seven p.m., Matt joined Beth out on the large deck, where she was sitting at a timber picnic table doing some work on her laptop. They made small talk, after Beth had gone to make them coffee. Initially, they discussed the sudden natural death of the local vicar, Simon Coulthard, who had suffered a massive cardiac infarction the previous day as he performed a marriage ceremony, causing him to drop his bible and fall like a felled tree between the would-be bride and groom; dead before his skull was fractured against the solid stone floor of the thirteenth-century church.

"Sounds like an omen," Beth said. "It might take the couple that were about to tie the knot quite a while to get over the trauma and set another date."

"True," Matt said. "Which brings to mind the fact that we seem to always be too busy to get hitched."

"What are you suggesting?"

"That I make an honest woman of you."

"And an honest man of you?"

Matt grinned. He doubted that he'd ever met a single person in his life who was *truly* honest. To his way of thinking, everyone, with the exception of babies and young children, had a cupboard with skeletons hanging in it of deeds done and untruths told, which they kept as secrets mouldering in dimly lit corners of their minds. Perhaps his outlook was tainted by the years that he had been a copper. Surely there were a great many honest folk in the world, with no unsavoury memories of past words or conduct to burden them with guilt.

"As soon as this case is put to bed."

"Any progress with it?"

Matt took a slim voice recorder from an inside pocket of the lightweight blouson jacket that he was still wearing and slid it across to her. "Put your criminal psychologist cap on and see what you make of this," he said. "It's a copy of an interview that Pete had with a young woman who was waylaid on Mitcham Common by an armed man wearing a balaclava, who we believe to be the Killer Clown.

Beth took a sip of her coffee and then played the recording. When it ended, she rewound it and listened to it again, as Matt had done. The main point of interest to her was the short conversation between the gunman and the woman. April Henderson said that the man had told her that if she attempted to run away or scream for help, he would shoot her. She had asked him what he wanted, and was ordered to walk into the woods, and that he kept his distance as they moved away from the path, to where he picked a spot and told her to stop, turn around, remove the bum bag, drop it on the ground and then step away from it.

He had then said that if she made any sudden move it would be her last, and that if she behaved, she would get to survive. He had then questioned her, asking what her name was, and whether she was single or married. She had told him her name, and that she *was* married, and he wanted to know if it was to a man or a woman. April said that it was to a man, to which he inquired as to whether they had any children. Her reply was, not yet, and at that point she had widened her eyes and stared over his shoulder, which caused him to turn and snatch a quick look behind him, giving her the opportunity to kick him in the head and run off into the trees.

Beth admired the way that April had kept her cool and used an inspired act of distraction to give her the chance to take proactive defensive action and turn the situation around.

"Any initial thoughts come to mind?" Matt said as Beth switched the recorder to off and placed it back in front of him.

"I'm amazed that she managed not only to distract him, but had the wherewithal to kick him in the head."

"She's into martial arts, taekwondo to be precise, and told Pete and Jeff that she was surprised that the guy had remained conscious, due to the force she kicked him with. He should have bruising and possibly a cut to the left side of his face, though."

"The questions that he asked her are a little bizarre," Beth said. "You have a serial killer who does not sexually assault or rob his victims, just shoots them. And I would take it as a given that he asked the first two women he murdered the same questions."

"Does that give you an understanding as to why he's doing it?"

"In all probability his questions are related in some way to whatever his motive is, but at the moment I can't fathom it out. I'll make a note of what he asked April, give it some thought and do some research."

"Okay, no more work talk for now. Do you want to go out for a meal, or stay home?"

"Home. I took some chicken out of the freezer last night and plan on grilling it with a spicy coating and serving it up with baked potatoes and a green bean salad tossed in a garlic dressing."

"Sounds good to me. I'll go take a shower while you work your culinary magic."

CHAPTER SEVENTEEN

DETECTIVE Chief Inspector John Stott was the SIO (senior investigating officer) of one of four major investigation teams, each consisting of fifty staff. The teams were part of the Specialist Crime and Operations Directorate's Homicide Command in London, which is split geographically into six units: West, Central, East, Northwest and South, each led by a Detective Superintendent. And each of the Command Units has four investigation teams under its wing. John Stott was leader of the South Unit, and the main thrust of his team's current interest was in – jointly with the Special Crimes Unit – identifying and apprehending the serial killer who had shot and killed DC Bill Spencer.

With copies from the SCU of all the paperwork and photographs relating to the serial murderer tagged the Killer Clown, John instructed members of his team to reinterview all the men that resembled the wanted man, to reassess their alibis for the pertinent dates, especially that of the fourth of May, when the protection officer had been murdered whilst on duty at the flat in Kingsley Hamlets. It was a task that would take time, due to the growing number of names and addresses involved.

It was the eighth of June. He had taken a few days off work, while the bruising to the side of his face, which had been inflicted by the bitch who'd kicked him on Mitcham Common, faded. The woollen balaclava had, to a degree, softened the blow, no doubt lessening the damage. His worry, initially, was that detectives would call to see him again, due to him being on their list of persons of interest. Thankfully they didn't.

Feeling totally safe again, he spent the evening at his girlfriend's flat, to enjoy a meal accompanied by a couple of glasses of what she considered to be an excellent Chardonnay, but in reality was an inexpensive Australian wine that he surmised she had picked up for six or seven quid from a supermarket or her local garage shop. After the meal, they went to bed, where he took her doggy style, holding her hips as both of them found a synchronicity of movement, with her shunting backwards against him faster and faster to fully encompass his turgid penis, as her shapely buttocks – the left adorned with the tattoo of a blood red rose on a thorny stem – repeatedly slapped into him until they both cried out simultaneously with pleasure and relief as they came.

Before leaving, he told her that he would have stayed over, but with having bookwork that needed doing for the next day, he couldn't. He also told her that he loved her, which he didn't, because he had never experienced that particular emotion in his life, and was positive that he never would. Saying that he planned on booking a table for Saturday evening at a swish restaurant, and that he would give her a call when he had, he drove towards home. On a whim, he parked next to the pavement seventy or eighty yards further along from the Wolf Trap, a recently opened pub in Tooting Bec that stayed open until midnight. He ordered a large brandy and dry ginger, to then sit on a stool at the long marble effect counter and people watch, giving young females the main focus of his attention, evaluating them in the same way he thought a big game hunter would view intended prey; for that was what he now was, a predator whose urge to kill had been instigated since he had found himself in possession of a gun taken from the mugger who, at a later date, he had located and killed. The handgun had been the catalyst which had driven him to risk everything, by letting his inner self – his subliminal innermost feelings – be liberated. Perhaps he lacked empathy in the way that Putin and the seemingly growing number of other homicidal autocratic psychopaths did. Everyone was programmed to follow their own path. His reasons to kill were not for profit, though. He had acknowledged years ago that he harboured an innate dislike of humanity in general. There were eight billion people in the world, which was far too many, and the projection was that the number would rise to almost ten billion by the end of the century. Pandemics, war, climate change, disease, famine and natural disasters could not stop the masses from procreating like rats or rabbits, and so he would – if only marginally – reduce the number of people on the planet by culling young women, who would therefore never bear children, which would stop the future generations that they would have been responsible for bringing into the world from ever existing. Plus, on an even more basic level he had – since becoming the owner of now two handguns – felt empowered by the cold, steel weapons that spat death and filled him with an incomparable rapture. Taking the lives of others, because he could, was as good as it got.

At a couple of minutes past eleven p.m. on the evening of the fifteenth of June, Melanie Parker and Jodie Coleman left the Stag Inn on the Brighton Road in Sutton, having been for a meal and just two small glasses of wine each. The two women ran a successful bridal shop, selling ready-made, made-to-measure and designer bridal gowns, as well as outfits for other members of wedding parties. Melanie waved as Jodie drove out of the gravelled car park at the rear of the pub to head for her home in Epsom. Thumbing the remote to unlock the diamond white Mini Countryman Hybrid – which she had only purchased the previous month – Melanie approached the vehicle. It had been a long day, she was tired and looking forward to being back at her flat on Mill Lane in Carshalton, which was less than a ten minute drive away, but then, before she had time to reach the car a figure appeared from thick shrubbery which bordered the poorly lit car park. Stopping, she studied the man at the other side of her Mini. He was wearing dark clothing, some kind of mask, which she believed to be a balaclava, and was pointing a gun at her.

"Scream or attempt to run away and I'll shoot you," he said in a low, calm voice.

Melanie felt fixed in place, as if every muscle in her body had seized up, preventing her from doing anything but just stand in place. A myriad thoughts ran through her mind, the foremost being that this man presumably planned on raping or robbing her, or both. When able, and with a trembling voice, she said to her assailant, "Do you know who I am?"

"No," he said. "Tell me. But first I want you to walk into the bushes behind your car. Do it now."

There was nothing that Melanie could think to do but comply. He stood to the side as she somehow forced her shaking legs to move into the deeper gloom of the shrubbery at the side of the car park.

"That's far enough," he said. "Stop, drop your shoulder bag and key fob, turn around to face me, and then tell me your name."

"I'm Melanie Parker," she said after complying with his instructions."

"Well, Melanie, in just a few seconds time you'll be dead. How does that make you feel?"

"My father is Jerry Parker. Perhaps you've heard of him."

"Yes, if he's the fat cat businessman at this side of the river who is rumoured to also be a hoodlum. Should I give a shit?"

"He will pay you a great deal of money if you don't harm me."

"This isn't about money, Melanie," he said, before shooting her in the crotch, to relish the sight of her crumpling to the ground, to cup her groin with both hands as she curled up into a ball, mewling like a kicked cat as he knelt several feet away to, after several seconds, administer the coup de grace; a death blow of mercy as the French would term it, to end the suffering of a severely wounded person or animal. After being shot in the forehead she should have instantly died, but amazingly her blood-covered right hand left her crotch, to be raised up, fingers clawing jerkily at the air for no more than three seconds before her arm fell back to the ground, limp and lifeless. It was an out of the ordinary event that alarmed and amused him in equal parts. Had she still had, if only for a second or two, awareness of the fact that she was dying? And if so, he wondered what scrambled thoughts she took with her into oblivion. Time to go. He tucked one of his small cellophane covered signature pictures of a clown's face under the neckline of the blouse she wore, took time to remove the silencer from the pistol and pocket the two parts, thinking that they went together like fish and chips, bacon and eggs, or perhaps Ant and Dec, complementing each other perfectly.

Returning through bushes and trees to the three foot high wall at the rear of the car park, he swapped the balaclava for a baseball cap and removed the latex gloves he had worn throughout the event. Checking that there was no one in sight, he climbed over the wall and casually walked back the way he had come. He had not selected and stalked the young woman he had just slain. He had parked his car a ten minute walk from the pub, to prowl through back streets in the direction of the Brighton road, to pause as he passed by the rear of the Stag Inn, having spotted two women exit the back door of the pub and walk across the car park. One had climbed into a car and driven away, leaving the other to approach another vehicle, after waving goodnight to whom he supposed was her friend.

Moving fast, he had leapt over the low wall and made his way to the right into undergrowth, to don the gloves and balaclava before coming out at the other side of the car that the remaining female had already used her electronic fob to unlock. Now, having done the deed, unmindful of the two muted shots he had fired, due to the loud voices, laughter and music emanating from open windows of the pub, he sauntered back to his car and drove it to the lockup, which he thought of as being the Cortina's lair.

Once home, he showered, ate a large slice of pork pie with chutney and a bag of crisps, and washed the snack down with a tumblerful of Jack Daniel's, to drink in celebration of his latest conquest. It was very late when he masturbated in the shower with vivid thoughts of the young woman clutching herself, suffering shock and pain as she fell to the ground, to look him in the eyes as he aimed the gun at her head, knowing that she was about to die. He had not asked her the set of questions that he had put to his previous victims. There was no need to, because they were not going to survive the meeting whatever answers they gave. He decided to cool it for a while, enjoy the speculation of the media, and the actions of the police who would presumably be milling around like blind mice in a coal cellar, unable to find any clues that would lead them to him.

CHAPTER EIGHTEEN

THE owner of the Stag Inn, Ian Fowler, said goodnight to the last two customers and locked the entrance door to the pub and switched off the external lights. He then made his way to the rear door, to go outside and check the picnic benches on the wide patio that ran the full length of the building, knowing that some punters left their empty glasses for someone else, invariably him, to take inside. The sight of the white Mini Countryman parked at the rear of the car park concerned him a little. He knew that it belonged to a young woman by the name of Melanie, and that she called in a couple of evenings a week, to usually meet up with a girlfriend called Jodie. Perhaps she had felt unwell and called for an Uber. He walked towards the vehicle and then around it, feeling very uneasy. The woman was not in the car, and he had no way of knowing where she actually was, but entered the adjacent shrubbery to look for her, fearing that she had been taken ill and possibly entered the foliage to throw up, and may have passed out. Even under the cold glow from the moon above it was difficult to see any details on the ground. Only as his eyes adjusted to the semidarkness was he able to make out a shoulder bag and a car key fob next to the shape of a body lying on its side just a few feet away from him. Hunkering down next to it, he saw that the eyes were wide open, fixed, and that there was a small round dark hole in the forehead, from which a ribbon of blood had run down the side of her face to pool in her ear. Standing, fearful that whoever had shot her was still in the vicinity, he hurried out into the car park and ran to the pub door, to slam it closed behind him, lock it, and go behind the bar to pick his phone up off the shelf behind it and dial 999.

Within twenty minutes, half a dozen police vehicles and an ambulance had arrived, to park on the street outside the car park. Paramedics attended the body, to verify that the person was deceased. After viewing the corpse, a plainclothes detective interviewed Ian, to take an initial statement.

"What reason did you have to check the car park after closing time, sir?" Detective Sergeant Roy Lester said to Ian as they sat either side of a table in the bar. Ian was nursing a double brandy, and had already had one before the police arrived, due to the state of shock he had suffered on discovering the dead body.

"I locked the front door and then, as usual, I checked out back, because some customers leave their glasses on the picnic tables. That's when I saw that there was still a car out there. I recognised it as belonging to a young woman who calls in for a bar meal a couple of times a week."

"Why did you go into the bushes?"

"Because there was no sign of her and I reckoned that she must be nearby, so I decided to look for her, in case she was ill and in need of help. When I pushed through a gap in the bushes I saw a bag and key fob on the ground, and she was laid quite near them."

"Did you know the woman?"

"I knew that her first name was Melanie, nothing else."

"How did you know that she was dead?" Roy said.

"Because she wasn't moving, her eyes were wide open, and she had what I'm pretty sure was a fucking bullet hole in her forehead."

"Did you touch anything?"

"No. I came straight back into the pub and phoned the emergency services."

"Did you notice any guy in the pub taking a particular interest in her?"

"No. As far as I know she and her friend, whom I believe is called Jodie, didn't appear to talk to anyone else."

"Do you have CCTV cameras operating?"

"Only one covering the car park," Ian said. "As a general rule customers want privacy when they're out having a meal and a drink. They don't want to be videoed. We already live in an Orwellian, semi totalitarian state."

"Whatever," Roy said. "Whether it seems to be authoritarian to you or not, we need the tape or disk from this evening. And the pub and car park are now a crime scene, and you'll be required to give an official statement in due course."

"I live above the pub."

"No problem, sir, but you will not be able to open up to the public again until we give you the all-clear to do so."

"Does that mean you'll reimburse me for lost revenue?"

"Afraid not. Just consider it as being your public duty to comply."

"Like I said, shades of Orwell's 1984."

"A murder has been committed on your premises, sir. Forensic technicians will be here very soon to evaluate any evidence that has been left at the scene, and your cooperation will be highly appreciated."

There was no answer to that. The detective was just doing his job, but Ian couldn't help but wish that the young woman had not been murdered on his property, which he immediately felt guilty for thinking. If he closed his eyes he could see the total absence of expression in her eyes and on her pale, doll-like face. He had savings, and so a couple of days with the pub shut was manageable. And it dawned on him that now being the scene of a heinous crime, it would in all probability increase the number of patrons to his door. It would promote the Stag Inn in the media, which gave him rise to recall that the showman P.T Barnum had once said, 'There's no such thing as bad publicity.' It was a win-win situation which in time would give him a little celebrity status for being the guy who had found the murder victim, and that in turn would almost certainly bring patrons to his pub like ants to sugar.

Roy got up and made his way out into the car park, where he phoned DCI John Stott to inform him that the victim had with little doubt been shot to death by the perpetrator tagged as the Killer Clown, who had murdered their late colleague, DC Bill Spencer.

John picked his phone up off the bedside table and checked the caller ID before accepting the call. He and his wife, Faye, had only been in bed for thirty minutes, and he had been on the cusp of sleep, half dreaming when the phone had started buzzing like a wasp in an upturned jam jar.

"Make this good, Roy," John said as he switched on the lamp. "Tell me that something has happened that is so bad you felt the need to interrupt my beauty sleep."

"A fatal shooting at the rear of the Stag Inn on the Brighton Road in Sutton, boss. The victim, a young woman, was shot in the belly and the head. It's odds on that the doer was the guy who shot Bill. I took the liberty of checking the victim, and there was a small picture of a clown's face in a sealed packet tucked in the front of her blouse."

"Who else have you contacted?"

"CSIs and a pathologist, they're on the way. I thought that you'd want to visit the scene."

"You thought right," John said before ending the call.

"Work?" Faye said as he climbed out of bed and began to get dressed.

"What else? The serial killer who murdered Bill Spencer has been at it again. He's shot a young woman in a pub car park, over in Sutton."

"Do you want a coffee to go, in your thermal mug?"

"That would be good," John said as he finished dressing and brought up the number of DCI Matt Barnes on his phone, which was now in his contact list, to speed dial it.

Matt was burning the midnight oil, sitting at a table in the lounge and reading through notes on persons of interest who had either been unable to provide satisfactory accounts for the times of the previous murders, or whose only alibis had been furnished by wives, girlfriends or close friends, who may or may not have been telling the truth. Pete had obtained copies of photos from driving licences of all initial suspects, and they had been shown to Jasmin Walker by the Witness Protection Service, but she had not been able to positively identify any of them as being the man she had seen at the house in Bethnal Green, and subsequently at her mother's flat in Stratford. The problem with the photos was that they were in most instances dated, and people aged, changed hairstyles, and could look quite different to when they had been issued their licences. Matt had now amassed a personal shortlist of twenty individuals, though, and intended to reinterview both them and whoever had vouched for their whereabouts on the pertinent dates and times of the murders. Enough for now, he was ready to put the paperwork aside and go to bed, where Beth would no doubt be fast asleep. That was when his mobile rang.

"Hope I woke you up," John said when Matt took the call. "One of my detectives did the same to me, with good reason."

"Which is?"

"Another murder. Same MO as the two that landed the case on your desk, and he left a picture of a clown's face."

"Where?"

"In bushes at the rear of the Stag Inn on the Brighton Road in Sutton, at the side of the car park."

"I'll be there in approximately forty-five minutes," Matt said before ending the call.

Beth was coming out of the bedroom, pulling on her dressing gown, as Matt reached the top of the stairs.

"You look as if you've got a head of steam up," Beth said. "Why?"

"I just got a call from John Stott, the DCI of the major investigation team that we're working this current case with. There's been another murder, in Sutton, and John says there was a pic of a clown's face left on the body."

"Was it another female?"

"Yeah," Matt said as he went into the bedroom to change into street clothes from the shorts and tee shirt he was wearing. "Another young woman in the wrong place at the wrong time."

"Any other details?"

"Not yet. I'll find out when I get there."

Less than five minutes later, Matt gave Beth a hug and a kiss at the front door, climbed into his Vectra and headed for the pub in Sutton.

CHAPTER NINETEEN

JOHN Stott met Matt in the car park of the Stag Inn. John had reached the scene before him, to park up on the street behind a line of official vehicles. There was a Forensic Services transit van and a distinctive, instantly recognisable archaic yellow Citroën among them, which Matt knew belonged to Dr Roshana Anwar, one of the duty Home Office pathologists who regularly turned up at murder scenes. DS Roy Lester was in the car park and was relieved to see his boss, to figuratively hand over the baton for him to run with.

"Bring me up to speed, Roy," John said.

"The deceased is over there, behind the bushes at the edge of the car park. The pathologist is currently carrying out her examination as we speak, and the CSIs are searching the area."

"Anything else?"

"I'm advised that the victim's shoulder bag and her car key fob are on the ground near the body, and a CSI said that her mobile phone and purse are still in it, and that the bag was fastened, so it would appear it hadn't been touched. He also showed me the pic of the clown that was found tucked in the neckline of her blouse. I used my phone to take shots of the front and back of it. And there is a CCTV recording in the pub that includes what happened prior to the murder, but the quality is crap."

"Show me the pics you took, before I see the video," John said as he saw Matt Barnes climb out of his car on the other side of the street and make his way into the car park. He paused and walked towards him and they shook hands.

"What have we got?" Matt said.

"The trademark clown pic, which is with Lenny Newton, the lead crime scene tech. My DS got to take a couple of shots of it, which he was about to show me."

Roy brought the images up on screen. The first was of a clown's face, which was dissimilar to the ones left at the previous scenes. The unfunny visage was of some guy wearing a curly bright green wig, large pillar box red pompom nose, and white facial paint with rosy cheeks. He was smiling broadly, displaying a mouth full of tartar-coated teeth, and was winking at the camera that had taken the original photo. The second pic was of the message on the back, which read: **ON WITH THE MOTLEY, THE POWDER AND THE PAINT. DID YOU MISS ME? IS IT WORRISOME TO HAVE NO FUCKING IDEA OR CLUE WHATSOEVER AS TO WHO I MIGHT BE?**

"The callous, cold-blooded bastard thinks that what he does is bloody comical," John said. "But we'll have the last laugh when we take him down."

"Nothing else?" Matt said as Roy pocketed his phone.

"The CCTV footage of the car park," John said. "Let's go and see it."

Ian Fowler, the landlord, was sitting at a table in the large lounge of the pub with a freshly poured tumbler of brandy in his hand and was feeling half-pissed. The shock of finding the murdered woman was still as fresh in his mind as a newly laid egg. The alcohol was a buffer of sorts to the indelible image of her waxen looking face, and the empty vacant expression of total lifelessness in her sightless eyes, which bulged below the penny-sized bullet hole in her forehead. Violent death was not something he was familiar with. He had never served in the armed forces, and apart from the thankfully infrequent drunken scuffle, which usually took place between punters in the car park, he had not come face to face with anything as disturbing as what he had been distraught by tonight.

"Are you okay, Ian?" Matt said to the obviously shaken landlord, having been given his name by DS Roy Lester.

Ian shook his head, "No, far from it. I served that woman tonight. She was smiling and full of life, and now she's as dead as mutton, shot in the head by some nutter."

Matt put his hand on the man's shoulder, to give it a light squeeze. "Unfortunately bad shit happens every minute of every day," he said. "The only solace you can take from this is that she didn't suffer."

"Something like this makes me wonder what life's all about," Ian said after taking a gulp of the brandy. "You get up in the morning with no certainty of making it through the day alive."

"That's the cold hard truth," Matt said. "I guess we just have to live in the now and make the best of it."

Leaving the forlorn-looking man to hopefully assimilate what had happened and get past it, Matt joined John and Roy in the small office behind the bar, where the CCTV unit was set up.

"Any second now," Roy said as he played the footage.

The recording was low resolution, very grainy. Matt and John watched as two females came into view from the rear of the pub, to walk across the car park. One of the women climbed into a Kia and, after presumably saying goodnight, she drove out onto the street. The other woman waved and then proceeded in the direction of a white Mini.

"Run that again," Matt said.

Roy rewound to where he had started and hit PLAY. Matt pointed at the screen. "There," he said. "In the background behind the wall."

John and Roy looked at the scene beyond the two women, to where an almost indiscernible figure in deep shadow walked slowly along the pavement, to vanish from view, and as the Kia disappeared, the now lone woman stopped in her tracks as a masked figure appeared in front of her, holding a gun in his hand, pointing it at her. Whatever he had said to her would never be known, but she walked at gunpoint into the shrubbery. There was no sound on the recording, so the gunshots that had taken her life were not heard. Matt was positive that there would have been two, as had been inflicted on each of the previous female victims; one to the lower abdomen and one to the head. On screen approximately three minutes elapsed before the male figure reappeared, to climb over the wall, now wearing a baseball cap, not a balaclava. The man was almost a silhouette, and therefore the chances of being able to identify him were slim to none.

"The recording is shit," Roy said. "Not state of the art. You get what you pay for, and the camera outside is cheap and not fit for purpose. I would think the best our computer section can do is tweak the contrast and brightness, but that won't enhance the definition."

"The killer wouldn't have known that," Matt said. "He should have seen the camera fixed to the wall. He made a mistake because he's a risk taker."

"He was wearing a ski mask or balaclava when he came into view," Roy said. "He could have seen the camera but not been concerned, because his face was covered."

"True, but he wouldn't have known that the live feed wasn't being viewed. If someone had been watching it, they would have investigated what was happening, or phoned the police."

Matt had seen all there was to see. He left the pub and made his way across the car park, intending to have a word with Roz, if she had completed her examination of the corpse. He was approached by a CSI, who handed him a pair of plastic booties, which he dutifully pulled over his shoes before making his way past the Mini Countryman to enter the bushes, beyond which Roz was standing up, grunting as she placed both hands to the small of her back and massaged it.

"Hey, Roz," Matt said. "What's the problem?"

"I guess spending so many years bending down to examine bodies has caught up with me, Barnes. My back is in half. I need a hot Radox bath and a couple of large Bacardi and Cokes. How are you and the lovely Beth doing?"

"We're both good. Just getting on with getting on."

Roz peeled off her latex gloves and said, "This young woman was shot twice. The kill shot to the head had been from three or four feet away. It was through and through and blew a portion of brain tissue with bone fragments out of the back of her skull. The one to her groin had been taken from further away, to hit solid bone and be deflected out of her left hip. I can see no other injuries or signs of sexual assault. Same as the other two that I performed autopsies on. Looks like you have another sick fuck who won't stop killing until you collar him."

"True. We *will* apprehend him, but if we did tomorrow it wouldn't be soon enough. He doesn't touch or rob his victims. It would appear he is simply a thrill killer with no apparent motive."

"Seems like murder is on the increase, whatever the stats say. I'm called out to more fatal urban stabbings and shootings every year. Back in the day I got breathing space, but now I'm doing more slicing and dicing than ever, and we always seem to have a backlog of homicide and suicide victims on ice, so to speak, waiting to be dissected."

"At least you know that you'll never be made redundant," Matt said. "A large number of people, the vast majority being men, will always have the proclivity to commit murder. It's part of the human condition; an inbuilt malevolent part of some unhinged minds."

"It's pretty depressing to know that serious crime is so rife. The world would be a far better place if people had more respect for each other and could live in harmony."

"I doubt that day will ever come," Matt said. "Good and evil go hand in hand. The law is almost ineffective, and opponents to violence and war are basically pissing in the wind."

"You know how to cheer a girl up, Barnes."

Matt grinned, "I try my best."

"Will you be attending the autopsy of this woman?"

"No, I'll pull rank and send Pete Deakin along to watch you dismantle her."

"Okay. As usual I'll get the results to you in a few days. I doubt that there'll be any surprises. She was shot twice. End of."

As Roz placed her bloodied gloves into a cellophane packet and tossed it into the metal case – that she referred to as her portable morgue – and closed the lid, Matt used his phone to take photos of the corpse, which would soon be A4-sized colour photocopies tacked to one of the whiteboards in the squad room.

"See you around, Barnes," Roz said as she headed for the street, to climb in her car and drive away.

Matt re-entered the pub, let John and Roy know that Roz had left the scene, and that apart from the two signature gunshots; one to the groin and one to the head, the pathologist had not found any other injuries and was almost certain that she had not been sexually assaulted.

"There was nothing else notable on this evening's footage," John said. "The best we can hope for is recovery of the slugs and casings, which will only tell us what we already know, that this was the work of the Killer Clown."

Matt nodded and said, "No one said that catching him would be easy. All the original persons of interest will have to be looked at again, in depth. I daresay that the shooter has been interviewed and provided us with alibis that need to be broken if possible. A family member or co-worker could have lied for him, probably because they believe that he is innocent. Most of these monsters live a double life, and the people closest to them have no idea who they really are."

"Okay, Matt. When I correlate everything available on what went down here I'll get copies of it to you."

"Thanks. Will your detectives inform the next of kin of their loss?"

"Yes. Roy here can have the displeasure of organising that. There should be contact info on her phone. And we can run the plates of her car if need be but I don't think that her identity is in question. What will you be doing?"

"Giving my DI a very early wake-up call, to fill him in with what little we have so far."

Before leaving the scene, Matt located the lead CSI, Lenny Newton, to see if the investigator had found anything worthwhile.

"Hi, Matt," Lenny said. "How come you're out and about so late? Doesn't being a Detective Chief Inspector now cut you some slack?"

My oppo, DCI Stott, heads up the Major Investigation Team that we're working this serial case with, as you no doubt know. He gave me a call, and so here I am."

"Well, all I can tell you is that we haven't found a smoking gun or anything else yet. This shooter is very careful, so any trace evidence we get will be a pleasant surprise."

After a little small talk, Matt left the scene, avoiding the now gathering media people, to climb in his car and speed-dial Pete's number.

The call was accepted after only three rings. "It's late. What's hit the fan, Matt? Are you and Beth okay?"

"We're fine. We have another victim of the unfunny clown, though. I got a call from John Stott, so attended. I took some photos at the scene, which is at the rear of a pub in Sutton, and I'm about to head for the Yard."

"Was it another young woman that got topped?"

"Yeah. Same MO. Shot twice. Nothing taken, and no sign of molestation."

"I'll see you in the squad room, and you can give me all the gory details."

"As usual there are none, Pete. He just shoots them and walks away."

CHAPTER TWENTY

HAVING retrieved phone numbers and addresses from Melanie Parker's smartphone, DS Roy Lester, accompanied by DC Marion Farrell, drove to Copsem Lane in Esher, to stop at a large detached residence which was located in isolation, with grounds of several acres surrounded by a ten foot high wall. Tall brick pillars topped by what appeared to be bronze lions stood either side of fancy wrought iron, electronically operated gates. There was an intercom system set on the right hand pillar, next to a plaque with the inscription Millfield House on it.

"This guy must be seriously rich to own a place like this," Marion said.

"He's Jerry Parker, and owns companies here in the UK and in several other countries," Roy said as he got out of the car and stepped up to the intercom box, to press the stainless steel button below the grill of the speaker.

"Speak," a crackly voice said after five seconds had passed.

"Police," Roy said. "We need to speak to Mr Jerry Parker."

"Hold your ID up to the camera on the pillar."

Roy complied.

"Okay," the disembodied voice said. "Tell me what it's about, because Mr Parker is in bed."

"We have some urgent news that he'll want to be made aware of."

"What news?"

"For his ears only. Do yourself a favour, open the gates and then wake him up."

There was a long pause and then the gates rolled back, their wheels squealing on tracks that needed spraying with WD-40.

Roy drove the unmarked pool Honda through the gates, to follow a long and winding drive that was flanked by mature conifers. Rounding a curve, his headlights illuminated an extremely large regency property, and on reaching it he parked at the foot of wide stone steps leading up to an impressive front door that he decided was no doubt solid oak.

In an annexe at the side of the house, Dean Miller was monitoring screens which displayed live feed from a dozen cameras covering the house and grounds. After opening the gates, he phoned the extension in the first floor master bedroom in which his boss was sleeping.

"Yeah?" Jerry Parker said. "Why the call, Dean?"

"You've got the filth on their way up to the house, boss. The one I spoke to held his ID up to the camera. He's Roy Slater, a detective sergeant with the Met, and he told me that he has some urgent news that you will want to be made aware of."

"What news?"

"He wouldn't say. Said it was for your ears only."

"Okay, I'll talk to them in the lounge. And record it, Dean."

The front door was opened to Roy and Marion by a young geeky looking guy dressed in a tee shirt and jeans. He was of medium height, had longish fair hair, a straggly goatee beard, wore old-fashioned Buddy Holly type glasses with thick lenses, and looked totally unconcerned as to why they were at the house.

"Mr Parker will be with you in a minute," Dean said as he showed them into a large reception room and gestured for them to take a seat, before leaving them and making his way back to the annexe.

"Nice furnishings," Marion said. "There's nothing in here that I could buy with a month's salary, apart from maybe one of the table lamps."

They remained standing until a grey-haired, middle-aged man of medium height and weight entered the room wearing a paisley patterned silk dressing gown and a pair of white moccasin style slippers.

"It's very late, officers. What's the urgent news you've got for me?" Jerry said as he sauntered over to a drinks cabinet and poured a large measure of French cognac into an iconic Bombay Sapphire balloon glass, to swirl the deep reddish brown liquid around before taking a sip.

"There's no easy way to say this, sir. Your daughter, Melanie, was murdered at approximately eleven p.m. last night."

Marion noted that Parker's face was instantly drained of colour, and that the hand he was holding the glass with was trembling, causing the cognac inside it to become agitated.

"I don't believe it," Jerry said in a hardly audible voice. "You must have made a mistake."

Roy withdrew his phone, brought up the picture he had taken of the victim's driving licence, and held it out for Jerry to study.

Jerry took a large gulp of the cognac, set the glass down and approached Roy, to look at the pic and details on the licence and shake his head as his eyes filled with tears. "Did you personally see her body?" he said.

"Yes, she was shot, sir," Roy said as he replaced the phone in his pocket.

"Where did it happen?"

"At the rear of a pub in Sutton."

"Have you caught the shooter?"

"Not as yet."

"What was the motive? Was she robbed and raped? I need to know the truth."

"It is not believed that Melanie was sexually assaulted," Marion said, taking over from Roy. "And nothing appears to have been stolen. We don't yet know the motive for why she or others have been murdered."

"Others?"

"The killer has fatally shot two other young women to our knowledge. He's the perpetrator that the media have tagged the Killer Clown."

"Jesus Christ," Jerry seethed, his cheek muscles bunching and his fists clenching. "You've got a fucking homicidal maniac on the loose, picking women off with total impunity. Why haven't you lifted him?"

"Because he doesn't have any physical contact with his victims, or leave any trace evidence. As far as we know they are complete strangers to him," Roy said.

Jerry took three deep breaths, before turning away from Roy and Marion, to stride back to where he had set his glass down. After picking it up and draining it, he threw it full force at the mirror behind the drinks cabinet, to shatter it, sending countless shards of glittering glass fanning out from the gilt-edged frame. Some hit him, but he took no notice as the main shower of them fell to the carpet.

"I need to see her," Jerry said, turning back to face them. "Where is she?"

"They'll have to perform an autopsy on your daughter, sir," Marion said, noting several cuts to Parker's face from small pieces of the broken mirror. "We'll inform you the second that you or another family member can visit the mortuary to formally identify her."

The now cold gaze that the man fixed Marion with was disconcerting. Gone were the tears, replaced by a totally dispassionate expression.

"It will be me that will identify her," Jerry said. "My wife, Gayle, is currently abroad with a couple of girlfriends, staying at our villa in Marbella. I trust that Melanie's name will not be given to the press until I have had chance to make calls."

"That's a given, sir," Roy said. "Did your daughter have a boyfriend that we need to notify?"

"No. She broke up with a guy over a year ago. As far as I know there was no current man in her life."

"We'll need her ex-boyfriend's name and address if you have it," Marion said.

"His name is James Carter, and he used to live in a mews house on Cavell Place in Highgate, number seven. Maybe he's moved, but I doubt that he's suddenly lost the plot and gone on a killing spree. James was a vegan, pacifist, and a Green activist as I recall, an all-round snowflake."

"Thanks," Marion said as she jotted the information down in her notebook.

"Is that it?" Jerry said. "I've got to phone my wife, and I know that what I have to say will totally destroy her."

"We'll be in touch," Roy said.

"You do that, detective. This fuckwit needs a lot more than being locked up in a maximum security prison for the rest of his life, though. Breathing is too good for him."

"I understand how you feel, sir, but—"

"You have no fucking idea how I feel, son, unless someone that you loved beyond words has been brutally murdered."

Back in the car, heading for the gates, which were opened electronically as they approached them, Marion said, "Parker doesn't strike me as being the type to sit back and let us get on with it."

"Rumour has it that he's his father's son, if you know what I mean," Roy said.

"Who was his father?"

"Vincent Parker; a gangster back in the fifties and sixties. He had a firm operating south of the river during the same period that Charlie and Eddie Richardson had a gang on the same patch. He had legit businesses and kept a very low profile, unlike the Richardson brothers, and also Ronnie and Reggie Kray who ran the East End. Vincent paid his taxes and couldn't be linked to organised crime. His name came up from time to time, but he remained untouchable, up until a car pulled up as he was leaving his office in Croydon with one of his minders. A hitman shot them multiple times. They both bled out on the pavement. That was way back in nineteen sixty-nine."

"Jerry Parker has got to be over sixty years old," Marion said. "He will have only been a kid when his dad was murdered."

"He had a much older brother, Christopher, who took over running the firm, along with their mother. Skip forward sixteen years. Jerry had been educated at an expensive private college and was a city trader with the London Stock Exchange. He had kept straight, but when his brother died from a brain aneurysm, he stepped into the breach and has been the top banana ever since."

"You seem to know a hell of a lot about Parker."

"You've only been with the team for a few months, Marion. Apart from the current ongoing investigations we're working, we also keep tabs on villains like Parker, hoping to pin something on him. When you have the time to, spend it going through the files of individuals that we have a year-round open season on; those that we know are big players, but don't have enough to lift them."

"I'll do that. In the meantime what are we going to do about Melanie's friend, Jodie Coleman? We have her address; it was listed in Melanie's smartphone."

"What do you suggest?"

"I'm not sure. It's very late to doorstep her."

"I think we should. Bad news travels fast. There will be outside broadcast vehicles at the scene by now. We don't want Jodie to get up early to switch on her TV and find out from the mouth of a news anchor that her friend has been murdered, do we?"

"Thoughtful of you, Sarge," Marion said. "But her identity will not be released to the media for the time being."

"Perhaps you're right, but why put off 'til tomorrow what you can do today, especially as Epsom is just a short drive from here?"

CHAPTER TWENTY-ONE

JODIE was startled from what had been a deep sleep, to look at her bedside clock and see that it was almost two-thirty a.m. There was nothing but silence for a few seconds, and then the sound of someone knocking loudly on her front door caused her to become wide awake. Shrugging her dressing gown on over her nightie, she made her way out into the hall, thumbed the outside light on, looked out through the narrow window in the top half of the door, and was faced by a man and woman that she did not recognise.

Taking the lead, Marion held her warrant card up to be examined and said, "I'm Detective Constable Marion Farrell, and my colleague is Detective Sergeant Roy Slater. We need to have a word with you, if you are Jodie Coleman."

"I am," Jodie said. "What is this about?"

"About your friend, Melanie Parker."

Jodie unlocked the door and opened it. Jumbled thoughts began to collide in her mind like bumper cars, and the main one was that she imagined Melanie had been in a road accident on her drive back to her flat in Carshalton.

"What's happened to her?" she said in little more than a whisper as the two detectives entered the bungalow.

"Can we sit down and talk it through?" Marion said.

Leading them into the lounge, Jodie sat in an easy chair, wringing her hands, wanting to hear what she knew would be bad news, but at the same time not wanting to know, because she knew that whatever had happened would be dreadful.

Marion and Roy sat side by side on a two seater sofa, and it was Roy that said, "Can you confirm that you were in the company of Melanie Parker until approximately eleven p.m. last night at the Stag Inn on the Brighton Road in Sutton?"

"Yes. Why?"

"I'm sorry to have to inform you that Melanie has been murdered."

Jodie said nothing. The premise that her best friend and business partner was dead did not compute. It had to be a case of mistaken identity.

After ten seconds of near silence, broken only by the humming of a fridge or freezer emanating from the partly open door that led into the kitchen, Jodie said, "Mel can't be dead. This is totally fucking crazy."

Roy once more withdrew his phone, brought up the image of the victim's driving licence and stretched his arm out to show the photo to Jodie.

"How? Why?" Jodie said as she stared at the screen.

"She was shot," Marion said. "At this moment in time we don't know why, or who did it. Do you know of anyone that would wish her harm?"

"To my knowledge, Mel had no enemies."

"Did a guy bother either of you in the pub earlier in the evening?"

"No. And I don't understand how it could have happened. We left the Stag together, and I got in my car. As I drove off, Mel waved as she walked over to her car."

"She was accosted before she had chance to get into it," Roy said.

"It's my fault," Jodie said as tears began to run down her cheeks. "If only I'd waited until she'd got in her car, Mel would still be alive."

"*If only* is not the way to think about it," Marion said. "It's easy with hindsight to wish you'd done something differently, which could have made it possible to avoid unpleasant events from happening. If Melanie had driven off first, then I've no doubt whatsoever that it would have been you that was murdered. We can't see the future, to be able to side-step whatever's up ahead of us."

Jodie shot up out of her chair to run into the kitchen, from where Marion and Roy heard her throwing up, hopefully having made it to the sink.

Marion felt impelled to follow her, to offer some measure of comfort, but didn't. Puking was an act which most people preferred to do without an audience.

Jodie leaned over the sink, clinging on to it with both hands, to vomit until her stomach muscles ached. Eventually, when there was nothing left to bring up, she ran the cold water and wiped the strings of bile from her mouth and chin. What the two police officers had told her was all-consuming. It was virtually impossible to process the heart-breaking news of Melanie's sudden and violent demise. One second, everything in her personal universe had been just fine, and now she was in a world of torment and tears, finding it totally unbelievable, almost surreal to acknowledge that she would never see her friend again.

After a while, when the sound of Jodie being sick had ceased, Marion went through to the kitchen to find Jodie standing motionless next to the sink, looking as sad and lost as a kid that had been separated from his mother in a busy shopping mall.

"Can I get you a drink of water or anything?" Marion said.

"A large vodka might help, but I doubt it," Jodie said, her voice a little croaky from retching so hard that her throat hurt.

"Where is it?"

"In the wall unit next to the fridge," Jodie said.

Marion found the bottle of Smirnoff on one shelf and an assortment of glasses on another, to pour a large measure of the clear, distilled alcohol into a long, straight glass and hand it to Jodie, not even bothering to ask if the distressed woman wanted a mixer with it.

"Thank you," Jodie said, gripping the glass as if for dear life with both trembling hands.

"Do you live here alone?" Marion said.

"Yes, why?"

"Because having company at a time like this would probably be a good idea."

"I'll be okay. In the morning I'll phone my mother. Have you contacted Mel's father yet?"

"Yes."

"Good. He'll see to whatever needs to be done. All I have to do is somehow find the strength to open the shop tomorrow. We, Mel and I, own a bridal gown business, and we employ half a dozen people. I've got to keep it going for them, although I know how badly they'll take the news. Perhaps I'll close the shop for a few days. I don't know. With Mel gone, I'd rather not face the place without her being around."

"I hope you find the strength to move on," Marion said. "Working through grief can be beneficial for some people. It helps to alleviate the initial deep sense of loss."

"Life really is a bitch," Jodie said. "It turns on you out of the blue and rips your world apart. If you live long enough, then you get to lose everyone that matters to you."

"It's all we have. We come and we go. The best we can do is make the most of each and every day."

"I know that you're right, but at this moment in time I just want to get as pissed as a rat and hopefully sleep until dawn."

"I'll leave you my card," Marion said. "If you feel the need to talk, don't hesitate to give me a call. I'll be seeing you again within the next forty-eight hours, because we'll need to take an official statement, and now isn't the time to do it."

Marion and Roy left the bungalow in Epsom and headed back to the city, to write up reports before heading for their respective homes after having worked very long shifts. To Roy it had just been another day at the office, so to speak, but Marion was more empathetic in her reaction to those who had lost loved ones to violent crime. She still had the capacity to care deeply. Apprehending murderers was imperative, but her foremost thoughts were always with the bereaved and their mind crushing loss.

CHAPTER TWENTY-TWO

BACK at headquarters on Victoria Embankment, Matt parked his Vectra and gave Beth a call before leaving the car, to tell her that he would be at the Yard throughout the night, due to the fatal shooting.

"Was it the same perpetrator?" Beth said.

"Definitely. It was a carbon copy of the other murders, and he left his calling card."

"Any clues?"

"There's CCTV footage of him, but it's poor quality, and he wore a mask when he approached her."

"Where did it happen?"

"At the side of a pub car park in Sutton. It was closing time and the landlord was locking up. He went out back to collect any glasses that had been left on tables and saw that there was still a vehicle parked up, that he recognised as belonging to a young female customer, so investigated. He found her body in shrubbery behind the car, and called it in."

"These are almost certainly random killings, Matt. I have the feeling that he just prowls around an area until he has the opportunity to approach a solitary female and shoot her."

"All we know is the where and when he does it, not the who or why. If the crime scene investigators don't come up with any trace evidence, then we're no nearer coming up with a prime suspect."

"That's four attacks he's made on women, resulting in three of them being murdered and one managing to get away from him. Have you had a geographic profile of the murders done yet?"

"One of the team, Jeff Sewell, has taken courses in the subject. He's already working on what we have. I'm hopeful that this latest murder will aid him to determine the most likely area of the offender's base of activities. That will help us to eliminate a lot of the persons of interest that we've already interviewed, and leave us with just a few suspects living in a relatively small district."

"Sounds like you could be closing in on him."

"I've got everything crossed."

"That sounds painful."

"Funny girl."

"That's me. I love you, Barnes. I'll see you when I see you."

"Love you, too. I'll make a point of being home tomorrow evening as early as possible."

"Keep me posted. If you land before eight, you can take me out for a pub meal."

Ending the call, Matt exited the car and made his way to the rear staff entrance of the building, to punch in the current four digit code to gain entry. Making his way through a maze of corridors, he took the lift up to the third floor and walked past half a dozen offices before reaching the squad room, where Pete, Marci, Jeff and Tam were discussing the case as they waited for him to arrive.

"It's already breaking news," Pete said to Matt, glancing at the wall-mounted flat screen TV. "Someone obviously tipped off the vultures. The media vans are at the scene, and a so-called crime correspondent has been running off at the mouth."

"Bad news always travels fast," Matt said. "What has been said?"

"Just that it is believed the body of a young woman found at the rear of a public house in Sutton had been fatally shot. Her name, Melanie Parker, has obviously not been released, but it has been reported that a reliable police source has informed them that the woman is believed to be another victim of the Killer Clown."

"I think it's a bloody crime that the press and TV stations are not legally bound to divulge the identities of their sources," Marci said.

"That will never happen," Pete said. "They pay their thirty pieces of silver without always knowing whether what they're told is fact, fiction or something in-between. But, love 'em or hate 'em, we need them at times to report what we want released. A lot of cases are solved due to information received from the public at large, having seen or read news reports."

"Here's something they *won't* get to see," Matt said as he took his mobile phone out of a pocket and handed it to Pete to view the photos he had taken of the corpse in situ at the crime scene.

Pete looked at the images of the victim, then handed the phone to Marci, for her to look at the pics before passing it to Jeff, for him and Tam to see the shots of the dead victim.

"DCI John Stott will arrange for us to have copies of all reports raised," Matt said. "Including the names and addresses of individuals that have been visited and informed of the late Melanie Parker's death, plus a copy of the grainy CCTV footage of the masked perpetrator approaching Melanie and obviously instructing her to enter the shrubbery, which is where he shot her."

As Matt informed his team of all the details he knew, Jeff went across to the map of Greater London, where he had already pushed a red-headed pin at the location of the latest scene in Sutton.

"Anything stand out like a beacon in the night?" Matt said to Jeff.

"No, boss. Apart from the murders of the three women being south of the river, there's no pattern to follow," Jeff said. "The first victim, Brenda Cummings, was murdered in Peckham Rye Park. The second, Natalie Swift, in Oxleas Wood in Eltham. The next attack was against April Henderson on Mitcham Common, but she managed to escape from him unharmed. The third and current killing of Melanie Parker was committed in Sutton.

Pete went to stand next to Jeff, putting glasses on which he had only been prescribed with six weeks previously and was still unhappy at having to wear for reading and working at his computer. "Peckham, then Eltham, followed by the failed attack on Mitcham Common, and last but not least, Sutton," he said. "Doesn't look like there's a pattern to me. Do you see one, Jeff?"

"Nothing obvious. Just a hunch that he lives somewhere between the first two crimes, in the Lewisham area," Jeff said, sticking a blue coloured pin into the map. "I have the feeling that he started up not too far from home, but being blindfolded and pinning a tail on the picture of a donkey could be just as close to the mark."

Matt joined the others in front of the eye-high map, and armed with a marker pen he drew an elliptical shape that encircled an area south of the Thames that took in all the crime scenes with room to spare.

"That's a pretty wide area to cover," Marci said.

"Not really," Matt said. "It narrows the field. Any phone calls that we've had from the public identifying some guy who lives in that patch is potentially the perpetrator. How many is there?"

"I'll check," Jeff said, going to his desk and bringing up relevant files on his computer.

"What about the Major Investigation Team?" Tam said. "Your oppo, DCI Stott, has fifty detectives under his wing."

Matt shrugged and said, "Let's first see how many possible suspects Jeff comes up with in the area we've highlighted. If there are only a few, we'll make first contact with them, check out their alibis and see what comes of it."

"We could have already interviewed some of them," Errol said.

"True, but if we have, it won't harm to put them under the microscope again."

Apart from Jeff, they drank coffee and discussed all aspects of the case, including the anomaly of the killer murdering two guys north of the river in Bethnal Green. The reason for his failed attempt to eliminate Jasmin Walker in Stratford was obvious; she had seen him, described him, and was the only person, to date, who could stand as a witness against him in a court of law.

It took a while, but Jeff came up with a list of names and addresses within the range in which the team believed the shooter was based. All of them had been interviewed previously.

Studying the existing details, including the men's backgrounds, and the alibis that they had given, they decided that early morning would be the best time to start knocking doors. All of the SCU squad were qualified firearms officers, cleared to carry them while working a live case. Especially when, as in this particular case, the offender was known to be armed and highly dangerous.

Sitting in near darkness, with just the flickering light from the TV screen, he fed off the news of his latest escapade in Sutton. Just the sight of the flashing blue lights and the milling coppers was a real turn on. And the media were there in force. One of the cameras caught a glimpse of a guy in civvies; a detective he recognised as being a DCI who had interviewed him several weeks previously, whose name was Barnes. Perhaps it would be fun to contact the copper and goad him. Raising the stakes was what any gambler worth his salt, did. *The higher the risk, the greater the emotional reward.*

CHAPTER TWENTY-THREE

ON the evening of the fourth day after the fatal shooting outside the pub in Sutton, the team were no further on. Each of the men that Jeff had pinpointed as living within the area that Matt had drawn on the map had been contacted and reinterviewed, to be asked where they had been on the evening of the fifteenth of the month. Nothing gave rise to any of them being thought of as a worthwhile suspect, and the people who'd provided them with alibis stuck steadfastly to the original statements they had given.

"That boat didn't sail," Pete said to Matt. "We're no further on."

"It's a step in the right direction," Matt said as he walked across the squad room to refill his mug with coffee that had been freshly brewed a few minutes previously by Errol. "He could have slipped through the nets of your boat that hasn't sailed yet, but there are still four of them that we can keep flagged, because they couldn't furnish credible alibis."

"Which leaves us at a standstill."

Matt shook his head and made his way across to the map tacked to a whiteboard, to pick up a marker pen and draw a fresh egg shape around the original one, to encompass more territory. "We can check on how many persons of interest that Joe Public fingered in this area now, and keep widening it until we strike gold."

"Sounds like a plan," Pete said. "Although we have no actual evidence that the Clown even lives south of the river. He could be using misdirection by concentrating the kills well away from where he lives."

"True, but we can only work with what we've got, Pete. I'm ninety-nine percent positive that he's committing the crimes in an area that he knows well. He's savvy. The concept that there is always a transfer of trace evidence between a perpetrator and victim doesn't apply, because he has no physical contact with the people he shoots. To date we have nothing but some blurry and totally useless CCTV footage of him, and he was wearing a ski mask or balaclava."

"He'll be revelling in the knowledge of what he does being such a big and ongoing news item. The headlines will just encourage him to escalate."

"Someone out there who has seen the sketch of him on TV or in a newspaper knows him. Could be a wife, parent, friend or workmate who has an inkling that they are trying to ignore, because no one wants to consider a loved one or friend as being a serial killer. Perhaps he wasn't where he should have been when Melanie Parker or one or more of the previous victims were murdered. If somebody is wrestling with their conscience, then there is a good chance that if another woman is slain and the perpetrator's location at the time it happens cannot be accounted for, they'll pick up the phone and voice their suspicion."

Pete shrugged. "What about the two cousins that were murdered in Bethnal Green? They were male. We know that the same handgun was used to shoot them, but it doesn't fit with what is nothing less than the executions of the women."

"When he's lifted, we can ask him. Until then, I suggest we concentrate our efforts wholly on the area that he has been most active in."

"We need some downtime to chill out for an hour or so," Pete said. "Let's go and have a pint and see if the beer gives us more insight and a eureka moment."

"That sounds like a plan," Matt said. "You're driving."

"Fine. You're buying." Pete said as he walked over to where Marci was working her computer, to tell her to hold the fort for an hour or so while he and Matt visited the Kenton Court Hotel to shoot the shit with Ron Quinn.

"Well, if it isn't Morse and his sidekick Lewis gracing my lowly hotel with their presence again," Ron said, grinning broadly through the beard and moustache that had once been red but was now ribboned with grey.

"Not funny, big guy," Matt said to the gentle giant who he considered to be one of his best friends. "Just pull two pints of your best bitter, and make it quick because we don't have time for your second rate banter."

"You do realise that this is a residents lounge, and that neither of you are booked in, so will only be served out of the kindness of my heart, should I choose to be benevolent."

"Bollocks" Pete said. "Behave, or I'll give you a slap."

Ron laughed aloud. He was built like a rugby prop forward – which he had been in his younger days – and stood at least six inches taller than Pete.

With pints in hand, Matt and Pete settled at a table next to a window at the rear of the lounge.

"Cheers," Pete said, and they clinked glasses.

After staying for a second pint, and passing the time of day with Ron for a while, they returned to the Yard. When Pete parked the pool car, Matt told him that he was calling it a day and going home.

"I'll give you a bell if anything breaks," Pete said as Matt headed over to his Vectra, needing time out to be with Beth and let his subconscious wrestle with the complexity of the ongoing case.

Beth was working her laptop, writing a weekly report on one of the children who had only been at Morning Star for several weeks, when her phone rang. It was Matt calling to let her know he was on his way home.

"Are you hungry?" Beth said.

"Yeah, I guess so. I had a break earlier, went to the Kenton Court with Pete for a couple of pints and decided that I'd had enough of work for one day. The beer has made me a bit peckish."

"How peckish?"

"My stomach's growling. Do you still want to go out for a pub meal or shall I pick up a takeaway?"

"Chinese, please. Sweet and sour chicken with noodles, and a portion of fried mushrooms. I haven't eaten since lunch, and I only had a tuna salad sandwich."

"I should be home in less than an hour. It will give you time to open a bottle of red to breathe, and to heat the plates."

Later, after Matt had arrived home with a plastic bag packed with containers full of steaming food, they ate it and drank a full bottle of Cabernet Sauvignon between them, before washing the dishes and going through to the lounge.

"Any updates on the case?" Beth said.

"No. We're focusing our attention on an area south of the river, expanding it as we reinterview any guys we had calls from the public about. Unfortunately the sketch Dick Curtis worked-up of the suspect, who Jasmin Walker saw, fits a great many men with dark hair, dark eyes and even features. There was nothing exceptional about him."

"You'll find him," Beth said. "It's just when, not if."

"I'm banking on that, and hope we finger him soon, because he'll keep on killing until we do. Have you had any revelations that could help?"

"Nothing definite. Just the belief that even if he has some emotionally screwed-up motive for selecting and killing, it will be no more than a reason he's conjured up to validate his actions. He doesn't rob or physically assault the women he shoots, and so his behaviour appears to be that of a man who is killing for the pure thrill and pleasure he derives from doing it."

"What are you saying, that he's a misogynist? A guy who hates women?"

"I would go further than that. I believe he's a misanthrope, and dislikes or despises humanity in general, but like a chameleon he probably appears to those he knows or works with as being a regular guy."

"A Jekyll and Hyde type?"

"Exactly. Someone who can separate the two sides of his nature and probably appear to be a kind and ostensibly pillar of the community most of the time, while in reality he is a cold-blooded killer."

"What leads you to that conclusion, Watson?"

"Elementary, Holmes, although not necessarily on the money. It's speculation based wholly on what little you currently have to go on. I believe that his MO tells us a lot about him. He is ultra-cautious, cunning, and is well prepared when he hunts what he considers to be prey. The mask he wears is to protect him from being seen, and the gloves are to ensure that he does not inadvertently leave prints at the scenes of his crimes. Plus, it's not about sex. He doesn't rape his victims, ergo, no DNA. And he doesn't take their mobile phones or money. There is no physical contact with them. He gets off on instilling a high level of fear prior to shooting them. That's what floats his boat."

Matt frowned. "To our knowledge, the first victim was Brenda Cummings, and she was murdered at lunchtime on a bright December day, not far from public toilets in Peckham Rye Park. That doesn't sound like the act of an extremely cautious person."

"Could be that if, as you just said, she was his first victim, then he realised that his act had been very impulsive and not well thought out, and so he upped his game and gave his subsequent actions far more due care and attention."

"Any idea why he would leave the pictures of a clown at the scenes?"

"Playing to the gallery; the media, police and public are his audience. He gets two hits for the price of one. His notoriety and being tagged the Killer Clown will give him a great sense of power."

"And like all of these nutjobs, he will no doubt keep on doing what he does."

"Right. Worst case scenario is that he'll escalate, become too self-assured and evolve."

CHAPTER TWENTY-FOUR

THE next morning at eight a.m., Matt walked into the squad room to be told by Errol that the head of the SCU, Detective Superintendent Julia Stone, had phoned ten minutes previously and asked him to tell Matt to go up to her office as soon as he arrived.

Armed with a mug of hot but stale coffee that tasted bitter, Matt took the stairs up to the next floor, after telling Errol to make a fresh pot of java.

Julia's door was open, and she beckoned Matt in and gestured for him to take a seat.

"One of the Assistant Commissioners, Ralph McBride, came down from wherever he perches up on the top floor, Matt, to ask me if we had something better than nothing in regard to the current case to tell him," Julia said. "The media, like clouds of blood-sucking mosquitoes, are tearing the Met to bits over the lack of progress with this so-called Killer Clown. Have you got *anything* at all that I can use to fend off the slings and arrows of outrageous fortune that are reigning down on me from a great height?"

"And good morning to you, Julia," Matt said, a little concerned that his boss had not taken the few seconds necessary to greet him before diving in at the deep end. "You know what I know. In conjunction with the Major Incident Team headed up by John Stott, we're working on it around the clock. We believe that the perpetrator lives in an area of south London, and so every initial person of interest in that patch is being reinterviewed, and their alibis for the pertinent times and dates will be scrutinised to the nth degree. Apart from doing that we have, as yet, no other avenues to explore. The Clown leaves no physical trace evidence."

"We need to close him down quickly, Matt. It's been several months now since he started up, and apart from the mugshot sketch we haven't got one solid lead. And we don't even know for sure that the man the girl saw leaving the house in Bethnal Green and described to the police artist, is in fact the killer. That's an assumption, not a definite known fact."

"I hear you loud and clear," Matt said. "But if the sketch hadn't been near the mark, then the perpetrator would have had no reason to find and attempt to kill her. Apart from that we can only follow what little we've got. I'm positive that he will escalate and make a mistake that will lead us to him."

A knock at the office door broke the tension of the discussion.

"Come in," Julia said.

The door opened to reveal DCI John Stott. He was looking casual, wearing a white short-sleeved shirt, black slacks and grey trainers. In his right hand he held a brown A4 size envelope.

"Speak of the devil and he doth appear," Matt said. "You look as happy as a dog with a fresh knuckle of pork to chew on."

"I've got something that will hopefully put a smile on both of your faces," John said. "Offer me a halfway decent cup of coffee and I'll give you the name of someone who is most likely responsible for the murders we're investigating."

"All I've got is Earl Grey tea," Julia said. "But I'm sure that after you share what you have, Matt will then furnish you with coffee in the squad room downstairs."

John placed the envelope on the top of Julia's desk. Removing four sheets of copy paper from it, she saw that two of the sheets had notes on them, and that the third was a photocopy of a colour photograph showing a small sealed plastic bag with what appeared to be a cigarette end inside it. The fourth had the image of a photocard driving licence. After initially speed reading the notes and studying the images, she handed them to Matt. When he had processed the content he turned his attention to John with his eyebrows raised.

"Tell me that you want to stick your clenched fists in the air and shout YES," John said, speaking to both of them.

"You've got the name and address of a guy, and what appears to be forensic evidence linking him to the scene of Melanie Parker's murder," Julia said.

"Exactly. And the photograph of him, and confirmation that he, Darren Selby, is living in a terrace house in Tooting Bec. One of the crime scene investigators lifted the cigarette end from the ground just three feet from the woman's body. Martin Frost, the head of the forensic science section, says that the DNA from saliva on and in the filter is a match to Selby, and that there is a partial latent print on it, which is also a match."

"Where did you get Selby's DNA from?" Matt said.

"From the National Database. He was charged with rape four years ago, and although he was found not guilty and walked, he's on file. As you both know, not only samples from convicted criminals or people awaiting trial are stored. Just being charged with a serious sexual or violent offence these days means that DNA can be kept for up to five years after acquittal."

"That makes him a prime suspect," Julia said.

"Recovering his DNA at the scene doesn't prove that he was present when the crime was committed," Matt said, playing devil's advocate.

"It will be interesting to hear his explanation for how it turned up at the rear of the pub on a cigarette end, just a few feet from the body," John said.

"He needs to be lifted before he has chance to increase the body count," Julia said.

"No time like the present," John said. "Being as how this is a joint operation, I suggest that Matt and I organise a team to stake out his address, if he isn't there, and arrest him when he appears."

Darren Selby took a break from delivering packages, to drive the FedEx Ford Transit van from a location in nearby Brixton to the terrace house in Tooting Bec, where he lived with his disabled father. It was almost midday, and rather than stopping at a burger van for a sandwich and coffee, as he frequently did, he decided to call home and have a bite to eat with his dad.

As Darren stepped out of the vehicle and closed the door, a man's voice said, "Hey, Darren, how're you doing?" Turning to his right, he was faced by a slender guy wearing a tee-shirt, lightweight jerkin and jeans, who was a total stranger to him.

"Do I know you?" Darren said.

"Not yet," Detective Sergeant Roy Slater said as DCs Errol Chambers and Jeff Sewell rounded the rear of the van and physically restrained the suspect, to firmly apply wrist locks and forcibly guide him into a facedown position on the pavement.

With another four plainclothes detectives standing by, including Pete Deakin, Roy frisked the man hoping to find a firearm, but didn't. All he found in his pockets was a mobile phone, a wallet and a set of keys.

"What the fuck is this all about?" Darren shouted as he was handcuffed. The cuffs were hurting his wrists, and his face was less than twelve inches from a pile of what appeared to be recently dumped dog shit.

"I'm Detective Sergeant Slater," Roy said as he squatted down in front of the suspect and held out his open wallet to show the man his warrant card. "I'm arresting you on suspicion of murder. You do not have to say anything, but it may harm your defence if you do not mention when questioned something which you later rely on in court. Anything you *do* say may be given in evidence. Do you understand the caution I have just given you?"

"No," Darren said. "I don't understand why I've been assaulted by a bunch of violent fucking coppers. I haven't murdered anybody."

"Is there anyone in the house?" Roy said.

"Yes, my dad, and he's disabled. I want to speak to him."

"That isn't going to happen," Roy said as Errol and Jeff hauled their prisoner to his feet and propelled him to a nearby unmarked car, to bundle him into the rear seat, next to Matt, who had watched the arrest being made.

Even as Darren was being driven directly to the Yard, Pete, Errol, Jeff, Roy, and two other detectives entered the suspect's house, having knocked on the front door, which was answered by a balding, middle-aged man wearing a dressing gown that was in dire need of a date with a washing machine. He had a pronounced limp and, judging by his expression, appeared to be in a great deal of pain.

"Who are you?" Bert Selby said to the officers.

"Police, sir," Pete said to the man as he showed him his ID. "Who are you?"

"I'm Bert Selby. Why are you here?"

"We have a warrant to search the house, Mr Selby."

"Looking for what? And where is Darren? That's his van at the kerb?"

"Is Darren Selby your son?"

"Yeah. What have you done with him?"

"He has been taken in for questioning."

"About what?"

"I'm not at liberty to discuss it with you at this time," Pete said.

"And I take it that you'll force entry if I don't let you in?"

Pete just gave him a hard look and held up the search warrant, and the man stood aside without even asking to look at it.

"An officer will stay with you, sir," Pete said. "I'm going to have the kitchen searched first, and then you'll be able to enter it and stay there until we've finished."

Bert said nothing, because he knew that to argue would be a total waste of time and breath. Whatever they were questioning Darren about didn't worry him, because his son was a law-abiding citizen, as straight as a die. When allowed to enter his own kitchen, Bert would make a cup of tea, read the newspaper, and when the coppers finally left empty-handed, as he knew that they would, he would give his solicitor, Sidney Reynolds, a bell and ask him to find out what the hell was happening.

CHAPTER TWENTY-FIVE

WHILE Darren Selby was incarcerated in a holding cell, Matt, Pete and John were in Julia Stone's office, discussing the best way to interview the prime suspect, and who would conduct it.

"I think that Pete and John should question him," Matt said. "This is a joint case, so both teams should be in on it. We have his DNA, and he looks reasonably similar to the sketch described to Dick Curtis by Jasmin Walker. If he doesn't have an alibi that is indisputable, and doesn't admit to being the Clown, then we can always arrange for Jasmin to be brought in by protection officers and hopefully identify him beyond any doubt, after first taking a photo of him and sending it to her via the officers that are guarding her and her mother."

"I don't expect for a second that he'll confess to being a serial killer," John said. "It would be contrary to the rule. These monsters very rarely give us anything but bullshit and bad attitude. They habitually deny any culpability."

The cell he was ushered into was small, dimly lit and cold, and made Darren feel more than a little claustrophobic as the solid door was slammed shut and locked, to leave him standing and looking around the confined space. There was a raised concrete pad on one side of the room with a wafer thin mattress on top of it, and a stainless steel, lidless toilet bowl at the rear. The handcuffs had been taken off, and he had been told to remove his shoes, belt and wristwatch before being locked up by a uniformed copper who would not answer any of his questions. After a while, he lay down on the mattress and decided to just keep calm and not worry unduly. This would soon be resolved, and he would be released, because they had nothing to hold him for.

After an unknown period of time passed, the cell door was unlocked and he was escorted from the holding cell area by three officers, along a narrow corridor to a door that had a sign on it, designating the room beyond as being Interview Room 2.

"Take a seat," Officer Chris Peterson said as he opened the door and pointed to a steel table that was bolted to the floor, as was the chair behind it which Chris intimated that Darren should sit on. Two of the three officers stayed in the room, but did not speak to him or to each other.

"Any chance of a cup of coffee?" Darren said.

"Maybe later," Chris said. "For now just relax. Someone will be here shortly to interview you."

"About what?"

Chris ignored him.

It was at least twenty minutes later when Pete and John made their way to the interview room. Outside it there was a switch on the wall next to the door at shoulder height, which John flicked on before he and Pete entered. It started a video running which was streamed directly to the department servers. It was now written policy to record sight and sound when any of the interview rooms were being used.

Pete intimated that Chris and the other officer should leave the room.

"Mr Darren Selby," John said to the man, who was sitting with his head lowered, as if asleep.

Darren opened his eyes and raised his head, to look from one to the other of the two men dressed in street clothes, who were obviously detectives.

"Yeah, that's me. Why am I here?"

"I'm Detective Chief Inspector Stott, and my colleague is Detective Inspector Deakin," John said. "This interview is being recorded and as you know, having been cautioned, anything that you say can be used in evidence at any subsequent trial."

"Just who exactly do you believe that I'm guilty of murdering?"

"We'll get to that in due course, Darren," John said. "What I need for you to do now is tell us your whereabouts on the evening of Thursday the fifteenth of June."

"I want to call my solicitor before I tell you diddly-squat."

"You've been arrested on suspicion of murder, Darren, but not charged with anything specific as yet. If we do charge you, then you'll get your phone call. Okay?"

Darren thought it through for the best part of a full minute. "Fine," he said. "But I need a cup of coffee, my mouth is as dry as bone."

Pete turned around, looked up at the wall-mounted camera and nodded. He knew that both Julia and Matt would be watching the live feed on a monitor as it was being recorded, and that they would arrange for coffee to be brought to the interview room.

Darren didn't say a word until the drink was delivered and he had taken a couple of sips of the hot beverage from the disposable cup.

"What date did you say?" Darren said as he set the cup down on the tabletop.

"Last Thursday, the fifteenth," Pete said.

Darren's brow furrowed as he appeared to have difficulty recalling the evening in question. He then said, "I finished work at six p.m. and drove home from the depot, stopping once to pick up fish and chips for me and my dad. At about eight I walked down to the pub, the Wolf Trap, had a few beers and got back to the house at ten-forty-five. My dad was watching the telly. I told him that I was knackered and went to bed, mainly because I was due to be in work at six-thirty on the Friday morning. Does that satisfy you?"

"Not really," John said as he took a folded sheet of paper from the inside pocket of his jacket, to open and push across the table to Darren. "Take a look at this picture."

Darren frowned as he studied the colour image and shrugged his shoulders. "It's a fag end," he said. "What's that got to do with anything?"

"A lot," John said. "It has your DNA on it."

"Meaning?"

"That it was found at a murder scene."

"That's impossible."

"No, it's a fact."

"Who exactly do you wrongly believe I've topped?"

"Have you seen the news over the last few days?"

"Yeah, but I still don't know what you're on about."

"A young woman was fatally shot in the car park of the Stag Inn on the Brighton Road in Sutton, and you made the mistake of leaving the cigarette end near the body."

"That didn't happen, and I'm not the psycho that you lot call the Killer Clown," Darren said as he came up off the chair with his fists clenched.

John didn't flinch, but Pete stood up and said, "Calm down, Darren. Get a grip or you'll be restrained and returned to the cell."

Darren took deep breaths and stood frozen in place for a few seconds before regaining his composure and slumping back onto the chair.

"I haven't shot anybody, and it must be a couple of years since I was in the Stag. It wasn't my kind of pub, and is a bit too far to walk to from home."

"So explain how your DNA got there," John said.

"I can't. There must be a mistake."

"The only mistake is that you were careless and left evidence at a murder scene," Pete said. "Isn't that the truth of it?"

"No. This is a mistake on your part, or a fucking stitch up."

"Okay, Darren. We'll take a break. We have more dates that you'll need to come up with an account of your movements on. We'll have you taken back to the cell to mull it over, and will resume later."

"You have no right to—"

"We have the right to hold you for questioning for twenty-four hours before having to charge you with a crime or release you," John said. "And if we need to we can apply to hold you for up to thirty-six or ninety-six hours if we strongly suspect that you have committed a serious crime, which would apply in your case."

After Darren was returned to the cell in a state of mind that was both downcast and angry, Pete and John met up with Matt and Julia to view the recording and pause it at times of particular interest in the suspect's demeanour and answers to certain questions.

"What do you think?" Julia said to the others.

"He could have left the pub in Tooting Bec a little earlier than he told us he did. It wouldn't have taken him long to leg it over to Sutton," Pete said.

"We'll hopefully get CCTV of him leaving," Matt said. "As for him saying that he walked home at ten-forty-five and had a word with his father before going to bed. Who knows? His dad would most likely cover for him."

"It gives us a couple of things to be going on with, though," Pete said. "I'll send Tam and Kelly to both the pub and his address."

"I suggest we let him sweat for a couple of hours, and then you two can hit him with the times and dates of all the other related murders, plus the assault on the one that got away from him on Mitcham Common, April Henderson," Julia said.

Back in her office, Julia got a phone call from Ralph McBride, the assistant commissioner who had been hassling her for updates at least twice a day.

"The grapevine says that you have a prime suspect for the Killer Clown murders in custody, Julia. Can you verify that for me?" Ralph said.

"That's correct, sir," Julia said, purposely not addressing him by his Christian name, due to the fact that he was one of those touchy-feely types that gave her the creeps. Rumour had it that, given the chance, he would bed any female with a pulse.

"That's good news. Has he admitted his guilt?"

"No. After an initial interview concentrating on the latest murder in Sutton, he has claimed that he is innocent and given us an alibi that is currently being checked. He will be interviewed again shortly over the other shootings."

"How sure are you that he is the perpetrator?"

"He stated that he had not visited the crime scene, but his DNA was on a cigarette end just a few feet from the victim's body."

"Excellent," Ralph said. "I shall arrange for you to give a statement to the media at, let's say at seven this evening. They are slagging us off big time over this serial killer case."

"At the moment he's just a suspect, sir. We have nothing concrete to tell journalists and TV interviewers."

"He's a *prime* suspect, Julia. That will cool the heels of the newshounds until we wrap this up by charging the guy."

"If he can substantiate that he *wasn't* at any of the scenes, then we'll have to release him."

"Let's have a little more positivity over this for God's sake," Ralph said. "You've got his DNA, which was discovered next to the corpse of one of the victims. What more do you want?"

"A random cigarette filter won't prove his guilt beyond doubt if he can prove he was somewhere else at germane times on any of the dates we're interested in. The Crown Prosecution Service will drop any charges against him if they decide that there is a lack of evidence, or if they believe the prosecution would not be in the public interest."

"Let's hope that he isn't able to come up with anything good enough to cause the CPS to block us, then."

"I have officers searching his address as we speak, looking for a balaclava, handgun, latex gloves or anything else that would give us enough to make it a done deal."

"Good. I'll be sure to watch the statement and following question and answer session on the TV. Will you front it?"

"No, I'll let DCI Matt Barnes and DCI John Stott handle it."

"Fine. Have a productive day, Julia," Ralph said, and then abruptly ended the call.

"Wanker," Julia said to the humming line before placing the handset back in its holder.

CHAPTER TWENTY-SIX

IT was five-thirty p.m. when Pete and John adjourned the interview with Darren Selby and he was taken back to his cell, where he would stay for at the very least one night in custody. They had questioned him at length for a second time, to ask him to tell them his exact whereabouts on all the dates that the murders had been committed

"He didn't do too well," John said as he and Pete made their way back to the squad room. "The only date he could give us a definite alibi for was the seventeenth of April, which was when Sonny Mason and Francis Dawson were murdered at two separate addresses in Bethnal Green."

"Easy to check out what he told us. He said that he had attended the funeral service and cremation of a family friend who'd been killed in a road traffic accident, and that it had taken place on the afternoon of the sixteenth of April at the Vinters Park Crematorium in Maidstone, and he also said he'd been accompanied by his brother and sister-in-law, and that they had stayed overnight at the Premier Inn on the high street."

"If he did, then there's no way he could have committed the murders in the East End. No one can be in two places at the same time."

"We'd better hope that he's lying and that no one will corroborate his story," Pete said. "If someone does, we'll have to release him."

"As far as I'm concerned he's as guilty as hell. The science says he was at the scene of a murder and that's good enough for me."

Back in the squad room with a copy of the afternoon's interview on a flash drive, the team gathered around a monitor on Marci's desk and Pete played the video for them to watch.

"Anybody got a take on whether this guy comes across as the killer?" Pete said while the video was running.

"I don't think he did it," Matt said. "There was no 'tell'. He didn't avert his eyes from you or John when he answered any of your questions. He came across as being exceptionally anxious but showed no expression or any other physical sign of guilt."

"He could just be a clever bastard," John said. "Anyone can watch TV crime shows and read up on shit like that."

"If he did stay overnight in Maidstone when the two black guys were topped, we've got nothing," Tam said.

At exactly seven p.m., John and Matt faced the throng of journalists, reporters, photographers and TV camera crews who'd gathered outside New Scotland Yard to be given an update on the ongoing serial murderer that they had tagged the Killer Clown.

"I'm Detective Chief Inspector Stott and head up a major incident team, and my colleague, Detective Chief Inspector Barnes, is the DCI of a special crime unit. In what is a joint operation we are investigating the case in question."

"Is it true that you have a prime suspect in custody?" Graham French of the Guardian said.

"We have a suspect that we are currently interviewing," John said.

"Does that mean he hasn't been charged as yet?" Donald Newman from BBC News asked.

"At the moment we have not ascertained beyond any reasonable doubt that he is the perpetrator."

"Am I right in my assumption that you have evidence linking this mystery man to the murders?" Caroline Maston of the Daily Mirror said.

"He is a person of interest, no more than that at this time."

"A question for DCI Barnes if I may," Steve Rigby of the Metro said. "Your specialised unit is renowned for investigating and apprehending serial killers. With that in mind, do you personally believe that you have the Killer Clown under lock and key?"

"I am not as yet convinced one way or the other as to his guilt or innocence," Matt said. "If and when he is charged with any crime, or released from custody, the media will of course be notified."

"Do you have any idea what type of perpetrator carried out the shootings?" Steve came back.

Matt decided to let the reporter draw him out. "I believe that the Clown is a pathetic thrill killer who gets his rocks off by committing murder for the pleasure he derives from doing it," he said. "These are stranger on stranger murders with no self-evident motive; not in furtherance of rape or robbery. Perhaps this particular homicidal maniac is impotent, and his inadequacy is the driving force behind his sick crimes. Or he may be a misogynist; a guy who hates women."

After three more questions, John ended what he always felt was little more than an interrogation by the fourth estate, telling them that they would be kept up-to-date with any subsequent progress made.

"The way you phrased your dramatic remarks over the killer make me think that you believe Selby is innocent," John said as he and Matt beat a hasty retreat to the safety of the building.

"I do," Matt said. "Watching the video footage of you and Pete interviewing him convinced me that he isn't a killer. I'm ninety-nine percent sure that his alibi for when the two men in Bethnal Green were murdered will hold up."

Darren slept fitfully. It was broad daylight when the door to his cell was opened and an officer handed him a plastic tray, cutlery and a mug. Two of the four compartments in the tray had scrambled egg and beans in them, and the mug was almost full of what appeared to be extremely weak-looking tea.

"What's happening?" Darren said to the stocky, bearded copper who handed him his breakfast.

"Fucked if I know," the constable, Travis Thompson, said as he closed and locked the door.

"What time is it?" Darren shouted.

"Probably later than you think," Travis chuckled. "Just eat your breakfast and shut the fuck up."

The egg and beans were barely warm; the tea was hot but weak. Darren sat down on the mattress, ate the bland food and drank the tea, due to having no idea when he would be fed again. *You need to go with the flow and make the best of the situation*, he thought as he lay back down, closed his eyes and dozed off.

At one p.m. in the squad room of the SCU, Matt discussed the current state of play with Julia and the team. John Stott had gone to update his own detectives.

"Much to my disappointment," Julia said, "Darren Selby's alibi is solid. We've confirmed that on the date of the late night murders in the East End, he had spent the previous day at a funeral in Maidstone in the company of his brother and sister-in-law, plus other mourners that know Darren. The Premier Inn also confirm that he stayed overnight. There is no way that he could be the killer."

"Which leaves us with the mystery of the cigarette end covered in his DNA," Pete said.

"It could have been planted," Matt said. "Let's not forget that the Clown is a game player. Ballistics have verified that the bullets which killed each of the victims were fired by the same handgun."

"We're back at Go on the Monopoly board, then, and Selby will be given a get out of jail free card." Jeff said.

"Not exactly," Pete said. "We get to throw the dice as many times as it takes to win the game, and we still have more persons of interest to interview in the area of south London that you zeroed in on. It would have been case closed if it *had* been Selby, but we'll find this scumbag. He's running out of time and space."

"If he stops now and doesn't kill anybody else, there's no saying we'll ever catch him," Errol said.

"He won't be able to stop," Matt said. "We all know that the need to kill spirals out of control with these serials."

He had watched the live coverage of the cabaret featuring two high-ranking detectives fending off the questions put to them by the media outside New Scotland Yard, and had enjoyed the show up until the point when Detective Chief Inspector Barnes of the Special Crime Unit began to badmouth him, calling him pathetic and insinuating that he was impotent. Barnes was well out of order. This was not personal, and the haughty cop had no right to make it so by assuming, wrongly, that he was incapable of getting a hard-on. The only reason he didn't rape his victims was because he had no intention of leaving any trace evidence at the scenes. Perhaps the stupid plod was ineptly attempting to draw him out. That could be a feasible consequence, but would not come to pass in the near future. Should it ever, then it would be at his convenience, on his terms, and when Barnes least expected it.

CHAPTER TWENTY-SEVEN

ACCOMPANIED by DC Kelly Day, Pete made his way down to the holding cell area to the interview room in which Darren Selby was now once more sitting at the far side of the table, expecting to be bombarded with more questions.

"We've checked out what you told us yesterday, Mr Selby," Pete said as he and Kelly sat down opposite Darren. "It would appear that you *were* attending a funeral in Maidstone on the sixteenth of April, and stayed overnight at a hotel."

"Thank God for that," Darren said. "Does that mean I'm free to leave?"

"You will be provisionally released on police bail, but will have to return for further questioning if required to do so."

"No problem, because I haven't committed any crime."

Pete hiked his shoulders.

"You still have doubts about my innocence, don't you?"

Pete said nothing.

"Once I leave here, the bloody press will be given my name by one of you lot, and they'll follow me home and be at my dad's door giving us both grief."

"Let's not forget that your DNA was found at a murder scene, so you obviously had to be questioned. And none of *our* lot have any reason to release your name to anyone."

"As you know, I was charged with rape, and although I was acquitted it didn't mean that I walked free and the episode was over and done with. Shit sticks. People always wonder whether you did it or not, you can see it in their eyes. However small, a part of them is left with lasting doubt."

"We're done here, Mr Selby," Pete said. "The items that were taken from you will be returned, and after you read through a form and sign it, you'll be free to go."

"You mean I have to walk out the front door into the waiting arms of the media?"

Pete gave what Darren said a few seconds thought and said, "No, I'll arrange for you to leave from the rear of the building, and a detective will drive you home."

"I'd appreciate that," Darren said. "Thank you."

Jerry Parker had watched and recorded the live outside broadcast of the interview between the detectives and the press, and was intent on finding out the identity of the prime suspect being held in custody. He called his chief of security, Larry Wade, on an extension, due to Larry living in a small bungalow that was situated in the grounds, screened by trees over a hundred yards away from the house.

"Yeah, boss," Larry said.

"Did you watch the press interview outside Scotland Yard?"

"No, I was checking security stuff. Why?"

"Because the filth have a prime suspect for the murders of Melanie, a copper, and some others."

"That's great news."

"It is, Larry. What I want you to do is find out the name and address of the suspect, in case they don't have enough to hold him. One of the two detectives was DCI Stott who heads up a Major Incident Team, and the other is also a DCI and his name is Barnes."

"I'll get on it. We have one or two MIT detectives on the books. I'm sure that one of them will be able to give us the info we need."

"Okay, Larry. Get back to me when you know who the guy is."

Larry Wade was an ex-professional boxer, stood six-two, and would have been quite handsome had it not been for the scarring around his eyes, and a nose that had been broken several times. It was now seven years since he had been paid handsomely by one of Parker's heavies to throw a championship fight, during which he had suffered a real beating and retired from what was little more than a blood sport. Parker had seen potential in the man, and had hired him as a security guard and driver. Larry had risen on merit to be Parker's personal bodyguard, and these days he was in charge of the gangster's/business man's security department.

The next morning, using a burner phone, Larry gave Detective Sergeant Noel Edwards a call and arranged to meet him in a city pub at noon.

Noel was nervous as he entered the Morpeth Arms on Millbank, which was off Vauxhall Bridge Road and had a view across the river of the MI6 building on the Albert Embankment.

It was over ten minutes later when Larry arrived, to nod at Noel but walk past the table he was sitting at to reach the bar and ask for a bottle of non-alcoholic beer. He wore a grey lightweight blouson over a sports shirt, black jeans and tan slip-on loafers.

"How're you doing, Noel?" Larry said to the short, overweight detective, who was wearing a cheap and shabby brown suit, a grubby shirt, Slim Jim tie and scuffed leather lace up shoes that had probably not been polished since the day he had bought them. "You look overworked and underpaid."

"I'm getting by," Noel said. "What do you want?"

"What we pay you for, information. There'll be a decent bonus if you find out what we need to know in a hurry."

"And that is…?"

"You – the Met – have a guy in custody. He's being grilled as a prime suspect over the murders of several citizens."

"You're talking about the Killer Clown, right?"

"Yeah."

"I watched the press conference last evening."

"And so you know what I want; a name, address, what he does for a living and whether he gets charged and held or is released."

"No problem. I can already tell you that he has given them an alibi for one date when this Clown character killed someone. They're checking it out now."

"Why was he arrested?"

"They found his DNA on a cigarette end at a murder scene in Sutton. Since they took him in they've searched his house, but come up with nothing as yet."

"Anything else?"

"No. I'll find out the current state of play and get back to you as soon as poss."

"Later today would be good, Noel," Larry said as he took a sealed brown envelope from a pocket of his blouson and passed it to Noel under the table.

Noel got up and left the pub. He had never intended to be in some gangster's pocket, but it just happened that way. Gambling was an addiction, and it had cost him dearly. Only by being connected with

Larry Wade by a fellow detective had saved him from losing his house. He had cleaned up his act, quit throwing good money after bad, and was now okay for cash, but had become a bad copper; one of a growing fraternity of them. And once you were on the hook there was no way to wriggle free of it; you had been bought and were owned, and had to just pay the piper.

It was four p.m. when one of Larry's mobile phones rang. The caller was Edwards, the bent DS. Making a note of the details he was given, Larry made his way to the main house, from where he had been drinking coffee with two of the security team in one of the offices situated above a six-vehicle garage block.

Jerry Parker was on the phone, talking with his wife, Gayle, who was still in Marbella, but would be flying home the following day. Gayle was finding it almost impossible to accept that Melanie was dead.

"I identified her at the mortuary, darling," Jerry said. "There's no doubt, it was definitely Melanie."

As he finished the call, leaving Gayle to probably get pissed and then cry herself to sleep, there was a knock at the door of his study.

"Come on in," Jerry said, having seen on a monitor that Larry had been let into the house by one of the staff.

"I've got some info on the guy that was being held as a suspect, boss," Larry said as he took a seat in front of Jerry's desk.

"You just said *was being held*. Does that mean that they cut him loose?"

"Yeah. His alibi checked out," Larry said as he took a notepad out of a jacket pocket. "His name is Darren Selby, he lives in a terrace house on Stapleton Road in Tooting Bec with his father, and he's a delivery driver for FedEx."

"What reason did the filth have to arrest him?"

"They found a cigarette end with his DNA on it."

"So he obviously did it."

"The shooter has used the same handgun and MO for all of the previous murders, and it is a known fact now that on the time and date of one of them, Selby was out of town."

"*I* need to personally clear him of my daughter's murder beyond *any* doubt, Larry. Arrange for him to be lifted and brought here blindfolded in the back of a vehicle. I want him lodged in the boiler room next to the garage block, naked, hurt, and tied to a chair. Got it?"

"Yeah, boss, but he's out on police bail. He could be under surveillance."

"Perhaps. Have him tailed for a couple of days. If he isn't being followed he can be taken at some point on his delivery route."

"Do you really believe the filth would have sprung him if they thought he was a fucking serial killer?"

"I'm keeping an open mind. What if he has an accomplice? Remember the Morgan twins. They went on a robbery and killing spree in the late nineties, and took it in turn to do the burglaries and shoot the houseowners, so that each of them had alibis for one out of two of the jobs, but they both used the same gun. The Old Bill were looking for one perp, not two. If it hadn't been for a victim surviving and being able to identify the shooter from mugshots, they would have kept at it."

"I'll set the wheels in motion, boss."

"Do that, Larry."

CHAPTER TWENTY-EIGHT

BERT Selby was still as sharp as a tack. After Darren had been arrested, he not only phoned his solicitor to tell him what had happened, but gave the FedEx depot a call and told them that his son was ill with a stomach bug, and would hopefully be well enough to attend work within the next forty-eight hours.

After being released, Darren had decided to keep a day-to-day diary with entries of all his movements, just in case he was put in a position of having to provide an alibi in the future for dates and times which he would in all probability have no memory of where he had been. Being arrested on suspicion of murder had infused him with a total mistrust of the police, bordering on paranoia. God knows what would have happened if he hadn't been able to provide them with a solid alibi for one of the dates that they had questioned him about.

Two days after his night in a cell, Darren was back at work, and three days later at two-fifteen p.m. in the afternoon he was about to deliver a large package to a posh detached house on Ashfield Lane in Chislehurst. Leaving the radio in the cab on, he climbed out and opened one of the van's rear doors, to lean in and manhandle the quite heavy cardboard box towards him. With the radio playing, he did not hear the black Land Rover Discovery as it freewheeled to a stop behind him.

Larry Wade took personal charge of snatching Darren Selby. Two of his team, Tyler Barrett and Dean Miller, had monitored the FedEx driver's movements for three days and were convinced that he was not under police surveillance.

All three men exited the vehicle. Tyler moved in quickly from behind the mark and used a woollen sock full of glass marbles to swing with measured force against Darren's right temple, and as he fell to the ground senseless, Larry pushed the box back into the van and closed the door. Within seconds they had dragged him to the SUV, picked him up between them and lodged him in the spacious cargo hold. As Dean climbed into the FedEx van and drove off, Tyler got behind the wheel of the SUV, while Larry wrapped duct tape around the unconscious man's head to cover his mouth, to then cut another strip and place the strong, sticky tape across his eyes. Last but not least, he fastened their captive's wrists behind his back with a self-locking plastic cable tie, and used another to bind his ankles together, before covering him with a blanket, closing the boot lid and climbing in the front passenger seat of the Discovery. The entire operation had taken less than ninety seconds.

"That went according to plan," Tyler said as he reversed into a wide driveway, to head back the way they had come. "The guy didn't know what hit him."

"I just hope that you didn't tap him too hard with that homemade cosh," Larry said. "The boss wants him to be able to talk."

"He'll be fine, apart from a pretty bad headache and an egg-sized lump on the side of his head."

Dean drove to an isolated location not far from the Longreach Sewage Treatment Works near the Thames in Dartford, to dump the FedEx van in a reed-filled marsh, after wiping everything he'd touched, which was only the door handle, gear lever, steering wheel and ignition key. He then ambled back along the track he'd driven down to a road that led him to a more built-up area where, after calling in at a McDonald's for a quarter pounder with cheese and a cup of coffee, he phoned for a private hire cab, giving his location and that of The Wheatsheaf, a pub overlooking the village green in Esher, as his destination. From there he would phone Larry and arrange to be picked up and taken back to the house.

Darren came to slowly. His head felt as if it had been split by an axe, he couldn't open his eyes or mouth and his arms were pinioned behind him. He was confused and frightened. One second he had been dragging a large package out of the back of the van, and now he didn't know where he was or what had happened to him.

"He's awake, boss," Larry said over the phone to Jerry.

"Good. I'll be over in a few minutes, when I've finished my coffee. On second thoughts, I'll bring it with me."

Leaving the house and walking across to where the garage block and boiler house were located, with an upper floor of offices above them, Jerry paused to take a sip of his coffee and look up to where at least two dozen house martins were perched on an overhead telephone line. He liked birds, their habits were, unlike most humans, predictable and posed no threat to him. Putting on a pair of black 'Mr

Burbank' style Ray-Ban sunglasses, he entered the boiler house, to be greeted by Larry and Tyler. He studied the slim, naked man secured to a chair at the far end of the room, as he stayed back in the gloom and said to Larry, "Get rid of the tape from his mouth and eyes."

"But he'll see us," Larry said.

"Just do it. I want to look him in the eye when I talk to him."

Larry gave Tyler a curt nod, for him to approach the man and use a Stanley knife to cut through the tape that had been wrapped around his head and pull it free, unmindful of the pain it caused as it was removed, or of the shallow cut that was now dripping blood down his cheek. He then ripped the strip of tape from the man's eyes.

"Do you know why you are here?" Jerry said to Darren.

"No," Darren said. "Where am I, and who the fuck are you?"

Larry stepped forward and drove a clenched fist into Darren's stomach, causing him to double up, but only as far as the handcuffs around the chair's back would allow. He felt the steel of the cuffs bite into his wrists, adding to the other pain in his head, and now his stomach.

"First rule, Darren Selby," Jerry said. "I ask the questions and you answer them, comprende? You're in no position to run off at the mouth and annoy me. If you do, one of my associates here will seriously hurt you."

Gasping for breath, Darren sat up as straight as he could to take the pressure off his wrists, but said nothing.

"We know for a fact that you are the psycho piece of shit that the media are calling the Killer Clown, and that you were arrested and questioned by the police as a prime suspect, but somehow lied your way out of it. I want you to admit it to me."

"The police let me go because I was in Maidenhead at a funeral when one of the murders took place. They checked it out, were satisfied, and released me."

"I know that a cigarette end was found at the last crime scene in Sutton, and the DNA on it was yours. How do you explain that?"

"I can't. I was nowhere near the pub in Sutton when the woman was murdered. I was in a pub in Tooting Bec that evening."

"I think that you're lying to me," Jerry said, and gestured to Larry, who walked behind Darren, picked up a four-foot long piece of nylon rope from a metal bench and looped it over his head, to pull it tight around his neck, increasing the pressure gradually until Darren couldn't breathe and felt as though his eyes would pop out of their sockets. As his vision greyed and he was on the verge of passing out, the rope loosened. He coughed, drew in a deep breath, and then another.

Jerry waited until his captive appeared to be able to talk again. He drained the mug of now lukewarm coffee he had brought with him and said, "You're making this unnecessarily hard on yourself, Selby. You need to come clean. If you don't, I'll let the man standing behind you finish the job with the rope, after he's cut both of your ears off. How does that sound?"

"Terrifying, and also a total fucking waste of your time," Darren said. "The killer will still be out there and I will have died for nothing, because I'm not a homicidal maniac and haven't murdered anyone, ever. If the police had harboured any doubt about it, I'd have been charged and remanded in custody."

Jerry studied the man's facial expression and his eyes, which held a look of combined fear and sincerity in them. He had spent many years dealing with both good and bad men, and for the most part the truth or lies always shone out through their eyes with far more believability than any words from their lips. He decided that Darren Selby was not his daughter's killer, but was now left with what to do with him. The simplest way to deal with the situation would be to have him disappear, never to be seen again, because he had allowed the man to see him, though only at a distance in low light, and he was wearing shades.

"Okay," Jerry said. "At this moment in time I'm inclined to believe you are telling me the truth. I'll let you get dressed, and then, blindfolded, you will be placed in the boot of a car and driven to within a short distance of your house in Tooting Bec. I strongly suggest that your explanation to the police, and to FedEx, due to their van being missing, is that you were about to make a delivery, when you were obviously struck from behind. The next thing you were aware of was coming around to be questioned over the killings that you had been suspected of committing. The main thing for you to remember is that you were blindfolded throughout the episode and saw no one. Any problem with that?"

"No."

"Good, because if you decide to go off script and change the story, I'll have your father killed."

With the cuffs removed, Darren saw that his clothes were in a pile next to the chair with his socks and shoes alongside them. After getting dressed, his wrists were once again shackled, and another strip of tape was applied as a blindfold before he was taken out of the room and roughly helped into the boot of a vehicle.

Time was fluid. He didn't know how long the journey had taken. When the car stopped, he was manhandled out of the boot, and the handcuffs were removed. He heard a door close, and then the sound of the vehicle being driven away.

Only when he was as sure as he could be that he was no longer in imminent danger, did Darren remove the tape from his eyes. He guessed that it was maybe six or seven o'clock. To his surprise, his smartphone and wallet were still in his inside jacket pockets. He checked his phone; it was five-twenty p.m. Only three hours had passed since he had stopped in Chislehurst to deliver a package, but it seemed as if he had been abducted and held for far longer than that. Looking about him, he saw that he was in the yard of a small factory. Its windows were broken, and the faded and flaking white letters on the old brickwork above the double entry doors read: J Cavanagh & Sons. He knew exactly where he was. The paint factory had been closed for more than a decade, and was just a few minutes' walk from his dad's house on Stapleton Road. His house keys were still in his trouser pocket, and so when he arrived home he let himself in, to find his father sitting at the kitchen table eating something he'd heated up in the microwave oven.

"What happened to your face?" Bert Selby said as he looked up and saw the cut to Darren's cheek and the bruised lump on his temple. "Have you been in a fucking brawl?"

"No, Dad. I got lifted by some guys. They knew that the police had arrested me as a suspect of those murders, and that I was then released on bail. It was like something out of a gangster movie. I was tied to a chair bollock naked and blindfolded, with my wrists handcuffed behind me."

"What did they want?"

"To satisfy themselves that I wasn't the guy they call the Killer Clown. I don't know what their interest in the case is, and I don't care."

"Are you going to give the police a bell?"

"Yeah, I'll have to, because the FedEx van is missing. If it wasn't I'd put today behind me. I've got a card in my wallet that one of the detectives gave me."

"There's not a lot you can tell them if you were blindfolded, is there?"

"No," Darren lied. He had decided to tell no one that he had seen the three men who had held him. Even in what he believed to have been an ill-lit boiler room, he had been able to make out the features of the middle-aged guy who had questioned him. He had worn dark shades, presumably to hide his eyes, but he would recognise his face if he saw it again. Not that he ever wanted to. Had the guy not believed what he had told him, then he knew without any doubt whatsoever that he would have been strangled to death. His neck was still sore from the rope which had bitten into it.

CHAPTER TWENTY-NINE

PETE was going through case notes in his shoebox-small office when the landline phone on his desk rang. Picking the receiver up he said, "DI Deakin."

"This is Darren Selby. You gave me your card. I'm calling to let you know that I was abducted today. They knew that I'd been arrested as a prime suspect in the serial killer case you're investigating."

"Thanks for calling," Pete said. "What other details can you give me?"

"Not many. I was delivering parcels and stuff. I'd stopped outside an address in Chislehurst and was hauling a package out of the rear of the van when I must have been knocked out by something. I woke up naked and sitting in a chair, blindfolded with tape covering my mouth and my wrists handcuffed behind my back. Someone cut the tape free so that I could talk, and I was asked a few questions. At one point, what felt like a rope was placed around my neck and I thought I was going to be strangled to death. After a while the guy that was asking me questions seemed to believe what I was telling him. That was it. The cuffs were taken off, and I was told that my clothes were on the floor next to me. I got dressed and was cuffed again, taken outside, placed in the boot of a vehicle and driven to the yard of a small paint factory that closed down years ago. When I was helped out of the boot, the cuffs were removed. I waited until I heard the vehicle drive away and pulled the tape from my eyes. That's when I saw where I was, just a couple of minutes' walk from my father's house."

"Where are you now, Mr Selby?" Pete said.

"At home."

"Good. I'd appreciate you staying there. I need to take a statement from you, face to face, so should be with you within the hour."

"Okay," Darren said. "But I've just told you all I know."

"It's procedure. Run what happened through your mind. See if you can remember anything else, however irrelevant it may seem to be."

After ending the call, Pete went next door to where Matt was working his computer.

"You've got something, haven't you?" Matt said, looking up from the list of persons of interest on his monitor. "I can tell by the smirk on your face."

"I don't smirk," Pete said as he made a beeline to the metal table on which Matt's coffeemaker and a couple of upturned mugs stood on a tea towel, which had an image of the Tower of London on it, to pour himself a mugful before sitting on a chair facing Matt's desk.

"So give," Matt said. "Cut the suspense. What have you got to tell me?"

"That some other person or persons are very interested in the Killer Clown case."

"In what way?"

"I just got off the phone with Darren Selby. He told me that he was abducted today, taken to an unknown destination and questioned."

"By who?"

"He doesn't know. He says that he was coldcocked from behind and came around blindfolded and cuffed to a chair."

"What have you decided to do?"

"Go and talk to him, now."

"I'll come along for the ride, and you can give me the details on the way."

"Which of the murders were the guys that lifted Selby specifically interested in?" Matt said as Pete drove them across Westminster Bridge, heading south to Tooting Bec.

"He wasn't asked about any in particular. Just quizzed in general. They knew that he had been a prime suspect."

"That means it was probably somebody that has contacts in the Met."

"Looks that way."

Pete parked outside the house on Stapleton Road in just under an hour from receiving Darren's call.

It was Bert Selby that opened the door, to be shown ID by both the detectives before inclining his head down the hall, to where they found Darren sitting in an easy chair in the small living room, looking sorry for himself.

"This is Detective Chief Inspector Barnes," Pete said, introducing Matt to Darren. "We'd appreciate you telling us exactly what happened today. Please start with the time, place and what you were doing when you were abducted."

"Would you two like a cup of tea or coffee?" Bert said from where he was standing by the door.

"Coffee black for me, please," Pete said.

"Same," Matt said.

Bert headed for the kitchen, to leave his son and the detectives to talk.

"I'll be taping this," Pete said to Darren as he set a mini digital voice recorder down on a small glass-topped table and thumbed it on, to state the time, date, and who was present.

"Whatever," Darren said. "I was just making my deliveries. At about two-fifteen I stopped outside a house on Ashfield Lane in Chislehurst. The radio was on in the cab of the van, and so as I opened up the back doors and was in the process of removing a large package I didn't hear any vehicle noise or anything untoward. The next thing I knew was coming round with a thumping headache. My mouth and eyes were covered, and my wrists were handcuffed behind me. The tape was ripped off my mouth and someone, a male, started asking me about the murders you're investigating. He initially believed that I was the shooter, and I was hit in the stomach and had a rope pulled tight around my neck."

"Which of the murders was he interested in?" Matt said.

"He didn't say."

"Did he mention *any* names or dates?"

"No."

"Why do you think he let you go?" Pete said.

"Because I told him that you'd checked out my alibi for one of the dates, and that you were one hundred percent positive I'd been in Maidenhead when one of the victims was shot."

"Did you pick up on anything while you were being questioned?"

"In what way?"

"Any sounds, an idea of your surroundings, and the dialect of the guy who was questioning you?"

"Nothing much. At a guess I was in a garage or some kind of storeroom. The floor felt like cold cement on the soles of my feet, and there was the smell of what I think was fuel oil. As for the man's voice, it was quite deep, and he was well-spoken."

Matt was not convinced that Darren was telling them everything he knew. He was too nervous and wouldn't hold direct eye contact with him or Pete.

"I get the feeling that you're holding out on us," Matt said, "and that you know more than what you've just told us."

"I've told you all that I can," Darren said.

"That's a strange way of putting it. *All that you can* suggests to me that you could tell us more. I think that you got to see whoever had you abducted and questioned you, and that you were warned that something bad would happen if you told us more than you already have. Am I right?"

"No. I've told you what happened. There's nothing else."

"You told DI Deakin that you were dropped off in the yard of a nearby disused paint factory, and that you pulled the duct tape from your eyes. Is that correct?"

"Yes."

"What did you do with it?"

"I just crumpled it up and dropped it."

"Where exactly is the factory?"

Darren gave Matt directions.

"Fine," Matt said as he picked up the recorder from the table, switched it off and handed it back to Pete. "We're done here, Mr Selby."

"What now?" Pete said as they left the house; the coffee that Bert had brewed left untouched.

"Check the yard of the old paint factory. If we find the tape there could be prints on it."

Parking outside the building's open gates, it took them less than a minute to locate the scrunched up piece of adhesive tape. Pete pulled on a cellophane glove, picked the tape up and removed the glove by rolling it back to avoid spoiling any latent prints.

"I reckon that someone who was close to one of the victims wanted to have a word with Selby, to satisfy himself that his alibi was solid," Matt said as Pete drove them back to the city. "If he hadn't believed him, we would probably never have seen him again."

"Any idea who would have had the wherewithal to find out about Selby from some official source?"

"Jerry Parker comes to mind. He'll have more than a few contacts in the Met. It's of no real importance, though. Our interest is in

THE URGE TO KILL

finding the killer, not wasting time with some bereaved father whose daughter has been murdered. We'll log what Selby has told us, see if we get a result on prints, and leave it at that, for now."

"Where's our next port of call?" Pete said.

"Ron's place. I fancy a quick pint before you drop me back at base. Then I'll head for home, because Beth will be forgetting what I look like with the hours I'm working."

CHAPTER THIRTY

IT was ten-fifty p.m. when Matt parked in the drive and let himself into the cottage. Beth was in the kitchen, sitting in the nook, cradling a large glass, which was half full or half empty, of Yellowtail Cabernet Sauvignon, which was their current favourite.

"What?" Matt said as Beth stared at him with a look in her eyes that he recognised as being one of infuriation.

"You didn't mention that you'd done a press interview, Barnes. I just saw a replay of it on Sky News."

"It's all part of the job, love, you know that."

"Slagging off the killer you're looking for was totally out of order. You agreed a long time ago that you wouldn't go out of your way to insult them and bring trouble to our door."

"I don't think I went over the top."

"No? I do. To paraphrase what you said, you basically called him a psycho with a limp dick."

"I said that the killer could be a homicidal maniac who is impotent, and that his inadequacy may be the driving force behind his sick crimes. Or he may be a misogynist; a guy who hates women."

"Which in layman's terms *is* a psycho with a limp dick."

"You're no layman, Beth. Let me get myself a large Scotch before we go any further with this discussion," Matt said as he headed for the utility room, where an array of spirit bottles stood on a counter below the wall-mounted wine rack. When he returned to resume what was to him a verbal battle, Beth had emptied her glass.

"Do you want a refill?" he said.

Beth thrust the glass towards him, but said nothing.

"I'm sorry," Matt said when he returned with her replenished drink. "I have a habit of saying what I think to the media."

Beth took a sip of her wine, set the glass down and said, "Tell me about it. Too late now to unsay what you said, so there's no point in us arguing over spilt milk."

"Good. I love you," Matt said, holding his tumbler out to wait until Beth picked up her glass and clinked it against his. "Cheers."

"You're like an old leopard unable to change its spots," Beth said.

"Less of the old. And this big cat has still got sharp claws and healthy teeth."

Beth sighed, smiled, and just shook her head in despair. "You do realise that you could have pissed him off enough to start a war with you."

"I hope not."

"I know you better than that. A part of you always wants to get personal with these flakes and draw them out."

"Who am I to argue with that? You're the psychologist."

"Just promise me that if you front another press interview, you'll be more careful with what you say."

"I'll do my best to censor what I think before I speak."

"You'd better. Have you got any new leads?"

"No. We got a call from Darren Selby, the guy that looked good for the murders until his alibi for one of the times and dates cleared him beyond any doubt. He reported that he'd been abducted and assaulted by persons unknown. They questioned him over his guilt or innocence."

"Does he know who it was?"

"No. Long story short, he told us he'd been knocked out, and when he came around he was sitting on a chair, naked, blindfolded and handcuffed. After being questioned and assaulted, it's obvious that whoever had taken him was convinced that he was innocent, and he was placed in the boot of a car and brought back to a spot near his home."

"Have you any idea who did it?"

"Yes, but it would in all probability be impossible to prove. I know that Selby was holding some details back, probably because he was warned off with threats of what would happen to him, his father or both of them if he said anything more than he did to us."

"I'm going to have another glass of wine," Beth said. "Do you want topping up?"

"Of course," Matt said.

Beth went to pour the drinks. When she returned with them she said, "Satisfy my curiosity, who do you think was responsible?"

"At a guess, Jerry Parker; a wily old fox who is a gangster as well as a legit businessman. Up to now his criminal activities are no more than supposition, with no hard evidence to charge him with anything.

He pays his taxes, does a lot of charity work, and comes across as a pillar of the community. The last victim of the serial killer to date was his daughter, Melanie, which leads me to believe that he wants to identify and deal with her killer as much if not more than we do."

"How did he know that it was Darren Selby who had been a prime suspect?"

"Had to be from a bent copper, who will be on his payroll. All gangsters worth their salt have contacts in the Met."

"Sounds to me as though a lot of serious criminals get away with whatever illegal activities they are involved in."

"They do, Beth, but knowing that someone is guilty of a crime is never enough. The law needs proof of their culpability. The CPS are not going to put someone in a court of law in front of a jury if they don't have a cast-iron case that they expect to get a result from. Admission and confession are the two main ingredients they want, or forensic evidence that is beyond contradiction."

"Meaning that even if you identify this so-called Killer Clown, that will only be half the battle."

"Unfortunately, yes. All he leaves at a murder scene are bullets in bodies and the dumb pictures of a clown's face. Once we know who he is, we'll need to find the gun he uses, or more of the pics, because the chances of him admitting what he's done are infinitesimal."

"Let's hit the sack," Beth said. "I've had too much wine, and I don't want to wake up in the morning with a blinding headache."

"You go up, love," Matt said. "My mind is still whirling around like a spinning top. Maybe another drop of Scotch will help me sleep for a few hours."

Beth kissed him on the cheek before heading for the stairs. Knowing Matt, he would spend another hour or two mulling over the case, attempting to come up with something that would put him on the right track to find the as yet unknown killer.

Matt took Beth's empty glass through to the kitchen to place in the sink, and then poured himself another Scotch before sitting in the nook with only the hall light casting a shadowy glow across the tabletop in front of him. After a while he found himself rubbing his left thigh, at the point where an indented scar was an indelible physical reminder of where on a now long-gone day he had been on witness protection duty; the officer in charge of a team guarding a lowlife who had done a deal to squeal on his gangland boss. Early that morning, in a detached pebble dashed bungalow in Finchley, a hitman had broken in through the door leading from an integral garage and shot every member of the team, and the guy they had ostensibly been protecting. Only Matt had survived the brief encounter, but had been shot twice; one slug nicking his femoral artery to fracture his femur, the other pulverising his left kidney. He had recovered, slowly, but the events of that June morning still haunted him, and the names and faces of the officers who had died were still fresh, permanently branded on his brain.

"Fuck it!" Matt said to the ether. You couldn't erase bad memories, you had to somehow accommodate them, get past dreadful events and move on. You never got a second chance to go back and make a difference. Enough. Being morose was at best pointless, at worst a threat to mental health. Gulping down the Scotch, he left the empty glass on the table and went to bed. One day at a time was the only way to go.

CHAPTER THIRTY-ONE

HE left the house by way of the back door at ten p.m., leaving his car out front in the drive. The lights were on in his lounge, as was his desktop computer, on which he was streaming a movie. He had also placed his smartphone on the coffee table next to the TV remotes, because its location could be traced. He subsequently made his way along the path at the side of the narrow brook which ran behind the dozen detached properties on the dead end lane on which he lived. Fifteen minutes later he arrived at the lockup where he garaged the old Ford Cortina. Check. He had his latex gloves, balaclava, semiautomatic pistol, silencer, and a gizmo that he had bought with cash from a stall that sold second-hand electrical items at a car boot sale on a site on the outskirts of Bromley, which he was eagerly looking forward to using. He was ready to go, to be out on the prowl again, hunting for some female who had put herself in a vulnerable situation by being in a location which would give him the privacy he needed to kill her.

Almost forty-five minutes later, in near darkness, he drove slowly past Croham Hurst Woods in south Croydon, and through a gap in the crowded trees at the side of the road he saw a light; perhaps someone with a torch. His imagination conjured up a woman on her own, or walking a dog. It was too interesting to ignore. Stopping and reversing into a gap in the foliage, he walked back to where he had glimpsed the light. There was a furrowed track large enough for a vehicle to drive down, and so he walked along it and came to a grass-covered circular area almost surrounded by tall trees with, lo and behold, a car parked almost at the centre of it.

Stepping to the side of the clearing, he made his way to the rear of what was a black Toyota Corolla. There was movement inside it, and he grinned as he donned the balaclava and latex gloves, to then screw the silencer onto the gun and walk around to the driver's door.

Only five minutes earlier, Lucy Poulson had stepped out of the car to smoke a cigarette, causing the dome light to come on before she shut the door behind her. Both her and Andy Garfield had already had sex twice, and she had needed to cool down for a couple of minutes. What she was doing out here in the woods with Andy made her feel both ashamed and guilty, but not enough to stop her from doing it. They were both married, but not to each other. Her husband of twenty years, Bruce, had over the previous couple of years lost interest in her. The love had deserted their marriage, and both of her teenage sons were living their own lives. One of them, Stephen, was at university up north in Leeds, and the other, Luke, still lived at home, but when in the house, apart from joining her and Bruce downstairs for breakfasts and evening meals, spent most of the time upstairs in his bedroom on his computer. It was as if the good family times had come and gone in the blink of an eye. She was forty-four, knew that her youthful looks had faded, and was now reduced to sneaking around having an affair with the husband of her best friend. God knows what she would do if it ever came to light; it didn't bear thinking about.

Back in the car, Andy was ready to go again. He had moved over to the driver's seat to sit on their pile of clothes while Lucy had got out to have a smoke, unmindful of being naked, due to it being a warm summer evening. The back of the passenger seat was reclined as far as it would go, and when Lucy got back into the car she laid back and spread her legs, as Andy almost feverishly moved over her, to feel her hand grasp his turgid penis and guide it deftly into her slick vagina.

With the glow of moonlight illuminating the man's juddering buttocks through the window, he became hard as he watched the coupling take place. Being a voyeur was, he decided, a very stimulating pastime; an appetiser to the main course of murder.

As the driver's door was pulled open, Andy jerked his head sideways, to be faced by a man who was wearing a balaclava and pointing a gun at him. He froze, and slipped out of Lucy as his erection immediately diminished.

"Do anything rash and I'll put a bullet through your skull," he said to the naked man. "Twist around, reach up and switch off the dome light."

Andy was too shocked to move. He just stared wide-eyed at the masked man.

"The light. Turn the fucking thing off. Do it now."

Slowly, half turning, Andy stretched his arm up to find the switch with a shaking hand and clicked it off.

Lucy heard every word, but couldn't have moved a muscle if her life had depended on it, which in reality it did.

"What are your names?" he said to the couple.

"Andy and Lucy," Andy said, answering for both of them.

"Let me guess, Andy. You both look to be of an age at which you shouldn't have the need to find places like this to get it on, which means that you're both cheating on your spouses. Am I right?"

Andy nodded.

"The price to pay for such behaviour can be very high. Do you want to survive this meeting?"

"Y…Yes," Andy said.

"That's good to know. All I want from you both is your mobile phones."

"Mine is in front of you on the seat, in my jacket pocket," Andy said. "And Lucy's will be in her handbag, which is in the footwell."

"Okay, while I find them, turn back to face the whore beneath you, and feel free to get on with what you were doing before I rudely interrupted your carnal activity with another man's wife."

Having sex was now the last thing on Andy's mind. He faced Lucy and, in the ambient light that his eyes had now adjusted to, saw the fixed look of terror on her alabaster-white face.

With his left hand, he rummaged through the woman's bag, watching the man intently as with his right hand he kept the gun trained on him, ready to shoot if he made any sudden, untoward move. When he had found both phones, he pocketed them before saying, "I've decided that you both need to be punished for what you are doing, so I'm going to shoot you. Are you ready to die?"

Lucy attempted to scream, but all she could manage was a whimper. Andy flung himself off her, sideways, in a vain effort to grapple with the stranger, whose threat he believed to be real.

Killing people was almost too easy. Human beings were such fragile life forms, vulnerable to countless diseases, accidents, or the intentional taking of their wretched lives.

Andy's forward momentum was halted abruptly as a bullet drilled through his left eye, to pass through his brain and exit the back of his skull, taking with it a cloud of blood and matter. Falling back over Lucy, the head of her now dead lover settled in her naked lap.

"Nooo!" Lucy shouted, grasping Andy's shoulders and pushing him sideways with all her might, for him to topple onto his back over the centre console; the rear of his damaged head coming to rest on the pile of clothing on the driver's seat. Lucy was going into shock, quivering and gasping for breath, unmindful of the copious amount of blood spatter that peppered her from face to thighs.

"You should have booked in some seedy hotel for the evening." He said. "Shagging in isolated places like this is asking for trouble as, far too late I'm afraid, you now know."

He shot her in the dark triangle of her neatly trimmed pubic hair, to watch as she thrashed around in agony for more than ten seconds, before putting a second bullet in her throat.

Lucy began to choke. The slug had passed through her trachea, and she knew that she was dying, due to being unable to draw breath. Blood gushed from her gaping mouth as she instinctively reacted by clutching at the site of the entry wound, as if she could somehow prevent the inevitable from happening.

Her fear, pain and the brief struggle she made to thwart death was an entrancing sight to behold. After she had slumped back, lifeless, he used the man's smartphone to take three photos; one of the woman, one of the man and, stepping back a few feet, one of both of them together. He thought it would be amusing to send the graphic images to the errant couple's supposedly nearest and dearest. As almost an afterthought he fished one of his clown pictures from a pocket to toss into the car, where it landed on the dead man's torso to settle face up, adhering to chest hair now matted with blood.

Walking back along the track to the road, he removed the balaclava, and also the silencer from the pistol, to pocket them before sitting down with his back against the trunk of a tree, to look up the pertinent numbers in the contact lists of both the phones and send the photos. Imagining the mental devastation that they would cause was more thrilling than visiting Disneyworld in Florida as a child had been. Once done, he had one more very important call to make, to the detective by the name of Barnes, who had badmouthed him during a press conference held outside New Scotland Yard.

CHAPTER THIRTY-TWO

AT a little before midnight, Matt and Beth were watching a Jason Statham action movie when Matt's Samsung Galaxy phone started to buzz on the coffee table. Picking it up he saw that it was from an unknown caller. He accepted the call, and set it to record, but said nothing.

"Are you there Detective Chief Inspector Barnes?" A *woman's* voice.

"Yes, who is this?" Matt said as he increased the volume so that Beth could hear both sides of the conversation.

"That's for me to know, and for you to find out. I've just called to gloat. Firstly, I bet you thought you'd won the lottery when the cigarette end was found next to the body of the woman in Sutton. Be aware that I planted it. But the real reason for this call is to give you the heads-up on what I've been up to this evening. I'm about to send you three photos, which I know you will find extremely interesting. Once you've received them I'll leave the line open so that you can trace the phone's location."

Matt waited, and as he did he held the mobile at arm's length and whispered to Beth, "Phone the SCU. I need this call traced."

The photos came through. He opened them to be faced by the horrific images of a naked man and woman in the front seats of a car. There was a lot of blood.

"Are you suitably surprised and appalled at the pics of my latest victims?" the *female* voice said.

"Both," Matt said, working at keeping his voice calm and conversational. "They *are* appalling, and I am surprised because I would never have guessed that our male killer has a female accomplice as deranged as he is."

"We are *not* fucking deranged, Barnes. Just a modern day Bonnie and Clyde who kill people instead of robbing banks."

"I look forward to meeting you Bonnie, because you can count on it happening. When you're both in maximum security prisons serving whole life sentences, you'll know that I'll be smiling every day, thinking of you caged like animals in a zoo."

"In your dreams, Barnes. It won't happen. You couldn't put a kid's eight piece jigsaw together without trace evidence or information from the public. You sad lot aren't fit for purpose. And now I'm going to loathe you and leave you. I need to quit the scene and let you get on with mopping up the mess I've made."

"Before you leave, tell me why you're doing it?"

"Because we can," *she* said, before leaving the two phones on the ground, removing the latex gloves and heading back to where the Cortina was parked, to then drive to a twenty-four hour McDonald's at the Colonnades off Purley Way in Croydon, to park in deep shadow at the rear of the car park and walk around to the main entrance. The adrenaline surge from the double killing and subsequent phone call to the detective had waned, leaving him famished. He ordered a Big Mac, fries, BBQ dip and a large cup of black coffee. As he ate, he reflected on his actions of late; the evening of the fifteenth of June, had been very rewarding. He had called in at the Wolf Trap pub in Tooting Bec, to have a drink before beginning his hunt, and noticed that a man of similar age standing at the bar had a slight look of him; same height, dark hair, and comparable facial features. Taking his pint glass with him, the man left the lounge by way of a door which led outside to a lighted Perspex-roofed smoking area, where he sat at a table and lit a cigarette.

Watching through the window into the yard, an idea came to mind. He waited until the man came back in and returned to the bar, before going out and casually looking in the large glass ashtray on the table where the look-alike had been sitting, to see that there was only one cigarette end in it. There was no other customer in the yard, and so using a tissue as a buffer, he picked it up and pocketed it. Later that night, after carrying out the shooting of the woman in thick shrubbery at the side of the Stag Inn's car park in Sutton, he had left the filched cigarette end on the ground, just a couple of feet from the corpse. It would have the guy's DNA on it, and with any luck a partial fingerprint, and voila, it had led to the police making an arrest, and for a short time believe that their prime suspect was the Killer Clown. That he, whoever he was, must have been able to provide an irrefutable alibi for the time and date when at least one of the murders had taken place was of no real concern. To confound them for a while had been the aim of the highly entertaining exercise. He grinned as heard the sound of police sirens in the distance, and ate his last fry, after first plunging it into the almost depleted container of BBQ dip.

With the meal finished, and just a mouthful or two of coffee left in his cup, he reviewed the phone call he had made to the DCI, using the second-hand compact voice modulator he had purchased at the car boot sale in Bromley. With the included cable and USB Micro-B connector, he had been able to plug it into the dead man's smartphone. The sound of his voice could be altered according to preference, changing the pitch, cadence and even the gender. He had chosen to sound like a woman, which had obviously given the detective much food for thought. Ah, well, time to go. He left the Mac's and drove back to the lockup to garage the Cortina and then walk home. It had been a terrific evening. He had enjoyed his phone call to Barnes as much if not more than the killing of the couple. Now, for a while, he would back off and lead what was his *normal* life, until the urge to kill once more became too powerful to suppress. It had all started with the young black guy who'd attempted to mug him at gunpoint in a multistorey car park in the city. He had overcome him and taken the handgun, and could not resist using it, again and again.

"Did you get through to the squad room?" Matt said as Beth returned to the lounge.

"Yes. I used my mobile. Pete took the call and said he would get back to us when they have a location for the phone."

"Listen to the conversation I had while you were in the kitchen, and tell me what you think," Matt said as he replayed the recorded call.

Beth listened intently and then said, "First impression is that it could have been a man attempting to sound like a woman. Show me the photos."

Matt brought up the grim images one by one for Beth to inspect.

"Whether you've got a single killer or a double act, he or they appear to just be murdering people for the hell of it, because they want to."

Beth's mobile rang. It was Pete, and so she mouthed his name to Matt and handed him the phone.

"Yeah, Pete. What have you got?"

"The phone that was used to call you is at Croham Hurst Woods, next to Upper Selsdon Road in South Croydon. There are local units on the way to the spot now. What has gone down?"

"A couple have apparently been shot to death in a car. The perpetrator phoned me and told me what he or she had done."

"He or she?"

"Yeah. I'm not sure which. I'll play the recording of the call to you later. Who's with you in the squad room?"

"Just Tam."

"I take it that you'll both be attending the scene."

"Yeah. Will you be turning up?"

"Definitely. I'll meet you both there."

"Could be a hoax."

"I very much doubt it. I'll send you pics that I received from the caller, now, and then let you phone John Stott and tell him what we know."

"Looks like a double hit out of a Yank gangster movie," Pete said as one by one he studied the photos from Matt on his mobile's screen.

Five minutes later, with his car keys in one hand and a lidded thermal mug of coffee to go, courtesy of Beth, Matt was leaving the cottage.

It was almost twelve-fifty a.m. when Matt parked his Vectra behind one of the police cars. Pete and Tam met him at the gap in the foliage behind which a short track led off into the darkness.

"What have we got?" Matt said.

"Exactly what was on the photos you sent me," Pete said. "I've taken a few more for our whiteboards. There's a black Toyota Corolla in the clearing at the end of the track with the bodies in it. And the first uniforms to arrive at the scene found two smartphones on the ground, halfway between here and the car. I've requested CSIs and a pathologist to attend."

Matt began to walk along the rutted track, passing where the phones had been left, to approach the car. Both the driver's and front passenger doors had been opened by the first attenders, to satisfy themselves that the couple inside were beyond the need of any medical attention.

The bodies in the car were lit by the soft glow of moonlight, and Matt stared at the chilling scene of the dead couple, covered only in their own slowly drying blood. The smell of shit assailed his nostrils.

The woman's bowels had loosened as she fought for life, and the cardboard, pine-scented air freshener hanging from the rearview mirror could not combat the malodorous stench. Looking almost directly down, his gaze met the eyes of the man, his head resting on a pile of clothing on the driver's seat, eyes wide open and rolled back in their sockets to show the whites. On the dead man's chest was a small, familiar translucent packet containing the image of a grinning clown, which was the killer's trademark.

Turning to where Pete and Tam were standing over six feet from the car, keeping their distance from the repugnant odour that had filled the vehicle, Matt shook his head at the pointless and brutal slaying of the couple. It was impossible to understand the workings of some people's minds. Throughout history a small percentage of human beings had cold-bloodedly used violence, torture and murder against others. Good and evil had existed side by side for as long as humanity had, and it still did and always would.

"I'll let you two wait for the troops to arrive," Matt said as he made to leave the scene. "Whoever turns up from the MIT on DCI John Stott's behalf, tell them that we'll be holding a case meeting at nine a.m. in the conference room on the second floor, and make sure that all our team members are there."

"Pulling rank, eh?" Pete said.

"Of course. If you've got it, flaunt it," Matt said as he walked off towards the road, knowing that within an hour the clearing and track would be lit up like an evening game at Wembley by arc lamps that would turn night to day for crime scene investigators and a Home Office pathologist to properly carry out their respective duties.

CHAPTER THIRTY-THREE

THE full team of SCU detectives gathered in the squad room at eight-thirty a.m. on the morning after the couple had been shot to death in south Croydon, in what had been an execution style slaying. As per usual, nothing appeared to have been stolen and there was no evident motive for the double murder.

Standing in front of the whiteboards, dressed in her trademark outfit of fitted black skirt suit over a white high-necked silk blouse, and wearing practical low-heeled black leather court shoes, Detective Chief Superintendent Julia Stone faced the small assembly of her elite squad to address them.

"You've all seen the pictures, and listened to the recording of the phone call between Matt and the shooter, who sounded like a woman." Julia said. "Any initial views on the crime?"

"It could be a copycat killer started up," Kelly said.

"The perpetrator left a picture of a clown's face, and also stated that he, *or she*, had planted the cigarette end found at the scene of Melanie Parker's murder," Julia said. "And I am convinced that when the bullets are recovered and examined they will be a match to the pistol used to commit the previous crimes."

"How did the killer get your smartphone number, boss?" Errol said, addressing his question to Matt.

"The only logical way is that one of the persons of interest that I've interviewed and left a contact card with is the perpetrator."

"Do you know how many you gave cards to?"

Matt smiled. "Yes, I made a note of the names. There are fourteen in all."

"That's the break we needed," Pete said. "It narrows the field."

"Picking one out and finding proof of his guilt, or even being able to get a search warrant for his house and car could be a non-starter," Jeff said. "If his original alibi holds up, all we would do is scare him off."

"That would be a start," Julia said. "If he knows that we suspect him and he isn't totally stupid, he'll stop killing until he believes at some point that he isn't a suspect under surveillance."

"What about the phone call from the woman?" Marci said.

"Could be an accomplice," Julia said. "Which complicates things, if there is two of them."

"I still believe that it's a lone wolf killer," Matt said. "After the meet with DCI Stott and some of his team at nine, I intend to take my phone over to Kenny Ruskin in Computer Crime Section. Hopefully he'll be able to run the call through whatever tech necessary to assess if it was tampered with."

"Tampered with?" Tam said. "In what way?"

"There is a very low but continuous background noise throughout the call. I believe that the caller was male, and that he was using a modulator plugged into the phone to alter his voice to sound like a woman."

"That's a novel theory."

"I looked it up on the net. You can buy those devices."

"He really *is* a game player," Errol said.

"That's his weakness," Matt said. "Communicating with us will be his downfall. We now have two leads to follow."

"Two?" Jeff said.

"Yeah," Matt said. "He, and I'm sure that it is a man working alone, should have thought it through and not phoned my mobile number. He obviously didn't realise that the only way he could have gotten it was from a card I'd left him."

"What's the other lead?" Pete said.

"He told me that he'd planted the cigarette end at the scene, which means he saw Darren Selby discard it, and we know that Darren was in the Wolf Trap pub in Tooting Bec on the evening that Melanie Parker was murdered."

"Ironical," Jeff said, "that your supposed lone wolf killer was in the Wolf Trap that night."

"Define lone wolf for me," Kelly said.

"As most of you know, Beth was a member of a CPP (Criminal Personality Programme) team at the Northfield Hospital for the Criminally Insane for a number of years, and for a while also consulted with the police on serial killers, trying to give an insight as to the personality of the offender," Matt said. "She analysed violent repeat crime and attempted to predict facets of an unknown subject's character. She was adept at interpreting and building a profile to gain an insight as to the personality disorder the individual suffered from. I've obviously learned a lot from her, and we have discussed the current case. In her estimation the definition of a lone wolf is someone who is not *usually* antisocial or a danger to others. They are just very private individuals and do not easily let others into their lives, having very limited interest in building any meaningful relationships with other people. Beth says that there are exceptions to every rule, and that in extreme cases they can be highly dangerous."

"Is that what Beth thinks the man we're hunting for is?" Pete said.

"With what evidence we have of his actions to date, yes."

"Does that in any way help us?" Marci said.

"A lot," Matt said. "We're looking for an antisocial guy who isn't the happy family type. I think he will be single, which immediately cuts down the number of individuals that I handed cards to. Five of them live alone, and didn't have what I deem to be solid alibis for any of the dates we're interested in."

"How do you want to play it?" Pete said, addressing both Matt and Julia.

"Interview all of the persons of interest that I handed cards to," Matt said. "Plus whoever gave them an alibi, if they had one. And we need to visit the pub in Tooting Bec along with Darren Selby, later. It's a longshot, but they may still have CCTV footage of the night when Melanie Parker was murdered."

"What now?" Darren said as he opened the door to Matt and Jeff, having just finished eating lunch with his dad.

"We'd appreciate it if you would accompany us to your local pub, Mr Selby."

"Why?"

"Because we believe that the killer lifted your cigarette end from there on the evening of the fifteenth of June."

"It'll cost you a pint of bitter," Darren said.

"No problem."

When they reached the Wolf Trap, Matt ordered the drinks; bitter for Darren and him and half a pint of shandy for Jeff.

"Which table were you sitting at?" Matt said.

"None, I was standing at the bar, and then went out through the door at the rear. It leads out to a smoking area."

"Show us."

Darren led them out to the roof covered yard and indicated the table that he had been sitting at.

"Was anyone else at the table?" Matt said.

"No. As I recall there was only one other guy out here."

"Can you describe him?"

Darren closed his eyes and gave it some thought before saying, "All that comes to mind is that he was maybe in his sixties, overweight, and had short grey hair. He went back inside the pub before I did."

"Were there any other cigarette ends in the ashtray you used?"

"No."

"Do you recall anyone else coming out here while you were smoking?"

"No. I put my cig out and went back inside. When I finished my pint I left and walked home."

Back in the pub proper, Jeff asked the guy behind the bar if he had CCTV footage from the relevant date.

"There's no footage from *any* date," the barman said. "We have two cameras; one out front and one out back, but both of them are fake. The boss doesn't spend a penny on anything he doesn't have to."

It had been a waste of time. All they were now sure of was that the killer had been in the pub and witnessed Darren go out back for a smoke, to watch as the man who had a slight look of him put the cigarette out and leave. He no doubt took the butt from the ashtray in a spur of the moment act, with the sole intention of amusing himself by leaving it at a murder scene to confuse investigators for a while, and he had succeeded.

Finishing his pint, Darren said, "Is that it, can I go now?"

"Yeah," Matt said. "Are you still working for FedEx?"

"No, they let me go. Said it was just cutbacks, but it was because I'd lost the van, and they weren't convinced with my story of being abducted."

"Have you got another job lined up yet?"

"I've got an interview with a second-rate security company. Long hours and low pay, but it'll put me on for a while."

"Best of luck with it," Matt said. "Thanks for helping out, and give us a call if you decide to tell us more about the guys who lifted you."

Darren gave Matt and Jeff a solemn look before showing them his back and leaving the Wolf Trap to return home. The man who had questioned him had made threats that he knew would be carried out if he said any more than he already had to the police. He had been hurt, even half-strangled, and if what he had said to the man had not been believed, then he was certain that he would have suffered a great deal of pain and then been murdered.

CHAPTER THIRTY-FOUR

JERRY Parker was sitting at a table on the patio outside the rear of the house. The heat of the midday sun was kept at bay by a large motorised blue and yellow striped awning that was fixed to the wall. Jerry was drinking cognac and reflecting on the most horrendous day in his life, to date; the day on which he had attended the police mortuary to formally identify the body of his daughter, Melanie. Larry had driven him into the city, to park in a space on the street, unmindful of the double yellow lines, to wait for his boss to return.

Once inside the mortuary and showing photo ID to a receptionist and stating why he was there, Jerry had, after a five minute wait, been led along a corridor by a bespectacled young man wearing a white coat over a tee shirt, to an office that had a couple of chairs, a desk with de rigueur computer, printer and phone on its top, and a large wall-mounted monitor. The nerdy looking guy used a remote to bring up a live feed on the screen, which revealed what was a viewing room. The walls and floor were stark white, as was the sheet that clearly covered a body on the wheeled gurney which stood in the middle of the room.

"Is that my daughter under the sheet?" Jerry said.

"Yes Mr Parker."

"Take me to see her."

"I'm afraid that's not protocol."

"I don't give a fuck about your protocol," Jerry said. "I want to see my daughter up close and personal, not on a fucking TV screen."

"I'll need to go and ask if—"

"You don't need to do anything but take me to her, now, Jon Barton," Jerry said as he lifted up the ID card, which was clipped to the ball chain around the young man's neck, to inspect the details on it. "Be aware that I am not someone that you would want to upset. Show some consideration and empathy, or suffer the consequences."

"Are you threatening me?" Jon said, finding it hard to believe that this grieving man was being so outrightly hostile toward him.

"I'm giving you the opportunity to do the right thing, son. The guys that work for me would probably be in touch with you if I left here without spending a minute or two with my daughter, and you really wouldn't want to meet them."

Jon looked into the man's dark eyes and saw the menace that radiated out from them. He didn't need this shit in his life. Sometimes you had to back down and use common sense when faced with adversity. Some people were genuinely dangerous individuals, and this guy definitely was.

Coughing nervously and using the zapper to switch the monitor off, Jon headed for the door and said, "No problem Mr Parker. Follow me."

Jerry was led to the next room, to feel a tightening in his gut and a chill run up his spine as he was faced by the covered corpse.

Jon walked across to the gurney, to grasp hold of the sheet and look at the man, who nodded, giving him the go ahead to pull the sheet down and reveal Melanie's face.

Seeing is believing. Although he knew that his daughter had been murdered, a small part of his mind still had the impossible notion that it was a case of mistaken identity, which he knew was foolish.

She looked to be at rest, which was at least a little heartening, but not much. There was a small white towel folded and draped across her forehead.

"Why the towel?" Jerry said, even though he was sure he knew.

"Your daughter was shot in the forehead," Jon said, not offering up the fact that she had been shot in the crotch as well.

Jerry stepped up close to the gurney, to bend forward and kiss Melanie's cheek. The expression on her face was peaceful, as though she was just sleeping. He said nothing aloud, but in his thoughts he told Melanie that he loved her, and vowed that whoever had taken her life would pay the ultimate price.

"Thanks, Jon," Jerry said. "When will I be able to have my daughter transferred to an undertakers?"

"I'll liaise with the police and give you a call, Mr Parker."

"I'd appreciate it being sooner rather than later."

"I'm on it," Jon said, having decided that this was not the kind of individual to fall foul of.

Back in the moment, sitting out in the sunshine, having dragged his mind away from the glaring white confines of the viewing suite, and the – in some way – surreal sight of Melanie's corpse laid out on a gurney, Jerry drained the glass, to refill it from the now depleted bottle of Courvoisier XO cognac that he had brought outside with him. Shit! His brain seemed to be scrambled of late, full of grief and of recent images of his daughter that he could not dispel. The current thoughts running through his mind were of when Melanie's body had been released to the funeral director of his choosing, and the morning that he and Gayle had gone to view her in the chapel of rest. It was amazing how alive she had appeared to be, and Jerry was relieved to see that there was no towel on her forehead, due to the expert application of mortician's wax and makeup, which had totally masked the bullet hole. He also recalled that with legs gone to jelly, Gayle had grasped the edge of the open coffin in a steely grip. Had she not, then she would have no doubt collapsed to the floor.

Leaving the sombre, oak-walled room, on what would be the final time they would see their late daughter in the flesh, anger had taken pole position in Jerry's mind.

And now it was over. The funeral had been a nightmare to live through, as was the following gathering in the function room of a local hotel, where people offered their awkward condolences as they drank alcohol and ate their way through a mountain of sandwiches, sausage rolls and other assorted canapés that had been served up. Jerry and Gayle hadn't stayed long. They hadn't thought of Melanie's funeral as a celebration of her life, it was no more than a final farewell.

Larry drove them home, where Gayle went up to the master bedroom to cry her eyes out in privacy, as she sat on the edge of the bed holding a framed photograph of a smiling Melanie in one trembling hand and a glass of neat gin in the other.

Before Larry left the house, Jerry had told him to get back in touch with his contact in the Met, to lean on him hard for more information with regard to the case of the psycho who had been tagged the Killer Clown.

"He knows that I want to know about any new leads, boss."

"Offer him a big payday to keep on top of it. Greed tends to concentrate the mind. This is personal. I want the piece of shit that murdered Melanie to be lifted by us, to be brought to the boiler room so that I can dismantle him over a lengthy period. What I *don't* want is for the filth to arrest him. Being given life in some cushy nick wouldn't settle the score for me."

"We have contacts doing bird," Larry said. "He wouldn't last long in prison."

"Like I said, this is as personal as it fucking gets. I want to be his one-man judge, jury and executioner. Do you get that?"

"Loud and clear. I'll have another meet with the MIT copper on the take and impress on him that it would be in his best interest to keep me up to date with any new leads they have, and let me know immediately if they come up with another prime suspect."

"Tell him that if we beat his lot to the killer's door, there'll be a twenty grand bonus for him. That should be incentive enough for him to pull out all the stops."

After Larry had left, Jerry made his way to the bar in the lounge, to take a fresh bottle of cognac from a shelf of the wall cabinet and begin to unscrew the cap, only to stop, give it some thought, and put the bottle back. Booze wasn't the answer, and didn't change a damn thing. The bitter truth was that life moved on through thick and thin. Nothing stayed the same. All he could do was get on with it. He had wealth, business interests both legal and otherwise, but at times like this it all counted for nothing. He couldn't bring his daughter back, but could and would avenge her death.

Heading for the kitchen, he decided to have a cup of coffee, and then get back to work. There were people he needed to discuss ongoing deals with, and at this moment in time, hanging one on and brooding over his loss would do nothing but take him into mental meltdown.

Before making phone calls and sending a few emails, Jerry went upstairs, to find Gayle sprawled out diagonally on top of the king size bed. She was asleep and had no doubt cried herself out. Next to her slack right hand was a gilt-framed photo of Melanie standing in front of their swimming pool at the villa in Marbella, with a smile on her face that would light up the darkest night.

Shaking his head, now back in the present, he put thoughts of Melanie's recent, tragic murder and all that had ensued to one side. What was keeping him going now was the hot wire of hatred running through his brain, and the determination to at some juncture have his daughter's killer tied to a chair suffering unimaginable torture before finally, after several days, having petrol poured over him and being set alight. He had always believed in an eye for an eye, and would relish exterminating a man who did not have the capacity to show any degree of mercy to others.

CHAPTER THIRTY-FIVE

"**I** guess that we should share details with DCI Stott of the fourteen guys that you handed out cards to," Pete said as they discussed the way forward.

"Okay, do that," Matt said. "But I intend to personally interview the five single guys again, starting just as soon as I finish my coffee, because not one of them had alibis that were bulletproof."

"Fine," Pete said. "I'll ride shotgun with you, just in case you meet up with the Clown. We can let some of John Stott's detectives team up with our squad and doorstep the other nine."

The five single men that Matt intended to talk to again were: Trevor Finlay, Gordon Lucas, Nathan Edmonds, Carl Gibson and Peter Willis. Two of them had been given alibis by girlfriends for one or more of the significant times and dates. The other three had not been able to account for their whereabouts on any of them, which did not imply guilt, but had given the team reason to red flag them.

Matt had all the information on the suspects printed up, and Pete went through it word by word.

"Let's start with the three who couldn't come up with anything we could check out previously," Matt said. "We can run through all the dates with them again and see if there are any variations from what they initially told us."

There was no answer to the door of Trevor Finlay's second floor flat in Walworth, and so Pete drove to a nearby fresh fish and seafood market where Finlay worked as a porter.

"Help you?" Barney Glover, a burly florid-faced man wearing a stained white coat and a straw boater's hat said as Matt and Pete entered the large building and tapped on the open office door.

"We'd like a word with Trevor Finlay," Pete said as he held up his ID for the fishmonger to inspect.

"What's he done?"

"We just want to ask him a couple of questions," Matt said. "Is he here?"

"Yeah, he'll be in the cold room at the end of the building."

Trevor was packing crates full of whitefish with crushed ice and looking forward to lunchtime, when he would call in at Arments Pie & Mash Café on Westmoreland Road for a bite to eat and a mug of tea, which he did Monday to Friday every week.

"Mr Finlay, we'd like a word with you," Matt said.

Turning to face the two detectives, recognising the one who had spoken, Trevor said, "Not you again. Who's been topped now?"

"You watch the news on TV, don't you, Trevor?"

"No. I watch movies on Netflix. The news is just full of talking heads spouting shit."

"Do you own a voice modulator?" Matt said.

"A what?"

"A gizmo that you can alter your voice with."

"No, but I've got a pet unicorn that only I can see."

"Is that a feeble attempt at humour?" Pete said.

Trevor just shrugged his shoulders.

"We need to know where you were from after ten p.m. on the eighteenth which is just Tuesday gone," Matt said.

Trevor smiled and said, "That's one I *can* answer. I was in the

Phoenix Club on Heygate Street. It was quiz night, and I'm one of a

team called the Fish Market Four. I got there at just before eight and

didn't leave 'til after eleven. One of the team, Mal Kellet, drove me

home. Check it out."

"We will Mr Finlay, you can count on it," Pete said.

"Next up is Peter Willis," Matt said as they walked back to the car. "He's on benefits, hardly leaves the council flat he lives in on the Milford Heights Estate in Bermondsey, which is a high-rise due to be demolished soon, and he couldn't come up with his whereabouts on any of the significant dates. He told me that he doesn't keep track of time, due to the effects of the weed he smokes."

"Did you buy it?"

"I kept an open mind. He was either a very good actor, or was telling me the truth."

Peter Willis had just poured boiling water over the contents of an original curry flavour Pot Noodle when someone knocked at his flat door. He wasn't expecting company, so ignored whoever was there and stirred his quick snack with a fork. When the door was knocked again, louder, he made his way to it and shouted, "Who the fuck is it?"

"Police, Mr Willis. Open the door," Matt said.

Peter opened the door, but didn't invite them in, just stood his ground and asked what their problem was.

"We need a word with you," Matt said.

"About what?"

"Ask us in," Pete said. "We don't want to stand out here and entertain your neighbours."

"Show me some ID."

"Don't you recognise me?" Matt said as he produced his warrant card. "Last time I was here I asked you to provide proof of where you were on several dates."

Peter frowned. He had no memory of meeting the copper before. "I've no recollection of you, but come on in to my hovel if you have to," he said. "I've got a Pot Noodle going cold."

Matt and Pete followed the dishevelled guy through to a small kitchen. Willis was wearing a stained Guns N' Roses tee, frayed denim shorts, and a pair of oversize slippers on his bare feet, which appeared to make him shuffle like a penguin to stop them from falling off.

"What's this about?" Peter said as he picked up the plastic pot, to shovel dripping noodles into his mouth with a fork.

"The card I left you with phone numbers on. I believe you gave me a bell the other night, late. Is that correct?"

"No, and like I said, I don't remember ever meeting you. If you left me a card I probably binned it, or maybe it's in the living room among all the other crap I haven't got around to chucking out yet."

Matt had no doubt that Willis was not the man they sought, or that his addiction was restricted solely to smoking joints.

"Okay, have a good day," Matt said as he watched a cluster of soft noodles and juice break free from the fork, to dribble down the man's chin, drop onto the tee shirt and slide down it like a tangle of writhing worms.

"If he's the killer, I'm the tooth fairy," Matt said as they climbed in the car and Pete drove to the address of the next suspect on the list, Gordon Lucas, who lived in a terraced house on Southvale Road in Blackheath. Although Lucas was one of the two who'd given a girlfriend's name as an alibi, geographically it was nearest.

"I recognise you," Jill Hawkins said to Matt when she opened the door. "You questioned me a while back over where Gordon was on specific dates."

Matt was a little surprised to see the young woman. She had lived in a flat in Deptford and worked at a nail salon when he had last interviewed her.

"You look a little confused," Jill said. "I was seeing Gordon four or five evenings a week, and so when he got around to asking me to move in with him, it made sense, so I did, a couple of weeks ago."

"So you would know where he was on the evening of Tuesday just gone, the eighteenth."

"That's easy. We went to a birthday do at a nearby pub, the Hare and Billet. Got there at about eight p.m. and didn't leave until closing time, which was midnight."

Both Matt and Pete were inclined to believe her. Her relaxed, stress-free disposition was totally convincing.

"Is Gordon in?" Matt said.

"Yes, he works from home three days a week. What shit do you suspect him of being involved with now?"

"We just need to have a word with him, Ms," Pete said.

Gordon appeared at the end of the short hall, to shake his head with incredulity when he saw the detectives standing at the door. He had heard the knock and the murmur of voices, and had stopped working his computer to see if Jill was being harassed by some door-to-door salesman, or any other unwelcome caller.

"What now?" Gordon said. "Is this about the couple that got murdered the other night?"

"Yeah," Matt said. "We'd just like to dot a couple of I's and cross some t's, although your partner has probably done that for us."

"Come in and ask your questions, then." Gordon said. "I'll be over the moon when you catch the guy who I have a look of, to get me off the hook. Being suspected of being a fucking serial killer is no fun."

Gordon confirmed what Jill had told them. It would be easy to check out.

"Two birds with one stone," Pete said when they left the house. "We can call in at the Hare and Billet for a pint and a bar meal, and see if anyone remembers Lucas being there on Tuesday evening."

A couple of the bar staff confirmed that there had been a birthday celebration on the evening of the eighteenth. One of them knew Gordon Lucas and his girlfriend and recalled them attending, and staying until closing time.

"Three down, two to go," Pete said to Matt as they sat at a table and tucked into ploughman's lunches accompanied by pints of bitter to wash the food down with.

"Let's hope that either Nathan Edmonds or Carl Gibson look good for it," Matt said. "We need to come up with something positive and close this case."

Nathan Edmonds was up a ladder outside his two bedroom bungalow cleaning a gutter out when Pete parked the car alongside the kerb on Park Hall Road in West Dulwich. He was not one of the suspects who had given a girlfriend's name to furnish an alibi, and had not been able to account for his movements on any of the dates in question.

"Mr Edmonds," Pete called out from the concrete garden path that bisected the small front lawn.

Turning his head and looking down, Nathan recognised one of the men, who he knew from a previous visit to be a homicide detective. Climbing down the ladder carrying a trowel stuck in bucket full of detritus in one hand, he placed the bucket on the ground and said, "I saw on the news that your killer had been at it again, so half expected another visit from you. Now that you're here do you want a cup of coffee?"

"Why not?" Matt said.

"Come around the back then, while I dump this shit in the bin."

Matt and Pete followed Nathan down the passage at the side of the bungalow and waited while he got rid of the bucket's contents and removed the bright yellow Marigold gloves he had been wearing.

Once inside the kitchen, Nathan washed his hands, switched the kettle on and took three ceramic mugs from a wooden mug tree on a counter next to a bread bin.

"Tuesday evening you want to ask me about. Am I right?" Nathan said.

"Yeah," Matt said. "Where were you between nine p.m. and midnight?"

Nathan actually smiled as he spooned coffee granules into the mugs. "I was in next door's back garden, enjoying a barbecue with Jim and Christine Finch, my neighbours. They'd invited several friends."

"When did it start?" Pete said.

"Eight-thirty," Nathan said as he poured boiling water into the mugs. "And I stayed until just before eleven-thirty. Does that cover it?"

Matt and Pete picked up their mugs and sipped the hot brew, and Matt said, "Yes I reckon that puts you in the clear Mr Edmonds, if your neighbours confirm what you've just told us."

They made small talk, finished the coffee and left the bungalow, to knock at the door of the one next to it.

A thirty-something woman answered the door, and Matt showed her his ID.

"Wow!" Christine Finch said. "A real live detective. How can I help you?"

"We've just been next door talking to Nathan," Matt said. "He told us that on Tuesday evening he was at a barbeque in your garden."

Christine chuckled and said, "He was. He brought a bottle of Scotch with him, but drank most of it himself. When he left us he was more than a little tipsy."

"What time did he leave?" Pete said.

"Latish, about eleven thirty or so. Why?"

"Just routine inquiries," Matt said. "Thanks for your assistance."

"That's four down and one to go," Pete said. "We're not having much luck."

CHAPTER THIRTYY-SIX

DETECTIVE sergeant Noel Edwards had inveigled a place on the major incident team working the Killer Clown case, due to investigative work he had done several years previously with Specialist Crime and Operations Directorate's Homicide Command on the headline making case of Malcolm Sandler, a decorated veteran of the 2003 Iraq War, who had gone on the rampage and murdered a high-ranking drug trafficker and more than a dozen members of a sizable network of people that worked for him. Sandler's son, Sean, had overdosed on heroin, and Malcolm had found out the name of the scumbag pusher from a close friend of Sean, who had also dealt with the guy. Noel Edwards had spoken to one of his CIs, (confidential informants), who was also a drug addict, to follow a lead from him and find out that the ex-soldier's late son had dealt with one of the pushers who'd been murdered. That had put Sandler in the frame, and he had soon after been arrested. The MOD British Army survival knife that was found hidden in his garage still had traces of blood from two of his victims on it, and the DNA results had been enough to put him in the dock, where he was found guilty and given a life sentence. Noel, many other coppers, and the majority of the general public thought that Sandler had done society a favour, but the law is the law.

"What have we got on the Clown case?" Noel said to fellow detective sergeant Lloyd Marshall.

"A short list of persons of interest south of the river that the SCU are looking hard at."

"How many?"

"Fourteen in all, but the SCU are door-stepping the five with asterisks next to their names," Lloyd said as he brought the names and addresses up on his computer screen. "John Stott, isn't particularly interested. He believes that in all probability the perpetrator lives in the East End, and that he does his killing south of the city to throw us off the scent."

"Let me take a pic of the list," Noel said, taking his mobile out of a side pocket of his jacket. "I'll run the names and see if anything rings a bell."

"Whatever," Lloyd said, tilting his head towards the screen. "What's your take on it?"

"I haven't got one, yet. There are still a lot of call-ins from the public to be checked out. It could take weeks to interview them all."

Noel took an early lunch, and used a payphone in Parliament Square to call Larry Wade.

"What have you got?" Larry said.

"Five names, addresses and work places of guys that the Special Crimes Unit are taking a lot of interest in."

"Where are you, now?"

"In the city, Parliament Square. I'm about to walk to the Albert pub on Victoria Street and grab some lunch."

"Have you got the list with you?"

"Yes, on my mobile. Do you want me to send it to you?"

"No, I don't like sensitive shit on my phone. I'll see you at the pub asap," Larry said before ending the call.

Sammy Crowther drove Larry into town from Esher, to drop him outside the pub and find somewhere nearby to park.

Noel had ordered a pint and a roasted half chicken, dressed salad, rosemary & garlic mayo and fries. He ate slowly, but finished eating almost forty minutes before Larry entered the pub.

"Traffic was a little heavy," Larry said as he removed his shades and tucked one of their arms into the open collar of his sports shirt. It wasn't an apology, just a statement of fact. "Can I get you a drink, Noel?"

Noel had taken his time drinking two pints while he had impatiently waited for Wade to show up. "A Scotch with ice would hit the spot," he said.

Larry ordered a double for the scruffy little detective, and a spritzer with ice for himself. Placing both glasses on cardboard coasters, he took a seat opposite Noel and asked to see the photo of the list, and then for him to email it to the burner phone he'd brought with him.

"What does the SCU have on these guys?" Larry said.

"I don't know, but if Barnes, the DCI heading up this case, is interested in them, he'll have good reason."

"If something positive comes out of this you'll get your big payday," Larry said as he had another sip of his drink, before getting up to leave, having seen Sammy enter the front door of the pub. "You could spend a few quid of it on a new outfit, because you look like a fucking tramp from head to toe."

Noel gave it five minutes before draining his glass and leaving the Albert to walk back to the Yard. What he was doing went against the grain. He had been a decent honest copper for years, up until the compulsion to gamble had got him in its stranglehold. It hadn't taken him long to lose his proverbial shirt. The small wins he'd had were a drop in the ocean compared to the heavy losses he'd suffered. Now, although he'd quit being a fucking idiot and playing the tables and slots, the invisible ties that bound him were in some ways worse. Being a cop on the take helped pay the bills, but the fear of being caught was on his mind every second of every day. Too late now to wish he'd stayed on the straight and narrow, though. You've just got to get on with what is and not look back over your shoulder at what might have been.

"Anything worthwhile?" Jerry said to Larry, when his head of security had returned from the city and was now at the house.

"A few names, five of which the Serious Crime Unit appear to be very interested in and have flagged for their attention," Larry said. "I would think that they're interviewing them today."

"What does our cop on the take think?"

"That the SCU are closing in, because out of fourteen suspects they tagged, their concentration is narrowed down to just five."

"And you've got their names?"

"Yes, boss, plus home and work addresses for those that have jobs."

"If one of them *is* the killer, I hope that the filth don't have enough to take him in before we get to have a word."

"At a guess I would say that by this evening they will have interviewed them all, and it should be clear for me and a couple of the team to make house calls."

"Do that, Larry. And if you like one of them for it, bring him in."

CHAPTER THIRTY-SEVEN

"**LAST** but hopefully not least," Pete said as he drove the car through the large gates into the yard of CG Aluminium Products on the Stone Trading Estate in Brixton, to park in a slot outside the reception, next to the F-Type Jaguar that they both recognised as belonging to the owner of the company, Carl Gibson.

"Good morning. How can I help you?" a smart looking young woman with a dazzling Colgate-white smile and long, silken mahogany hair that matched the colour of her eyes said as they entered the building and approached the desk she was sitting behind.

"We're here to see Mr Gibson," Matt said, once more withdrawing and flipping open his worn leather wallet to show the receptionist his warrant card.

Denise Gardner examined the card, looked up at Matt to check his likeness to the photo, and said, "Would you like to take a seat while I contact him?"

Matt and Pete walked across to where three easy chairs and a couple of tall yucca plants in fancy pots were fronted by a large coffee table with a few magazines on its smoked glass top.

Carl Gibson entered the reception area from a door at the rear corner of the room with the sleeves of his open neck shirt rolled up to just below his elbows.

"How are you today, Mr Gibson?" Matt said to the businessman.

"I'm as fit as a flea, a fiddle or a butcher's dog," Carl said, looking from Matt to Pete and back again. "Come through to my office and tell me what's on your mind, as if I didn't know."

The office was at the end of a corridor next to a much larger general office occupied by at least half a dozen employees. Once seated with the door behind them closed, Carl offered them both coffee from a machine that was throwing out a strong rich aroma of java. They both accepted a cup.

"Let's get straight to it," Carl said, seemingly relaxed, showing no sign of anxiety. "You want to know where I was on the evening of the eighteenth, which was Tuesday. Am I right?"

"Spot on," Matt said.

"I was at home alone, but saw the news on Wednesday morning about a couple having been murdered in woods near Croydon."

"And that caused you to believe we would want to interview you again?"

"Yes, and I find it annoying that I have no decent alibi for when your killer struck. If he had the decency to let me know the times and dates on which he planned to commit his crimes, I could ensure that I had alibis that would satisfy you."

Matt sipped the quality coffee, gave the suspect a cold piercing look and said, "Humour us and run through your movements on that evening, Mr Gibson."

"I was here until after six p.m., I then drove home, had a shower, a meal, and caught up with emails and a little office work before watching a movie at nine o'clock. When it finished at a little after eleven, I went to bed. That's it, boring I know but just how I like to spend an evening after a long day at the plant."

"Did you make any phone calls?"

Carl gave it some thought and said, "No, I'm afraid not. I parked in the driveway, went into the house, and had no contact with anyone until the next morning."

"What movie did you watch?" Pete said.

"An ancient Eastwood western; The Outlaw Josey Wales. I must have watched it at least half a dozen times over the years."

"And your car was out front of the house all evening?" Matt said.

"Yes. I should garage it, but I usually don't bother."

"As I recall you have a camera above your front door. Does it work?"

"Yes, Why?"

"It would help to see footage of the evening in question."

"To check on whether I went out?"

"That's right. We need to eliminate as many people as possible from the list we have. Will you be home after seven O'clock?"

"Yes, but this is all unnecessary. You know where I was on one of the dates you asked me about. You interviewed my girlfriend and she confirmed that we were together."

Matt withdrew his notebook, flipped back a few pages and said, "That would be Bonnie...Sorry, wrong page, your girlfriend's name isn't Bonnie, it's Joanne Maguire, right?"

"Er, yes," Carl said, finding his eyes momentarily drift away from the unwavering gaze of the detective, which he believed was loaded with unspoken accusation.

"Fine. We'll have another routine word with Joanne, and call by your place this evening to check out the CCTV."

"The way you're talking, you still seem to consider me a suspect."

"We need to run a very thorough investigation," Matt said. "and take nothing at face value. You'd be amazed by just how many people are not what they purport to be."

"It must be dismaying to be so distrusting of citizens."

"*Some* citizens, Mr Gibson. Finding skeletons in the cupboards of homicidal psychopaths and proving that they are not who they pretend to be is what we do. Someone has to follow the horses and shovel up the shit they leave behind them."

"Rather you than me," Carl said as Matt and Pete stood up, ready to leave.

On reaching the office door, Matt turned and said, "Just one more thing."

Carl grinned. "Wasn't that what the shabbily dressed little TV detective Columbo used to say to his suspect every week?"

"Yeah, it's one of my favourite old shows. Do you possess a voice modulator?"

"A what?"

"A device that you can plug into a mobile phone and change the sound of your voice."

"The answer is no; I don't own one. Why do you ask?"

"Because the homicidal psychopath we are hunting for gave me a bell from the scene of his latest double execution, and attempted to con me into believing that I was speaking to a woman. I obviously recorded the call, and our CCS, Computer Crime Section, is currently analysing the voice, doing tests. Apparently you can change the pitch, cadence and even gender of your voice with those things, but our techno geeks have state of the art equipment that can, given time, unscramble voice frequencies and patterns of speech."

"Good luck with that. The quicker you catch him and stop harassing me the better."

"Luck doesn't come into it, Mr Gibson. We'll call at your home address at about seven-thirty this evening, if that's okay."

Carl nodded, and that was it. Matt and Pete left the factory and headed for the Fleur hair salon on Streatham High Road where Gibson's girlfriend worked, with the intention of reinterviewing her. Joanne Maguire had stated that on the night of the seventeenth of April, when Sonny Mason and Frankie Dawson had been murdered in the East End, she had been with the man Matt had now decided was the prime suspect.

"You gave Gibson a lot of info," Pete said as he drove.

"I know. Did you see the expression on his face when I mentioned the name Bonnie to him, before correcting it to Joanne?"

"Of course, I'm a detective, remember? His eyes widened a fraction and his cheek muscles tightened up. You hit a nerve."

"That's right, and when I mentioned the voice modulator he grasped hold of his right earlobe and rubbed it, which at a guess I believe he probably does whenever he has a complex problem or is put under any high level of stress."

"You like him for it, don't you?"

"Yeah, Pete, a lot. I think that we've just found the Killer Clown. All we need to do now is get his girlfriend to admit that she lied to us, and we can concentrate on finding enough proof to arrest him."

"That could be easier said than done."

"I realise that, but with Julia's all clear to put him under surveillance twenty-four seven we'll nail him. It's when, not if."

"Do you really believe that he'll carry on killing, now that you've basically tipped him off?"

"He may cool it for a while, but I doubt that he has the sense or capability to quit. Almost all serial killers are too overconfident for their own good. They think that they're smarter than us, which gives us the upper hand, because they're not."

Pete parked at the rear of the hairdressers, which was sandwiched between a carpet store and a small supermarket, and he and Matt cut through a nearby alley and entered the Salon, to be welcomed from behind a glass counter by a middle-aged woman wearing too much makeup and what looked to be a large platinum blonde wig reminiscent of those worn by Dolly Parton. The name tag pinned above her oversized left breast to a tight-fitting blue nylon overall bore her name, which was Marlene.

"Can I help you two gentlemen?" Marlene said with a false smile revealing teeth which were as false as her bouffant styled wig.

"I hope so," Pete said as he showed the woman his warrant card. "We'd like to have a word with Joanne Maguire."

Marlene's smile vanished with the speed of a light being switched off. "Joanne is off today and tomorrow," she said. "Is she in some kind of trouble?"

"No," Pete said, "We just need some information from her."

Matt and Pete left the salon, returned to the car and made their way to the ground floor flat on Wellfield Road, which was just a short drive from the town centre.

The front door was closed but not locked. Entering, Pete knocked at the door of flat two, but there was no answer. He rapped on it again, harder, only for the door to flat one being opened.

"There's no one in," a stocky and muscular guy with a shaven head, a mass of full sleeve tats on both arms and a suspicious expression on his rugged face said. "What do you two want?"

"Just a word," Matt said as he held up his identification for the man to see.

"Coppers," Clive Plummer said. "Joanne isn't in."

"Do you know where we can find her?"

"Yeah, up north. She told me that she had a couple of days off work and was going up to a friend's wedding in Liverpool."

"Thanks," Matt said.

"Now what?" Pete said as they drove away from the house. "We've got her phone number; shall I give her a bell?"

"No. If she lied over being with Gibson on the night in question, then she either knows what he's done, or is covering for him because he asked her to, due to his not being able to give us an account of his whereabouts. She probably just thinks that because he has a look of the killer, we're hounding him. I think it would be best to question her face to face when she gets back."

"Sounds the way to go," Pete said. "Although he will have no doubt phoned her by now and asked her to stick to her story."

"If she isn't complicit in his activities, and I don't think she is, then I'm sure that it won't take much for her to retract the alibi she gave for him."

"I'm hungry, are you?" Pete said, changing subject as his stomach growled loudly, as though he was a starving grizzly bear that had just emerged from hibernation.

"Peckish. What do you fancy?"

"I noticed a Wimpy next to Greggs on the main drag. I could murder one of their all-day breakfasts."

Pete found a parking place and they entered the Wimpy. Matt decided on a quarter pounder with bacon and cheese and a side of battered onion rings, and they both ordered large cups of black coffee.

While they waited for the meals, Matt phoned Julia, brought her up to speed and suggested that having Gibson under constant watch would ensure that if he was the killer, and Matt was sure that he was, then there would be no chance of him taking another life.

"Just how confidant are you that this guy is the Clown?" Julia said.

"A hairsbreadth off one hundred percent."

The line went silent for at least five seconds before Julia said, "I hope to Christ that you're right, Matt. When you've interviewed his girlfriend again over the alibi she gave him, and if she retracts it, I'll jack it up with John Stott and we can work out a rota between us and the MIT."

"We've arranged to call at Gibson's house near Clapham Common at seven-thirty p.m. to view some CCTV footage of the evening when the couple were murdered in south Croydon."

"Footage of what?"

"He said that his car was in the drive from when he got home until the following morning."

"Fine. I'll be here when you get back and we can go through it all in detail."

CHAPTER THIRTY-EIGHT

LEAVING the factory and driving home, he felt that the position he found himself in was untenable. The detective, Barnes, had somehow zeroed in on him, to do all but accuse him outright of being the serial killer that they sought. He had a hard choice to make; cut and run or stick it out. As yet they had no concrete proof of his guilt, but would now keep digging. Once home, he filled a tumbler with Scotch and drank it down neat in three gulps. The alcohol steadied him. He needed to keep his wits about him and act quickly. First thing to do was phone Joanne, to tell her that the police had questioned him over the murder of a couple in Croydon, and had told him that they would be contacting her again, to hopefully break the alibi she had given him for the night of the seventeenth of April.

"Hi, Carl," Joanne said after checking the caller ID before answering. "What's wrong? You know that I'm up in Liverpool at a wedding."

"Just a slight problem. The police are harassing me again. They called at the factory earlier and did everything but accuse me of committing murders in Croydon the other night."

"What do you want me to do, say that I was with you?"

"No. I told them the truth, that I was at home all evening, but I can't prove that I was. I just need for you to stick to what you told them about me being with you on that date in April, because they will do their best to talk you into going back on what you originally said."

"Why do they still suspect you, Carl? I thought that a great many people had phoned in and said they recognised the photofit or drawing of the man they're looking for."

"Because apart from the alibi you gave me, I couldn't account for my whereabouts on any of the dates they asked me about. You know that I don't socialise much, apart from playing golf a couple of times a week. When I don't see you, I stay indoors, do bookwork for the company, watch TV and read books."

"Okay, Carl," Joanne said. "I need to go now. I can hardly hear you for the music. I'm at the wedding reception in the Cavern Club."

"I thought I could hear background music. Enjoy. I'll see you when you get back."

The call from Carl unsettled Joanne. Why would the police be so interested in him? A moment of doubt crossed her mind. He was a very private person; the kind that she doubted she would ever fully know. They usually only saw each other one night a week, because neither of them currently wanted a commitment to anything more serious. Could it be possible that Carl was a Jekyll and Hyde type with two different sides to his character? Wouldn't she have noticed a darkness beneath the easy-going personality that he always displayed? Of course she would have. He was gentle, had a good sense of humour, and she had never even heard him raise his voice to anyone. There was no possible way that he could be a cold-blooded killer, so why was she even contemplating the idea?

Carl considered the likelihood of Barnes keeping him under surveillance. There would be no way that he could just take the large amount of money he kept in his home safe and catch a plane from Gatwick or Heathrow to some other country and start afresh. Vanishing was not as easy as it was made out to be in the movies, so was not a viable option. No, he would have to ride it out, stay cool and behave for the foreseeable future. They'd got absolutely nothing on him, because he did not believe for a second that some techno geek in a police computer department could do anything with the recording of his phone call to Barnes to identify his real voice. They were fishing with no bait on their hooks to catch him. Everything would work out. The handgun he had used, along with the ammunition for it, the voice modulator, balaclava, latex gloves and all other incriminating items were in the lockup with the Ford Cortina. He had nothing to worry about. The only item he had kept in the house was the second pistol, which he had not used, and a cardboard carton full of bullets. All he had to do was focus on the fact that they could not link him to any of the murders. Keeping the spare weapon and the box of bullets at home had been a mistake, though, because he had no knowledge of its history. Perhaps Frankie Dawson had used the gun to wound or kill somebody. He could always leave the rear of the house in the middle of the night and dump the weapon and ammunition into the brook.

At exactly seven-thirty on the dot, the doorbell rang.

Carl was in his study and turned away from his computer to view the CCTV monitor that was on another smaller desk. The image displayed Barnes and his partner standing outside, both looking up at the fisheye lens that gave a wide-angle view of the front of his property.

"Come on in, detectives," Carl said as he opened the door. "Hopefully you've caught the killer and are here to tell me that I'm no longer on your list of suspects."

Matt allowed himself a slow smile and said, "Afraid not, Mr Gibson. We just need to see the footage from the night in question."

Leading them into the study, Carl walked over to the system and brought up the images from the evening of the eighteenth on the large monitor.

"There you go," Carl said to Matt and Pete. "It's ready to play from just before I got home from work."

Pete started to play the footage, which was time and date coded. He fast forwarded until Carl pulled into the drive, exited his Jag and went into the house at just after twenty-five past six. Flipping through the evening on screen, the only movement was that of a fox loping across the large front lawn. Continuing to fast forward until one a.m. on the nineteenth, Pete then turned away from the screen, disappointed that Gibson had not appeared and driven off.

"Satisfied?" Carl said to the two detectives. "Or a little pissed off that I didn't leave the house waving a gun, to get in my car and drive off into the night to commit some heinous crime?"

"Have you got a camera covering the rear of the property?" Matt said.

"No. I keep meaning to have one installed and linked to this system. I just haven't got around to it, yet. Why, do you think I sneaked out through the back door and trudged through the dark to find a taxi and get a lift to the murder scene, to then shoot two complete strangers while the cab waited to bring me back home?"

"It's a stretch, I agree," Matt said. "Thing is, I never underestimate anyone, or wholly believe everything I'm told as being the gospel truth, until I have irrefutable evidence to support it."

Carl shook his head, "Do you honestly believe that I am guilty of the murders that you're investigating?"

"You are still what we choose at this moment in time to consider being a person of interest. That's as much as I will for now," Matt said. "You fit the description of the perpetrator. Someone who contacted us was certain that the sketch drawn by a police artist was you, so until we know that you're innocent beyond any doubt, you're still in the frame. As you will know your girlfriend, Joanne, is up north at a wedding, is due back home tomorrow, and will be interviewed again with reference to the alibi that she gave for you."

"This is beginning to feel like a witch-hunt. When you find the killer, I'll expect a full apology for your actions."

"There hasn't been any actions, Mr Gibson," Pete said. "We are just chasing down a sick fuck who we believe is shooting people dead purely for the thrill it gives him to do it. And it would appear that another person or persons unknown are also looking for the perpetrator; people whom we believe would almost certainly do a lot more to him than put him behind bars."

That was it. Matt and Pete abruptly and with no sincerity wished Carl goodnight and took their leave, believing that the man, if he was guilty, would now suspend his murderous activities for the time being, surely not foolish enough to kill again.

Were they bluffing? Carl thought as he made his way to the kitchen to pour himself another large glass of Scotch. Who else could be interested in him? He could only think of one man; the father of the bitch he had shot at the rear of the Stag Inn back in June. She had told him that her dad was Jerry Parker, an extremely wealthy businessman, who was also, if gossip was to be believed, a gangster with connections. To dump the gun and ammo was now out of the question, because he hopefully wouldn't, but might need the weapon for self-protection.

CHAPTER THIRTY-NINE

"NICE touch," Matt said to Pete as they drove away from Laburnum House. "If Gibson *is* the Clown, he must be more than a little troubled at the thought of not just us but another interested party attempting to identify him."

"If it was Jerry Parker that had Darren Selby lifted, then Gibson is toast if someone tips Parker off," Pete said. "And I suspect that some bent MIT detective will do just that."

"Yeah," Matt said. "Knowing that people are out to get him, other than us, will have left Gibson fearing as much for his life as for his continued freedom."

Julia was in the squad room when they arrived back at the Yard. "Did you get anything else to work with?" she said.

"No. The CCTV footage showed him arrive home and park his car at the front of the house on the evening the couple were murdered. It didn't move all night, and he didn't come out of the front door" Matt said.

"What does that tell you?"

"That he's a clever bastard. He could have left the house by the back door, stolen a car and committed the crime, before dumping the wheels and walking back home."

Julia didn't like it. "That sounds highly unlikely," she said

Matt hitched his shoulders. "I know, but he's a gameplayer. I can almost smell the guilt coming off him in waves."

"What's your take on it, Pete?" Julia said.

"The same as Matt's. If it wasn't for his part-time girlfriend's alibi, he wouldn't have any explanation for his whereabouts on any of the pertinent dates, and we could get a warrant to search his property, including his car for any evidence. He'll have a gun, balaclava, latex gloves and probably other incriminating stuff stashed away somewhere."

"We'll grill Joanne Maguire when she gets back from Liverpool tomorrow, to see if she thinks he's really worth lying for," Matt said. "If she doesn't want to be implicated, then she'll come clean."

"If she sticks to her story, we'll still have nothing, and I will not be able to authorise a round-the-clock stakeout on him. You do realise that, don't you?" Julia said to Matt and Pete.

Keeping his ear to the ground, Detective Sergeant Noel Edwards, the enemy within, kept abreast of all updates on the Killer Clown case. Latest news was that the SCU had come up with a new prime suspect, and had discounted four of the five names that he had given to Larry Wade. Word had it that a guy by the name of Carl Gibson was good for it, and subject to an alibi he had for one of the germane dates being broken, he would be subject to continuous surveillance.

Larry answered his mobile. The caller ID was of the detective, Edwards.

"Yes?" he said, recognising the nasally voice.

"Fresh off the press," Noel said. "The five names I gave you have now been whittled down to just one."

"I'll get straight back to you," Larry said and ended the call. He used a burner phone to call the copper back.

"Shoot," Larry said when Noel accepted the call.

"The name of the guy is Carl Gibson. He lives at Laburnum House on Potter's Way in Clapham. He owns a factory on the Stone Trading Estate on Milkwood Road in Brixton; CG Aluminium Products, and he drives a grey Jaguar F-PACE."

"Anything else?"

"Only that you'll have to get to him fast. His girlfriend gave him the only alibi he's got for one of the dates that they're sure he killed on. She's due back from a trip up north tomorrow. If they break her original story, then he will be under a microscope, day and night."

"Okay, Noel. Good job. Don't forget to delete this call. I'll be in touch."

Larry had been planning to leave the estate and spend a couple of hours at the Marquis of Granby on West Street, to eat a steak meal and down a couple of vodka tonics with slices of lime. The pub was only a couple of minutes' drive from Jerry's place, and he valued a change of scenery and time away from his security duties. The call from Edwards had changed his plan. He went to the main house to see Jerry and no doubt be given instructions as to what action his boss required to be taken.

Jerry met with Larry in his study, having left Gayle in the lounge where she was watching an episode of some romcom series, with a glass of gin in hand and a half full bottle of it on the coffee table in front of her.

"Our MIT snitch gave me a bell." Larry said. "He says that they have another prime suspect who they are convinced is the serial killer who shot Melanie. I've got his name and address."

"How come they haven't taken him in?"

"Because his girlfriend covered him for one of the dates that they're interested in. She's up north until tomorrow, and if she sticks to her story they'll have no cause to nick him. If she bottles and admits she was lying they'll have enough to watch him while they find some proof of his guilt."

"Now seems a good time to bring him in," Jerry said, "before it's too late to lift him."

"He could already be under surveillance, boss."

"Perhaps. Check it out before you make a move on him."

It was eleven-thirty p.m. when Larry, Dean and Tyler arrived at the head of the long cul-de-sac on which Carl Gibson's house was situated. Dean got out of the SUV with Vinnie, his pet dog, a German Shepherd that he always took to work at Millfield House. Vinnie was on a lead, and Dean set off walking down the dead end avenue, cautiously checking out the few vehicles that were parked outside houses. At the end of what was little more than a lane, and after Vinnie had stopped to lift a back leg and piss against the wheel of a car, he returned to the Discovery and told Larry that it was all clear; that there was no sign of the filth keeping an eye on Gibson's house.

"What if he doesn't open the door?" Dean said. "And there's probably a security camera above it."

Larry grinned. "I considered all contingencies. That's why I'm head of security and you two aren't," he said to Dean and Tyler as he opened the large glove box and withdrew a torch and a bulky item that looked like a heavy-duty staple gun, but was in fact a snap gun, also known as a lock pick gun; a tool made specifically to open a mechanical pin tumbler lock without using a key. The steel rod at the front of the gun is inserted into the lock and the gun fires the rod against all the lock pins simultaneously, to momentarily free the cylinder and enable it to be turned with a small tension wrench.

Parking in the relative darkness of the shrub-lined circle drive, Larry and Tyler quickly approached the front door, while Dean hung back to thumb on the torch and aim it at the camera that was positioned a few feet above it.

With the snap gun in hand, Larry rang the doorbell, almost certain that Gibson would open it, at which point he would immediately be felled by the sock full of marbles which Tyler was holding out of sight.

Carl was startled by the sound of the bell. It was after midnight and he had just switched off the TV and was about to go to bed. Hurrying through to the study, all he could see on the screen of the monitor was bright white light, and he believed that someone was intentionally disrupting the scene of his front garden by shining a torch at the wall-mounted camera.

CHAPTER FORTY

WITHIN seconds Carl retrieved the loaded gun from where he had concealed it in the hollowed-out space in the pages between the covers of a bulky hardback on a shelf of his bookcase, and the silencer from another. He could have put them in his floor safe, but that would have basically put them out of commission if he had, like now, needed them in a hurry. The bell rang again, and whoever was outside kept his finger on it for at least five seconds. Making his way into the hallway, fitting the silencer to the 9 mm Glock pistol, he looked through the peephole in the door to see who was outside. There were two men, both wearing jackets and ties. One was tall and quite good-looking, the other was shorter, more compact, and looked to be edgy, looking around him and chewing his bottom lip.

"Who are you?" Carl said, loud enough for them to hear.

"Police, sir," Larry said. "We need to ask you a few questions."

"It's gone midnight. I suggest that you call back in the morning."

"It's important that we talk to you now."

"Show me your ID."

Larry had thought that Gibson would open the door, but anticipated this kind of snag. Without any hesitation he pushed the rod of the snap gun into the lock and pulled the trigger.

Carl knew that they were not coppers, for if they had been they would have identified themselves as such. He also knew by the sudden sound from the lock of the door that it was being breached. Backing off to the far end of the hall, positive that these men were the ones that Barnes' partner had warned him about, he held the gun two-handed, waited for the door to be pushed open and shot the first man to enter, for the bullet to hit him square in the chest, stopping him in his tracks as the slug nicked his aorta before striking his spine, to be deflected and exit his back at an angle and bury into the wall.

Tyler felt nothing for a couple of seconds as his central nervous system attempted to unsuccessfully coordinate the sensory information, which was disrupted by the sudden traumatic event. The loaded sock that he had been ready to stun the man with fell from his limp fingers, and he was shunted forward as Larry, unable to stop quickly enough, crashed into him, causing both of them to fall down onto the paisley patterned carpet.

Larry rose to his knees and reached for the gun which he carried in a shoulder holster, only to be shot through his left eye, for the bullet to burst it and pass through his brain and the rear of his skull, to cross the garden and lodge in the trunk of a mature sycamore tree.

Larry died instantly, and fell forward over Tyler, who was bleeding heavily from his mouth and nostrils as he attempted to draw breath through the outflow of blood that was spouting into the air and falling back down like droplets of red rain to spatter over his face and hair.

Dean froze. The incident which had just unfolded in front of him when Larry had forced open the door and entered the house behind Tyler had lasted for no more than five seconds, and even as he thought to turn, run back to the SUV and drive away, a man appeared in the open doorway and pointed a gun at him.

"Any sudden move and I'll shoot you dead," Carl said to the slim, young bespectacled guy who was standing as if he was superglued to the tarmac-topped driveway, holding a large torch in his hand. "Switch the torch off, toss it onto the lawn, and then come into the house. We need to talk."

Dean looked behind the man to where Larry and Tyler were sprawled out unmoving on the floor in the hallway. He knew that getting away was not an option so did what he had been told to.

Carl backed up as the man reached the door, to tell him to come inside and close the door behind him.

"Now what?" Dean said. "Are you going to shoot me, too?"

"Not if you behave. What's your name?"

"Dean."

"Okay, Dean. First, take your jacket off to show me that you're not carrying a gun, and then dump your mobile and sit on the floor with your hands in your trouser pockets while I collect weapons, smartphones and wallets from your deceased associates. While I'm doing it, tell me why you came here tonight."

"Our boss wanted you lifted," Dean said as he followed the armed man's instructions

"Who's your boss?" Carl said as he squatted next to the bodies, keeping his gun and one eye on Dean.

"Jerry Parker. He's—"

"I know who he is," Carl said as he checked that both of the men were dead before going through their pockets. "What does he want with me?"

"His daughter was murdered, and a copper on his payroll said that you were a prime suspect for it."

"Let me guess, Parker intended to kill me."

Dean blinked rapidly and hiked his shoulders.

"You three stooges have not only fucked up, but I've now got two dead bodies to get rid of and a lot of blood to clean up with your help. Let's start off by bringing the vehicle you came in up to the house and loading these two into it."

With Dean six feet in front of him, Carl kept him at gunpoint as they walked down the drive to the 4x4. When they reached it, he saw a large dog in the rear, looking out of the slightly open side window.

"Is he friendly?" Carl said.

"Yes, unless I tell him not to be," Dean said.

"If I think he's a threat to me I'll shoot him."

"He won't be, will you, Vinnie," Dean said to the massive German Shepherd.

"Get in the driver's seat and pull up to the door with the rear opposite it," Carl said. "First thing I want you to do is drag these two out to it and dump them in the boot."

One at a time, Dean dragged both Larry's and Tyler's corpses out of the door by their ankles, and with a great deal of difficulty deposited both of them into the Discovery's cargo hold, while Carl stood by, not taking his gun off Dean for a second.

"Good job," Carl said as Dean closed the lid on his lifeless henchmen. "Here's the plan. You drive us to a place where we can dump those two and their possessions where they won't be found for a while, if ever. After that we come back here and clean up."

"Then what?"

"I let you give Parker a bell, to tell him that I wasn't at home, and that you and the other two intend to stay until I turn up."

"What do you plan on doing to me?"

"Nothing. After you've lied to Parker, I doubt that it would be safe for you to show your face again. Not only will I let you go, unharmed, but I'll even give you a few grand to sweeten what turned out to be a shit night for you. How does that sound?"

"Like it's the best deal I could hope for under the circumstances."

"It is. What's Parker's address?"

Dean told him, and was then instructed to go into the kitchen for a packet of wipes and use one or two of them to clean the now unloaded gun, and the phones and wallets. Dean was then told to take any money in the wallets for himself.

"You'd do better to use a pro to remove everything and get rid of the blood in the hallway," Dean said as he followed instructions.

"Meaning?" Carl said.

"There are what we call cleaners; guys that for a price will get rid of evidence, including bodies, no questions asked."

"And you know one?"

"Yes. Sometimes, as a last resort, Parker has people got rid of, and uses a guy by the name of Drake to do the business."

"Can you contact him?"

Dean nodded. "His number will be in Larry's phone contacts, under HD, for Howard Drake."

Carl initially thought it was too risky to involve strangers, but was it? It made sense to have professionals take care of the mess and make the bodies vanish. "Can you arrange it?" he said to Dean.

"Yes, he knows that I work for Parker."

"Okay, make it happen," Carl said. "Use your own phone and put it on speaker, so that I can hear both sides of the conversation."

Dean made the call.

"Yeah," a gruff voice said.

"It's Dean Miller, Mr D. Are you available to do an urgent job?"

"What does it involve?"

"Two items to remove, and a little residual leakage."

"Give me the address."

Dean did.

"I should be with you in less than half an hour," Howard said. "You know the score, cash up front. I'm estimating that it will be ten grand, give or take."

"No problem," Dean said before the line went dead on him.

"Okay," Carl said. "Switch all three phones off and dump everything in a plastic shopping bag that you'll find on a hook with others in the unit under the counter in the kitchen."

"Do you mind if I smoke," Dean said as he put the now wiped items in the bag. "My nerves are shot."

"As a rule I *would* mind, but I guess I can make an exception tonight. Where are your cigarettes?"

"With my Zippo lighter in the left side pocket of my jacket."

Carl handed Dean the jacket, after first checking the pockets for anything other than the cigs and lighter.

"Before you light up, lead the way through the door on your left."

They entered the lounge and Carl told Dean to sit on the floor, next to a neoclassical Adam Style fireplace, with his legs out straight and his hands once more in the pockets of his trousers. He then pulled the corner of a large rug back from the boarded floor and lifted up a trapdoor to disclose a steel safe set in a deep space beneath it.

"You don't need to keep pointing that fucking gun at me," Dean said. "I'm in this way too deep now to do anything stupid."

"Call me overcautious, but I guess I don't trust the majority of people, if any, especially if they've called uninvited to break into my house and abduct me."

"Circumstances change. I was just following orders from Larry, but now that he's dead I'm going to end up being on the run from Parker."

Carl said nothing, just warily knelt down to enter the combination, open the safe and withdraw four banded wads of banknotes, each containing five thousand pounds in twenty pound denominations. After relocking the safe, closing the trapdoor and straightening the rug over it, he said, "You can stand up now, pick up the money, carry it through to the kitchen and put it on the counter next to the coffeemaker. There's twenty grand there; ten for this cleaner guy and ten for you."

Once in the kitchen, now more relaxed and reasonably sure that Dean did not pose a threat to him, he tucked the pistol into the waistband of the chinos he was wearing and noted the look of relief on the younger man's face.

"Do you drink?" Carl said to the man who was now more of a partner in crime than an enemy.

"Not a lot, but I could use one now," Dean said before lighting a cigarette and taking a long, deep drag.

There was a knock at the door soon after they had both drank large brandies. Carl and Dean both went to the door, and Dean opened it to be faced by the tall, portly, ruddy-faced figure of Howard Drake, who was standing alongside a younger, smaller guy. To Carl, the surly looking twosome brought undertakers to mind, which he supposed that in an unofficial way, they were.

Howard nodded curtly at Dean, and with his son, Davy, who was also his assistant, entered the house and surveyed the pools of blood that had soaked into the thick pile of the hallway carpet. "Where are the DBs?" Howard said referring to the two dead bodies he had expected to be faced with.

"Outside in the back of the Discovery," Dean said.

That was the total sum of the conversation. Carl handed Howard the fee, and the two 'cleaners' donned hooded Tyvek jumpsuits, disposable overshoes and nitrile gloves from a large holdall, giving them the appearance of forensic investigators; the difference being that they were not searching for evidence, just removing it.

Dean led them out to the 4x4, opened the back and told Vinnie to stay and behave.

Howard and Davy removed the cadavers one by one, to transfer them in body bags to the Transit van they had reversed up the driveway. Back in the house, they spent more than ninety minutes removing all traces of blood from the carpet, wallpaper and paintwork with a mixture of hydrogen peroxide and other ingredients, and dug the slug out of the wall. Apart from the door lock being slightly damaged by the lock pick gun which the now late Larry Wade had used to gain entry, the hallway was almost restored to its former pristine state. All the owner would need to do was fill the small hole left by the bullet.

"That's it, all done and dusted," Howard said, taking the bag containing the incriminating evidence that had belonged to Larry and Tyler from Dean as he entered the kitchen, where Carl and Dean had retreated to while the cleaning was being done. "Come and check it out."

Carl was pleased with the result. There was no sign of blood anywhere. "Looks good," he said. "Thanks."

"You're welcome," Howard said before he and his son left the house, to drive away in the Transit, richer by ten grand.

"What will he do with the bodies?" Carl said to Dean.

"I've no idea. He owns a butchers shop. Larry used to refer to him jokingly as Sweeney Todd, and supposed that his wife had a bakery that among other stuff sold a variety of special meat pies."

Carl smiled, handed Dean the two remaining banded wads of banknotes and said, "Do you have a plan of what you'll do when you leave here?"

"Yeah, I'm going to go to my flat, pack, and drive up to Norfolk. My divorced sister lives alone on a houseboat moored on the Broads. She'll put me up for a while, until I get sorted."

"Take Barrett's phone and both of their wallets, and lose them. I'll keep the one that belonged to Wade."

"Stay safe," Carl said a couple of minutes later after Dean had put his blood-smeared jacket back on, stuffed the money into its pockets, said thanks and headed for the door. "And dump the stained jacket." Carl called after him.

After Dean had left the house and driven off into what was an unknown future for everyone, Carl had another glass of brandy and considered what *he* should do now. He had a decision to make, and not a lot of time to do it. If Joanne stood by him when Barnes interviewed her in a few hours' time, then he would be home free, but would have to stop killing people and get rid of all the incriminating evidence in the lock up. He had once been addicted to smoking, but given it up, due to common-sense dictating that it was potentially a serious health risk. And now he would have to suppress the urge to kill indefinitely, due to it being far too dangerous to continue with, because the dogged Detective Chief Inspector Barnes was positive that he was guilty.

CHAPTER FORTY-ONE

THE moon was, to Matt, a constant in life, seemingly floating impossibly above in the vastness of the cosmos, as cold and incomprehensible as the killers he hunted as though he was no more than a modern day bounty hunter. It had been three a.m. when he had given up on sleep, to get up and go downstairs to make coffee. When it was ready, he took a mugful out onto the decking, wearing the tee shirt and boxers that he had gone to bed in. Carl Gibson was on his mind. He was convinced that the man was the serial murderer the media had tagged the Killer Clown, which meant that his part-time girlfriend, Joanne Maguire, had lied through her teeth when she stated that she had been with him throughout the night when the two fatal shootings had taken place in Bethnal Green. If she went back on what she had told them they would still need some proof of guilt to obtain search warrants. Without evidence they would not be able to arrest him. Matt also believed that Gibson was intelligent enough to quit while he was ahead. The upside being that while they continued to somehow build a case against him, no one else would die by his hand.

"Do you want company?" Beth said from the open door behind him.

"Yeah. Did I wake you up?"

"No, I needed to pee, saw that you had gone, and so decided to join you. What is it, the case playing on your mind?"

Matt nodded.

Beth went back into the kitchen poured herself a cup of coffee and re-joined him. It was warm and so they sat at the table in the still night air.

"You told me earlier that you were ninety-nine percent certain you know who the killer is. Are you having doubts?"

"No. I'm certain that he's the perpetrator, but even if we break his one and only alibi, that doesn't give us reason to arrest and charge him. Sometimes not being able to prove where you were on given times and dates is as good as having false ones that can be disproved."

"You'll nail him, Matt. You're the Mountie who always gets his man."

"Always doesn't last forever. You can't win them all."

"Do you want more coffee?" Beth said.

Matt smiled and said, "Why not, with a drop of brandy in to liven it up."

They stayed out on the deck for another hour, talking about the woes of the world; of war, climate change, the cost of living, and how everything seemed to be going to hell in a wheelbarrow. As a welcome interlude, a large hedgehog shuffled into view from the orchard and made its way across the lawn towards the decking, before veering off to vanish under a flowering shrub.

"Let's go back to bed," Matt said. "Maybe I'll be able to nod off for two or three hours."

It was six-thirty a.m. when Matt rose again to meet a brand new day. He showered, got dressed, and was joined in the kitchen by Beth. They drank coffee again before both of them left the cottage; Matt to drive into the city, and Beth to head for Uxbridge to the Morning Star Children's Rehabilitation Centre.

South of the river in Clapham, Carl had not slept at all. His dilemma was what to do next. He had thought it through and decided that even if Barnes did break the alibi Joanne had given him, which he was confidant wouldn't happen, then the detective would still have no proof whatsoever of his guilt, and never would have, because he had no intention of killing again. No, all Barnes had was suspicion which without evidence counted for nothing.

After Dean had left, he used the remains of the night industriously, driving the Jag to the lockup, confident that he was not yet under surveillance, due to the fact that the late-night events, had they been observed, would have brought any watchers to his door at the gallop. Wearing latex gloves, he removed all incriminating evidence and drove back home to, under the cover of darkness throw the gun he had used to commit the murders, the ammunition and voice changer out into the middle of the brook at least two hundred yards away from the house. Even if it were ever to be found under mud at the bottom, it could not be linked to him. After that he had opened the windows in the utility room, placed the balaclava, gloves and a pair of trainers he had worn into the Belfast sink, and burned them. The big problem he was now faced with was not the law, but Jerry Parker, the gangster who had sent a three-man team to abduct him, positive that he had murdered his daughter, Melanie, which he had.

It was broad daylight before Carl decided on a course of action. All he wanted to do now was start over. Everything that he had done over the last few months seemed to be like a surreal dream which he had now awakened from. It was almost inconceivable to believe that he had become a serial killer. The evening back in December in the multistorey car park in the city had transformed his life. Defending himself against an armed mugger, and then taking the shithead's handgun had somehow rewired his brain. The pistol had given him an enhanced sense of power, and although it was no more than an inanimate object, it seemed to come alive and demand that he use it when he held it in his hand and curled his finger around the trigger. He had decided to use the gun to shoot young women, and to excuse his actions by convincing himself that he was just doing society a favour by reducing, however insignificant in the greater scheme of things, the possibility of his victims breeding and increasing an already overpopulated country, which did not currently have the necessary resources to adequately provide for the existing number of what in the main he thought of as the hoi polloi. The pictures of a clown's face being left at the scenes was just a frivolous touch, which amused him and had given him a high level of notoriety as the Killer Clown.

He had never even considered the possibility of becoming a prime suspect, and would not have been if he hadn't come face to face for a few seconds with the black bitch outside the house in Bethnal Green, after he had shot and killed Frankie Dawson. The only positive aspect was that it had been dark and he had been wearing a baseball cap. She had also seen him again momentarily at the flat she moved to in Stratford, where his attempt to kill her was thwarted when she locked herself in a bathroom which had been modified to double as a panic room. Logic told him that she would have been shown scores if not hundreds of mugshots of criminals loosely fitting his description, which would have surely clouded any definitive memory of him in her mind to a level that would make it impossible for her to be able to identify him with any measure of certainty. All in all, the police had nothing more solid than bullets retrieved from the murder scenes. The gun that they were fired from was now sinking into the sludge at the bottom of the deep brook.

At eight a.m., Carl used Larry Wade's mobile to call the number in the contact list for Jerry Parker.

Jerry had a cook on his payroll Monday to Friday; a local woman by the name of Diane Lowe, who arrived every morning on a bicycle and was now in the kitchen grilling a twelve ounce ribeye steak for him; medium rare, which she would serve up in the dining room along with scrambled eggs, toast, a carafe of fresh orange juice and a pot of coffee.

When the breakfast was served, Jerry picked up his knife and fork, to cut a piece of the steak, only to pause as his phone, which was on the tablecloth no more than six inches from his right hand, began to vibrate.

The caller ID was Larry Wade, and so he put his cutlery down and accepted it.

"What the fuck is happening, Larry?" Jerry said. "Have you lifted Gibson?"

"This *is* Gibson, Mr Parker. We need to discuss what you arranged to happen last night when your three goons broke into my house and unsuccessfully attempted to abduct me."

"Let me talk to Larry."

"He is no longer able to talk to you or anyone else. Think of him, Dean and Tyler as having vanished into thin air, because you'll never see them again. The important thing you need to know is that you were given false information that I murdered your daughter, and with no proof to support the accusation you intended to kill me."

"That's bullshit."

"Listen to this recording, and be aware that the phone and other items will be lodged with my solicitor and given to the police should I go missing or be harmed."

Jerry almost ended the call, but refrained from doing so, needing to obtain as much information as possible from Gibson.

The stammering voice of Dean Miller came on the line, sounding very scared: "I...I'm in a real f...ix here, Mr Parker. I've had to admit to Mr Gibson that you sent Larry, Tyler and me t...to abduct him and bring him back to the house. I also admitted that y...you intended to kill him."

"I think that's enough to be going on with," Carl said. "I fully realise that you are distraught at what happened to your daughter, but as I've already told you, I did not do it. I own a small company, have a girlfriend, and the most aggressive activity I indulge in is hitting a golf ball around a course a couple of times a week."

"You really don't have any idea of just who you're dealing with, do you, Gibson?" Jerry said in reply before ending the conversation.

Jerry's appetite was gone. He took a swig of the coffee and just remained sitting and thinking, wondering what Gibson had done with Larry, Dean and Tyler. He was also worried about the recorded message, which could be used in evidence against him in the event that Gibson *had* lodged the phone and other items with a solicitor. He had choices: take heed of a man who had somehow got the better of his three employees, leave it to the police to deal with him, or bide his time, and if Gibson was not arrested, send another more capable team to lift him.

Phoning an extension in the offices above the garage block, Jerry spoke to Randy Grant; told him that he did not expect Larry, Dean or Tyler to be back any time soon, if ever, and asked him to recruit another three guys from different areas of his enterprises, especially if they had security experience, could be trusted, and would have no qualms over some of the work that they might at times be called upon to carry out. He also offered Randy the position of head of security, with a fitting rise in pay to take over Larry's job, which Randy readily accepted.

Randy lit a joint and told the currently only other member of the team, Sammy Crowther, that they needed to select three suitable guys from other divisions of Jerry's varied illegal businesses, to transfer them to security, based at the offices of Millfield house.

"What the fuck's happened to the others?" Sammy said.

"The boss didn't say, and I didn't ask. If he'd wanted us to know, he'd have told me."

CHAPTER FORTY-TWO

IT was four p.m. when Joanne got back to her flat on Wellfield Road in Streatham.

DC Kelly Day was parked next to the kerb in a pool Kia between other vehicles when a minicab pulled up outside the house she was watching. Joanne Maguire climbed out and wheeled a trolley suitcase up to the open front door and vanished inside.

"Yes," Kelly said to herself as she plucked her phone from the built-in tray behind the cup holders in the centre console and speed-dialled a line in the squad room.

Marci picked up and said, "Yes, Kelly, has the eagle landed?"

"If you're referring to the bird of prey by the name of Joanne Maguire, then yes, she's back at her eyrie."

"I think that Pete intends to interview her, so stay put until he arrives, and you can handle it with him."

"Okay. I'll call back if she leaves the house for any reason."

"You've got each of the teams mobile numbers in your phone, haven't you?"

"Yes."

"Then contact Pete directly if she goes walkabout."

It was forty minutes later when Pete parked outside the house in Streatham. He had told Matt that the woman had returned from Liverpool, and Matt had said he would be happy for Pete and Kelly to grill her over the alibi, due to the fact that one of the detectives being a female would be less intimidating.

When Kelly saw Pete arrive, she got out of the Kia and joined him in front of the terraced house, which had been converted into flats.

"How do you want to do this?" Kelly said.

"There's no script, we'll just play it by ear and use measured verbal pressure," Pete said. "Feel free to jump in whenever you like."

After Pete knocked at the door of flat two, the door to number one opened and the muscular, shaven-headed guy with probably more tats than brains, who he had met the last time he'd visited with Matt, glowered at him and Kelly, retreated into his flat and slammed the door shut, having recognised Pete as being a detective.

As one door closes another one opens, Pete thought as Joanne opened hers.

"What do you want now?" Joanne said, recognising Pete from when she had been initially interviewed several months ago.

"We'd like to come in and go over the alibi that you gave for Carl Gibson with reference to the night of April the seventeenth."

Joanne tilted her head sideways to signify that they could enter.

The flat was brightly lit by sunlight streaming in through a sash window, and the interior of the small living room was minimally yet tastefully furnished with: a circular rug featuring what appeared to be a modernistic Mexican or Spanish motif, a two-seater settee, one wingback easy chair, light oak sideboard, glass-topped coffee table and the de rigueur big screen TV.

"You don't seem surprised to see us," Pete said.

"I'm not. I had two phone calls. One from Carl and one from Marlene at the salon, to let me know you wanted to talk to me, so why don't we sit down and get it done with?" Joanne said as she settled in the easy chair.

Pete and Kelly sat at the other side of the coffee table on the settee, and Pete began the interview without any preamble by saying, "Do you realise that if you knowingly gave Carl Gibson a false alibi for the date in question, then you will have aided and abetted him in respect of any crime that he committed when you said that you were in his company?"

Pete and Kelly saw the blood drain from Joanne's face as she began to chew at her bottom lip, but said nothing.

"We know for a fact that Carl was *not* with you when you said he was," Kelly said. "We have a reliable independent witness who saw him getting into his car in Bethnal Green after midnight on that date."

"As far as I remember I was with him," Joanne said in no more than a wavering whisper.

"That doesn't cut it, Ms Maguire," Pete said. "We now have every reason to believe that he is the serial killer who the media call the Killer Clown. If you did lie for him, then as far as the law is concerned you will be charged as an accessory to the murders which, if found guilty, could result in you being subject to a very long prison sentence. This is the last chance saloon for you. Tell the truth, now, or be prepared to suffer the consequences."

"I need a drink of water," Joanne said, standing up and heading for the kitchen.

Kelly followed her.

Joanne took a tumbler from the dish rack to half-fill it with cold water and drink it down in two large gulps. When she put the glass down and turned to face Kelly, her eyes were brimming with tears.

"Are you okay?" Kelly said.

"No, I'm fucking anything but."

"Come back into the living room and get it off your chest, love," Kelly said, acknowledging the anguish the other woman was suffering.

"In your own time, tell us the truth," Kelly said when they had retaken their seats.

"I lied," Joanne said, looking first to Kelly and then Pete. "Carl told me that because there was a strong likeness to him in the police artist's sketch, which was shown on the TV and in the newspapers, he was being treated as a suspect. He asked me to say we had been together on that night in April, and because I thought I knew him and could not believe he would harm a fly, I did."

"You've just put what was a wrong to right," Pete said. "I would suggest that for the time being you arrange to stay with a friend or family member, and take some time off work, just to be on the safe side."

"What are you saying?" Do you think Carl would hurt or kill me?"

"I doubt it, but it's always better to be safe than sorry. We have no idea what he might do. If he is the perpetrator we're looking for, and we are positive that he is, then he is highly dangerous. If he believes that his back is against the wall, he could be capable of doing anything."

"I hope that you're wrong about him," Joanne said. "I've never known him to be anything but gentle and thoughtful, with a great sense of humour. How could a person like that be the monster you're painting him?"

"Every coin has two sides," Kelly said. "You are on the side of it that he presents to those he knows. Think of an actor playing a part; assuming the opposite of his real personality and able to completely delude others. As for your safety, you do know the man, so I do not believe that he would harm you, because his victims have, as far as we can ascertain, been strangers to him with no link that we can find."

"You'll be required to provide a new official statement, Ms," Pete said. "And we'll need to know the address you decide to stay at."

"What do you think she'll do?" Kelly said after they had taken a written statement, which Joanne duly signed, and left the house.

"I think that one part of her mind will not accept Gibson as being the killer we believe him to be. I wouldn't be surprised if she gives him a bell and tells him about our visit, and the fact she admitted to us that they had not been together on the night she had said they were."

"Do you think that he'll panic and do a runner?"

"Who knows? He seems to be a smart cookie, and he's aware that if we had any proof of his guilt he would have been arrested by now. All we've done is confirmed that the only alibi he gave us is invalid."

"That gives us reason to interview him again."

Pete nodded. "We'll confront him with the lie he told us, lean on him hard, and hope he starts to break under the strain and attempts to do a Lord Lucan."

"If he is the Clown, then we know that he's armed and highly dangerous. If he begins to feel at risk he'll become more unpredictable than he already is."

"We'll just have to make damn sure that he doesn't vanish like John Bingham did after becoming a murder suspect."

"Who?"

"Lucan. His real name was John Bingham, and he disappeared way back in nineteen seventy-four, never to be seen again."

"I didn't know that."

"You do now," Pete said as he thumbed the remote fob to open the doors of the Volkswagen Golf he had signed out of the Yard's car pool, to climb in and head back to base, leaving Kelly to trot back to the Kia and follow on.

Inside the flat, Joanne phoned Carl, having decided to tell him that she had rescinded the alibi.

Carl had just arrived home from the factory when his smartphone trilled. Placing his briefcase on a counter in the kitchen, he accepted the call from Joanne, convinced she would tell him the police had quizzed her and that she had stuck to her story of being with him on the night he had told them he had been.

"Hi, Joanne," he said. "How was your trip up to Scouseland?"

"Fine, Carl. I'm calling to let you know the police have just left my flat. They told me that they have a witness who saw you getting into your car sometime after midnight on the date I said you'd been with me."

"They were lying to you, to break your story."

"One of them said that if you *were* guilty of the crimes, then I would be charged with being an accessory."

"I understand," Carl said, staying calm, considering the possibility of the call being monitored. "All I can tell you is that I haven't committed any crime, and that the police are grasping at straws, because as far as they are concerned I look like that guy in the bloody drawing, and have no alibis for when some lunatic murdered people."

"I'm sorry. I was under a lot of pressure."

"I can imagine. We'd better not see each other for a while. After they catch whoever *is* guilty, we can make up for lost time."

"Thank you for being so understanding, Carl. I feel terrible for letting you down."

"It's okay, don't worry about it. Goodnight, love."

Ending the call, he almost hurled the phone at the wall, but held back, took deep breaths and let an instant hatred for Joanne pervade his mind. The disloyal little slut was like everyone else; untrustworthy and beneath his contempt. She was attractive, been a good lay, and he had taken her to evening functions at his golf club and to the previous Christmas work do at a hotel in Croydon. She was little more than window dressing, to display a social side of his personality that in reality he was lacking. When this current problem with the law was well and truly over with, he would call to see her one final time, to cut her throat from ear to ear and make it look like a burglary that had escalated.

CHAPTER FORTY-THREE

KENNY Ruskin phoned Matt from the Computer Crime Section with expected but disappointing news. Kenny's tests of the recording of the call from the killer to Matt had, in his opinion, definitely been made by someone using a voice modulator. The problem being, there was no software programme available that could be run to reverse the altered voice to its original sound.

The good news Matt got was from Pete. Joanne Maguire had admitted to misleading them by providing a false alibi for Gibson, who could not now account for his whereabouts at the times and on the dates of any of the murders. It was no hard proof of guilt, but both Matt and Pete were convinced that he was the perpetrator.

When Pete got back from Streatham, he and Matt took the stairs and mugs of coffee up to Julia's office, hoping that she would now obtain authorisation for the prime suspect to be watched around the clock.

"You still haven't got a shred of evidence to link Gibson to the murders," Julia said after telling both of them to take a seat, to save her from having to tilt her head back and get neckache. All you have is a hunch, which could lead nowhere."

"It's not a *hunch*," Matt said. "When we questioned him again, his body language was screaming guilty at us. We saw behind the façade of innocence he attempts to project. If we don't keep him under constant observation he'll most likely kill again, and I would be pissed off to have that on my conscience."

Julia stood up and walked over to the small table in the corner of the office which had her: kettle, box of Earl Grey teabags, a cup and saucer, spoon, sweeteners and an open carton of milk standing on a tea towel. After switching on the kettle, she waited for the water to boil as she mulled over Matt's ardent request. She trusted him implicitly. He had a high percentage of successfully solved serial cases under his belt, and would not be asking for the surveillance on Gibson unless he was positive of his guilt.

Matt and Pete just sipped their coffee and waited, saying nothing as their boss weighed up a plethora of ifs and buts as she brewed her tea and retook her seat.

"Okay, Matt," Julia said after another short period of contemplation. "Organise it, with full observation being carried out on Gibson between the SCU and John Stott's MIT. I'll see to the necessary paperwork."

Matt just nodded. He fully intended to call and see Gibson again just as soon as he left Julia's office, with the intention of putting the man on edge by basically accusing him of the serial murders he was certain he was guilty of committing. The intense pressure of knowing he was under the microscope would, apart from ensuring that he did not kill again, mess with his head and hopefully feed the paranoid thought process which was now undoubtedly causing him to experience anxiety, suspicion and the fear of being caught. He would soon know beyond any doubt that everyone in law enforcement was definitely out to get him. Having gunned down a copper, they would be relentless in their efforts to apprehend him.

It was after nine p.m. when the doorbell rang. Carl checked the CCTV monitor, unsure as to whether Parker had decided to ignore his threat and send more of his thugs to abduct him. No need to get his gun, though, because it was Barnes and Deakin back again.

"What now? Is this another desperate fishing trip?" Carl said when he opened the door to them.

"It's just to keep you informed of the state of play, Mr Gibson. Ask us in."

"Why should I?"

"For us to sit down and talk the talk. You will definitely be interested in what we have to say."

Carl sighed theatrically, shrugged and stood aside, making sure he was standing on the still slightly damp area of the hallway carpet where two men had shed their lifeblood. "Okay, shoot," he said, once the three of them were sitting down in the lounge, with Matt and Pete facing Carl across a highly polished mahogany coffee table. "What is it you think I'll have the slightest interest in?"

"We know that you lied to us, and that you were not with Joanne Maguire on the night of the seventeenth of April," Matt said.

"Tell me something that I don't know. Joanne gave me a call and told me that you thought I was the killer, and that you had a witness who had seen me in the East End on the night she'd said I was with her. You even scared the shit out of her by implying that she risked being charged with being an accessory after the fact."

"The point being, you asked her to lie for you. Why would you do that if you're innocent?"

"Because I didn't like being a suspect without an alibi."

"Or you're as guilty as sin and hoped that conning Joanne into lying for you would put you in the clear."

"Fuck you, Barnes. This is nothing less than groundless persecution. You haven't got anything to implicate me with any crimes."

Matt smiled and said, "We know that you *are* a serial murderer, Gibson. Consider yourself to be on a very short leash from now on."

"What exactly do you mean by that?"

"Work it out. Your days of killing are over. Next time we knock at the door it will be with search warrants for your house, car and the factory you own, now that your one and only alibi has been broken."

"You have no legal right to do that."

"We'll do whatever it takes to find the evidence we need. And be aware that when our search teams do their work, they do it thoroughly."

"I'll instruct my solicitor to obstruct you," Carl said. "You have no right to do fuck all without proof that I've broken the law."

"Get real, Gibson. You and I both know that you're a homicidal psychopath. It won't be long now until we have enough to charge you with and take you off the streets. You will without doubt spend the rest of your life incarcerated, to die in prison."

That was it. Matt and Pete stood up and made their way out of the house without saying another word to the man who they intended to prove was the Killer Clown.

CHAPTER FORTY-FOUR

"WHAT do you think he'll do now?" Pete said to Matt as they sat in the car less than fifty yards away from Gibson's driveway, waiting for two of the team to reach them and take over what was now a live surveillance operation.

"He's got two choices; keep his cool, or run for the hills," Matt said. "I've got the feeling that his spirit will break and that at some point he'll attempt to do a runner. Paranoia will blossom like a black rose in his mind, now that we've told him we are convinced without any reservation whatsoever that he is the killer."

Jeff and Errol turned up, and Matt told them that Gibson had been left in no doubt that they were positive he was the Clown.

"Which means he'll stand his ground, keep his nerve, or attempt to escape," Errol said.

"Correct. He knows that we don't have any hard evidence to warrant charging and arresting him," Matt said. "But the vast majority of killers are basically insecure, full of uncertainty and self-doubt. I think he'll attempt to work out a way to evade us and leave London for pastures new. He probably won't do anything hasty, because he will assume, rightly, that he is now being watched continuously. But the burden of the position he's in will grind him down."

Shortly after Matt and Pete left, another unmarked car arrived at Gibson's house with two MIT detectives who liaised with Jeff and Errol before driving back to the main road and parking on the grass verge at a point where, should Gibson leave his house by the rear and follow a path to circle around, they would be sure to see him.

Carl couldn't relax enough to even sit down. His nerves were jangling and he knew that Barnes would not back off; the detective was absolutely certain of his guilt. His previously total anonymity was now a thing of the past. Going into the kitchen, he poured a large brandy to ease the stress which was making it impossible for him to decide on a course of action to take. He felt like a fly in a spider's web, just waiting to be taken. If he could not fathom out a way to somehow slip the noose which was metaphorically tightening around his neck, then he would lose everything: house, business, car, and the high standard of living he had grown accustomed to. But what was the alternative? Living with the threat of being locked up, growing old and dying in prison was an unbearable outcome to contemplate. What he needed was a plan to get out from under the watchful eyes of what he knew would be an unremitting stakeout by the police, with his every move being observed.

It was Saturday morning at seven a.m. Matt and Beth were drinking coffee and watching the early morning news on the TV in the kitchen, when Matt decided to reinterview the man who had contacted the police and said he was positive that Carl Gibson was the person depicted in the police artist's sketch. Gavin Shaw worked for Gibson as product manager at CG Aluminium Products in Brixton, and had done so for over a decade, so why would he choose to implicate the man who paid his salary, instead of just ignoring the fact that Gibson had a look of a murder suspect? Did he think that his boss was capable of being the killer, and if so, why?

"You've got a thousand yard stare, Barnes," Beth said. "That means you're thinking about the case, right?"

"Yeah," Matt said. "It's niggling me that it was one of Gibson's

management team who rang us to say he thought his boss was a look-

alike for the Clown. Surely he realised that his job would be on the

line if Gibson *was* guilty, because the company would probably go

bust."

"Perhaps he has some reason to believe that Gibson has the capacity to commit the crimes."

Matt phoned the squad room. Jeff answered, and on being asked, he came up with the address and telephone number of Gavin Shaw within seconds from the list of people who had phoned in to give names of men that they believed were spitting images of the killer.

"I shouldn't be long," Matt said to Beth as he grabbed a lightweight fleece from the back of a chair, and plucked his car key fob from one of the cup hooks under a wall unit.

"Pick up a litre of milk and half a dozen eggs while you're out," Beth said, kissing Matt on the lips before he left the cottage.

It was almost an hour later when Matt parked at the kerb on Hayter Road, Brixton, outside the bungalow owned by Gavin Shaw.

When the doorbell rang, Gavin was finishing washing up the breakfast dishes, cutlery and pans, after he and his wife had enjoyed a fry-up.

"I'll get it" Glenda said, dumping the tea towel she held, to walk out into the hallway and open the front door to a tall, craggy-faced man with short dark hair and penetrating slate-grey eyes.

"Can I help you?" Glenda said.

Matt took a step back to avoid invading the woman's personal space, and held up his open wallet for her to see his warrant card.

"I'd like a word with Gavin," Matt said.

Glenda's forehead furrowed with concern, but she invited the detective in as she turned her head and shouted, "There's a police detective to see you, Gavin," before leading Matt into a small lounge.

"What's the problem?" Gavin said as he appeared from behind them.

"Carl Gibson," Matt said. "You phoned us a while back and said that he looked very much like the serial killer we are attempting to find."

"Would you like a cup of coffee?" Glenda said to Matt, not wanting to hear the conversation. She had told Gavin at the time not to implicate his boss and risk losing his job.

"Please," Matt said. "Black, no sugar."

"What more can I tell you?" Gavin said when his wife left the room. "He looks a lot like the mugshot, that's why I phoned and said so."

"I see from my notes that you've worked at the factory for over ten years, so I take it you know Gibson well."

"You take it wrong. He doesn't let anyone get close to him. I don't know him any better now than I did the day I joined the company. All I can tell you is that he pretends to be a regular guy when it suits him, but has a dark side."

"What exactly do you mean, 'a dark side'?"

"An instance that stands out in my mind was five or six years ago. He had a short-lived affair with one of the office girls, and when she fell pregnant he paid her to have an abortion, and then fired her on the grounds that she was not performing her job to an acceptable level. He's got a mean streak."

"Anything else?" Matt said before pausing as Gavin's wife brought the coffee in and left the room again.

"Just the way he treats staff in general. He behaves as if they're slaves not employees; as if they are not worthy of his respect. That includes me. I remember him once asking me to go with him to his lockup to drop off some old and superfluous desktop computers, monitors and several filing cabinets. I dropped one of the monitors and he went apeshit, calling me a fucking clumsy retard. He then apologised for insulting me, but the damage was done, and I've never forgiven him for it."

"A lockup?" Matt said.

"Yes, it's at Clapham Junction at the rear of Dorothy Road, next to the railway lines."

"What was in it?"

"Just bits and pieces, and an old car covered with a semi-transparent plastic dust sheet."

"Could you tell what make, model and colour it was?"

"A classic seventies Ford Cortina. I guess it was plum or maroon coloured."

"I would appreciate it if you accompanied me to see the lockup," Matt said before finishing his coffee.

"Now?"

"Please. I'll have you back home in no time."

Less than twenty minutes later Matt parked on hardstanding ten yards back from a block of a dozen lockups.

"It's the fourth from the left," Gavin said. "The one with the dark green up and over door."

Matt took a photo with his phone. The hardly legible number eight was stencilled on the grime-covered metal door.

"I hardly need to say that it would be well out of order for you to mention to Gibson that I paid you a visit this morning," Matt said as he drove Gavin back to the bungalow.

"That's a given. He'd fire me on the spot if he knew I'd contacted the police over his likeness to the nutter you're looking for. Do you really think that he is the guy dubbed the Killer Clown?"

"All I'll say is we consider him to be a suspect."

After dropping Gavin back home, Matt returned to the cottage in Woodford Wells, where Beth was sitting in the kitchen nook at her laptop, catching up with reports on a couple of the children at Morning Star.

"Any luck?" Beth said as Matt entered the kitchen and headed for the coffeemaker. "The expression on your face tells me that you got lucky."

"Luck has nothing to do with it. I hoped that talking to Gavin Shaw, the guy that fingered his boss as being a dead ringer for the killer, would give me an insight as to what Gibson is really like, and he had nothing good to say about him, just painted him as being an overall nasty piece of work. The bonus was that in conversation it came out that Gibson has a lockup not far from where he lives, and that he kept what Shaw is certain was an old Ford Cortina in it."

"What does that tell you?"

Matt poured himself a cup of coffee and said, "It would explain why his Jag showed up on CCTV coverage outside his house at the time and date when one of the murders was committed. If he has an unregistered vehicle, it seems highly likely that he uses it when he's out hunting."

"Hunting?"

"Yeah. I think that when he has the urge to kill he goes to the lockup and uses the Ford to cruise around in until he finds suitable prey."

"Let me guess," Beth said. "You cannot legally force entry to the lockup without a warrant, which without any concrete proof against him you won't be able to obtain."

"True. We need more than belief in his guilt to search it, or his house and place of work. We have no evidence yet to give us legal cause to charge him with anything. As of now he is just a prime suspect under surveillance."

"And he knows that, does he?"

Matt nodded. "I told him that I'm positive he's the killer."

"Why?"

"To stop him in his tracks. He won't kill again, now that he knows we have him in our sights."

"Perhaps the pressure you're bringing to bear will be too much for him to handle. But if he just quits while he's ahead and withdraws into his shell, knowing that you have no solid evidence against him, he could remain beyond your reach."

"Is that what you think he'll do?"

"I think you will have no doubt caused him to feel extremely paranoid, which is an instinct or thought process that is believed to be heavily influenced by anxiety, suspicion, or fear. Gibson will have no doubt decided that he is being persecuted by the police, which makes you a threat to his continued freedom. It's an 'everyone is out to get me' frame of mind, which in his case is not irrational. Perhaps at some point, if he *is* guilty, he will attempt to flee, because the risk of being imprisoned for the rest of his life will be intolerable."

"At face value he appeared to be an unlikely suspect, Beth. He's a well-educated thirty-eight-year-old; a successful businessman enjoying a high standard of living, and the only law that we know he has ever committed is driving over the speed limit a couple of times."

"You told me he's a bachelor; basically a loner, and that he only saw his girlfriend once a week. He apparently has little time for other people, which is telling. If the young woman he murdered in Peckham Rye Park was his first victim, then the reason he started killing is a mystery. I can only assume that something happened in his life to set him off on what has become a killing spree. And he will without any doubt in my mind kill again if necessary to evade capture."

CHAPTER FORTY-FIVE

IT was eight-thirty on Monday morning when Carl drove into the yard of his factory on the Stone Trading Estate, to park the Jaguar in his slot near the main entrance door and walk into the reception area carrying a large leather holdall.

Two of John Stott's MIT officers were parked on Milkwood Road and watched from a distance with the aid of binoculars as the suspect arrived and entered the building, noting that he was wearing a dark grey suit, white shirt and poppy red necktie.

DC Stan Adkins made a note of the time and radioed in to report Gibson's current location.

"They've got nothing concrete on this guy," DC Wendy Moore said. "I think that having eyes on him twenty-four seven is over the top."

"I don't give a shit, love," Stan said. "As long as my salary is in the bank at the end of each month I'm a happy camper. Sitting here for a few hours with the radio playing and a flask of coffee is a cush number."

He waited until almost lunchtime before taking the bag from his office, to make his way to the rear of the factory, where he entered a storeroom to pull on a pair of navy blue coveralls and a baseball cap, both with the company logo on them. Slipping on a pair of mirrored sunglasses, he was all set to make his move. A couple of lorries were being loaded with product in the yard, and some of the transit vans were leaving to make local deliveries. He was blending in as he took a key fob for one of the vans, to walk out onto the loading dock and down the steps, climb into the vehicle and, after dumping the bag in the passenger footwell, follow a lorry around to the front of the factory and out of the main gates.

"I wonder if he'll leave for lunch soon," Stan said as he eyeballed the Jag, and Wendy took hardly any notice of the vehicles with CG Aluminium Product decals on their sides that passed by them.

"I could murder a pub meal." Wendy said. "A steak and kidney pie, chips, mushy peas and gravy would hit the spot. Are you up for it when our shift is over in a couple of hours?"

"Yeah," Stan said, "Although it would be cheaper to eat in the canteen back at base."

"You're a tight sod, Stan. A change is as good as a rest."

Parking the van on Dorothy Road at Clapham Junction, Carl walked to the nearby lockup, to enter it carrying the heavy bag which held the money from his floor safe and his remaining handgun, along with the silencer and bullets. Removing the coveralls and cap, he loaded the bag into the boot of the Cortina, drove out, and stopped briefly to get out and lock the door.

Driving west, he picked up the M4, having decided to head for Bristol and hole up in a cheap hotel for a few days while he attempted to come up with a long-term plan of action. He would start growing a beard, let his hair grow longer, and wear shades whenever he was out and about. The big problem was not being able to function normally. He didn't want to leave a trail, so had no smartphone or laptop, and could no longer safely use his credit or debit card. His only goal was to avoid being found. Somehow he would have to build a new life, and he knew that doing so would be a hard ask. The thought of going off the grid by being homeless and, worst-case scenario, sleeping rough was almost inconceivable. Where there's a will there's a way, though. He needed a new identity, and a passport to go with it so that he could in a few weeks' time leave the country, never to return. When ready, he would drive to Dover, board a ferry and sail off into a new life. He spoke decent French, so would be able to get by without drawing anyone's undue attention.

Stopping once at a service area to break the hundred and twenty mile journey, he had a sandwich and a cup of coffee, then used the loo before continuing on his way, to reach Bristol less than two and a half hours after leaving Clapham. It was southwest of the city in the Knowle West district where he found a seedy looking three-storey hotel off Leinster Road. It had a sign outside naming it as *The Grand*, which was a total misnomer, due to the fact that the windows looked to be coated with grime, fronting grey curtains behind them which had presumably once been white, gutters in need of repair with weeds growing out to hang over them, and the overall look of a dump with no amenities and the high probability of bed bugs to help guests make it through the night. The thought of his upmarket house, which he very much doubted he would ever see again, saddened him. He had at no time believed that he would ever end up being a serial killer, let alone a prime suspect for the murders he had committed. Being on the run was already no fun.

Parking on the street, Carl hefted his bag from the boot, along with a navy blue fleece which he pulled on over his suit jacket. He also removed his tie and loosened his collar before entering the door of the hotel into a small, gloomy reception area.

"What can I do for you, squire?" Dermot Harmon, the balding, grossly overweight owner of the Grand said from behind an open hatch which separated the reception from a room behind it, where Dermot spent a lot of his time watching sport on Sky, drinking cheap supermarket Scotch and reading sci-fi paperbacks.

"I'd like to book a room for a couple of nights," Carl said. "The best that you have."

"I've got a nice suite on the top floor for seventy quid a night, in advance. How does that sound?" Dermot said as he lit a cigarette, to take a long drag from it and immediately suffer a phlegmy coughing fit that turned his face as red as a beetroot's.

"Sounds fine," Carl said as he placed his bag on threadbare carpeting, took seven twenties from his wallet and put them on the counter. "My name is John Smith and I won't be needing a receipt for this, okay?"

"Excellent. I won't be needing any details, then," Dermot said as he counted the banknotes, folded them and stuffed them into a pocket of his trousers, to then produce a key with an overlarge yellow plastic fob attached to it with the number 14 printed on it with a black marker pen.

There was no lift. Carl carried the heavy leather bag up the stairs to the top floor, swapping it from hand to hand a couple of times on the way.

The suite was surprisingly clean looking, had a wall-mounted TV in the small lounge/kitchen, and another in the bedroom. The bathroom was pretty basic with a toilet, wash basin, and a shower on the wall above a bath enclosed by a plastic curtain.

Placing the bag on top of the bed, he removed a few items of clothing and the gun and silencer, which had rested on top of the stack of money. He felt relatively safe for the moment, but knew that he would, to a degree, probably be on guard for the rest of his life. It was normal to feel very paranoid when you knew that every copper in the UK was out to arrest you; especially the homicide detective, Barnes.

Walking across to the street-facing window, Carl looked out and down, to watch as light traffic and a few pedestrians passed by. He was overtired with stress from the day's hectic events, making his escape from the factory under the watchful eyes of plainclothes detectives, whom he had not seen but was positive would have been parked near the factory, ready to follow him when he left, expecting him to leave by the front door and drive home in his Jag. Stretching out on top of the bed he fell asleep, to wake up just after dusk with his stomach rumbling. He was hungry, so changed into jeans and a sports shirt, picked up the phone and pressed 0 for the front desk. He didn't want to drive again, or risk leaving the money in the room and walking to a nearby restaurant.

"Yeah," the raspy sound of the hotel owner's voice said.

"I don't want to go out again until tomorrow," Carl said. "I've had a long day, but I'm starving. Do you have room service?"

Dermot chuckled and said, "No way, José, this isn't a swanky five star hotel in the city. I have a few menus of local takeaways if you want to order some food."

"That will do. I'd be obliged if you would order something and have it collected for me."

"There will be an extra charge for that kind of service. I'd have to send my son, Mick, to pick it up. He works here with me, and time is money."

"No problem. I'd like fish and chips with mushy peas, and a large cup of coffee."

"There's a chippie just a five minute walk from here. Just give Mick fifteen quid when he brings it up to your room."

The line went dead.

Going through to the lounge, Carl didn't switch the light on. He walked over to the window and looked out again, as far left and then right as he could, and experienced the sensation of his stomach dropping as blood was redirected away from it to feed muscles with. Physiologically he was experiencing the fight or flight reaction as he saw a car pull in behind two others and stop, almost but not quite out of sight. More alarming was the fact that no one exited the vehicle. The paranoia he was suffering from caused him to believe, for no logical or obvious reason, that he had somehow been followed to Bristol, and that it was Barnes, his nemesis, out there in the gloom; one of the two figures sitting in the front of the last car in line.

CHAPTER FORTY-SIX

BARELY a minute after Carl had parked on a side street just past a grotty-looking hotel, whose owner had apparently had the temerity to have a large sign above its front door proclaiming it as being *The Grand*, two MIT detectives drove by, noting that their suspect had retrieved a large bag from the boot of the Ford, and was about to enter the hotel.

Pete and Marci were in another car, but had hung back on Leinster Avenue, to be given Gibson's current location by DC Fred Hilton. In the third car, the last of the vehicles that had tailed Gibson to Bristol, were Matt and Errol. The SCU detectives had been given the details of the suspect by DC Hilton, who with his partner DC Dale Clayton, had been surreptitiously watching the lockup in Clapham Junction, to see Gibson arrive in one of his companies vans, enter the lockup, and drive off in a maroon Ford Cortina less than five minutes later.

They waited until the sun dropped away in the west, before all three cars parked on the street where the hotel was situated.

The plan was simple enough. Matt and Errol would enter the hotel by the main door and subsequently arrest Gibson, while Pete and Marci remained outside on the pavement, and the MIT officers would keep watch on the rear door and fire escape.

"A guy booked in a few hours ago," Matt said as he held his warrant card out through the open hatch of what appeared to be an office separated from the dowdy reception area. "What room is he in?"

"Number fourteen on the top floor," Dermot said. "Is he in some kind of trouble?"

"You could say that. Did he give you his name?"

"Said it was John Smith."

"Give me a spare key for the room."

"Don't you need a warrant to—?"

"Behave," Matt said to the man he assumed to be the owner of the dump. "I reckon that you didn't register him as a guest and most likely charged him over the top in cash and pocketed it, which could get you closed down and the taxman looking at your books long and hard. Is that the way you want to play it?"

"Okay, no sweat," Dermot said as he produced a key and placed it on the counter, just as Mick entered the hotel swinging a plastic bag in his hand and headed for the stairs.

"Hold it, Mick," Dermot said. "There might be a problem."

"Who's this?" Matt said as the teenager approached them.

"My son. The guy in number fourteen asked for room service, which we don't provide, but I said I could get Mick to pick him something up. He wanted fish and chips."

"Let's go up and deliver it, then," Matt said to Mick. "No need to keep a hungry man waiting."

"Will my son be safe?" Dermot said as he lumbered out of the office door to face Matt and Errol.

"He'll be fine," Errol said. "All he has to do is tell the guy that he's got his food. We'll take it from there."

Following Mick up to the top floor, Matt rapped on the door, and the lad said in a loud voice, "I've got your fish and chips, mister."

Matt gently pushed the boy to the side, for him to be out of any line of fire, motioning for him to go back downstairs, before knocking again as Errol used the room key to unlock the door, twist the brass-plated doorknob and push it back. Both he and Matt had drawn their handguns and were ready for any hostile reaction. The room was empty.

Matt and Errol searched the small suite. No one was in it.

Carl didn't hope for the best, he expected the worst. He was positive that the police had somehow found out about the lockup, to observe him arrive at it and then drive off in the Cortina. Perhaps he was totally wrong, but was not prepared to ignore his gut instinct, which was no more than a rapid evaluation of the circumstances around him. Many of his decisions were intuitive, and he was invariably driven to act on them. Being on the top floor, there was no apparent escape route. Backing away from the window he considered his options. His pursuers would more than likely be now exiting their cars and approaching the hotel, to soon be climbing the stairs. He bolted into the bedroom, retrieved the silenced pistol from beneath a pillow and stuck it into the waistband of his jeans. There were two windows in the room; one on the far wall facing the rear, and one on the side wall, from which he looked out and down at the large flat roof of the two-story building abutted to the hotel.

The wooden sash window appeared to be jammed, but it was only flaking, yellowing paint holding it in place. Forcing it open took less than thirty seconds. He knew that if he jumped there was the risk of injury, perhaps a sprained or even broken ankle. No time to linger, though. He lifted the bag of money from the side of the bed, to drop it out of the window, before climbing out, to first sit on the ledge and then turn, grasp the concrete sill with both hands and lower himself against the wall before letting go. Bending his knees and rolling sideways on impact, he grunted with pain as the butt of the gun dug into his stomach. Sitting up slowly, he took a few deep breaths before climbing to his feet and picking up the bag and walking across to the edge of the roof, hoping that he would find a drainpipe to climb down.

"In the bedroom," Matt called out to Errol, who was checking the bathroom.

From a window, Matt could see Gibson making his way across the flat roof below, which was obviously that of a business premises, due to it being the size of a tennis court.

"Armed police. Stop where you are, drop the bag and lay face down with your hands joined behind your neck, fingers linked. Do it now."

Carl looked up towards the window he had dropped down from to see Barnes and another detective framed in it, both aiming handguns at him. He had choices; jump off the roof, to probably break his neck or legs, draw the pistol from his waistband and start shooting at them, or do what he'd been told to. He let go of the bag, but just stood there, arms by his sides. He had to believe that they still did not have enough to charge him with.

Errol kept his gun unwaveringly trained on Gibson's chest as Matt holstered his gun and did what the fugitive had done; lowered himself down from the ledge outside the window and dropped the few remaining feet, to turn and face the suspect, who he was positive was the serial killer they sought.

The light from one of the side facing hotel rooms and the moon above illuminated the scene. Drawing his gun, Matt walked towards Gibson and said, "Are you deaf, stupid or both? I ordered you to hit the deck and—"

"Fuck you, Barnes. I've done nothing wrong. All you've got is suspicion, which counts for shit."

"I see that you've got a handgun tucked in your jeans. Take it out with your left hand, using your finger and thumb only, and toss it away from you."

"It's for self-protection," Carl said as he drew the weapon but kept hold of it, ignoring Matt's instructions. "I've never fired it, so don't get a hard-on thinking that you'll be able to get a ballistic match to the murder weapon, because you won't."

Matt shrugged. "Doesn't matter, now that we've got your Ford Cortina. If just one single fibre inside it is a match to the hundreds that forensic officers gathered from the murder scenes, then you get to die in a maximum security prison."

"Whatever," Carl said. "We're all just statistics; here today and gone tomorrow, so why sweat it? You've got to give your inner self its head, and fuck the consequences."

"Why did you do it?"

"I'm not admitting to doing anything. But if I *had* murdered those muppets, it would have been because I was bored rigid with the life I was leading and needed a little drama to spice it up."

"Well you've got a lot more drama now, Gibson, because if you don't drop the gun and step away from it, I'll shoot you where you stand, so use it or lose it."

Carl wanted to take his chance and do the unexpected, but the other copper was above him at the open bedroom window of his suite, still pointing a gun at him. He decided to drop the gun, jump off the roof and take his chances, because he was definitely between a rock and a hard place. Surely neither of the lawmen would shoot if he got rid of the weapon, turned his back on them and leapt off the building.

CHAPTER FORTY-SEVEN

OTIS Crawford knew that a DCI by the name of Barnes was heading up the squad which had Carl Gibson under round the clock surveillance. That had made his job easier. All he'd done was keep Barnes under his watchful eye, to follow the homicide detective wherever he went. Doing so had now brought him to Bristol, where he had watched the three-car police tail pull up on a street where the maroon Ford Cortina driven by Gibson was parked a little way past a third-rate hotel. Waiting in a murky corner on the third level of a multi-storey car park just one hundred and fifty yards away, he had a side view of the Hotel's main entrance, which gave him a good enough view of all movement in and out.

Matt gave Gibson a few seconds to come to a decision, and kept the Glock pistol aimed at his chest, tightening his finger on the trigger, not knowing what action the desperate man would decide to take, to be surprised when the suspect who he knew to be the killer, let the gun slip from his hand, to then turn and walk the three steps to the very edge of the roof with his hands raised in apparent submission.

"Stop where you are," Matt said as he also approached the edge of the flat roof, keeping at least twenty feet between them. "Jumping from this height isn't going to do you any good. There are other officers down below, so even if you were lucky and the fall didn't kill you, you'd be detained."

"I'm thirty-eight-years old, Barnes," Carl said as he swayed a little in the late evening breeze. "I have no intention of spending the rest of my life locked up like an animal in a fucking zoo."

"Is that an admission?" Matt said. "Do you confess to being the so-called Killer Clown?"

"I'm not about to say anything that would make your job easier. In fact I'm *not* going to jump, because until you can prove I did anything illegal you've got nothing but straws in the wind."

Carl half-turned, and Matt saw the small green dot of light dancing on the man's chest and knew instantly that it was coming from the laser sight scope of a rifle.

Carl lowered his head, noticing the bright moving beam as Matt shouted, "Get down now, Gibson. Someone is targeting you."

As the penny-sized dot steadied and began to rise up the front of his shirt to his face, Carl dropped to his knees, but not fast enough to dodge the high velocity polymer cased bullet that was travelling at more than three thousand feet per second. As the trigger was pulled, the crosshairs of the semi-automatic Heckler & Koch PSG1 sniper rifle's scope had been centred on the middle of the mark's forehead, but the figure's sudden downward movement altered the destination of the bullet, for it to enter Carl's head higher, drilling a pathway through the scalp and bone to graze the dura mater, the first and tough outer membrane of three layers which protect the brain.

Otis saw the splash of blood fan out from his mark's head as Gibson was blown back from the impact of the slug to lay supine on the flat roof which abutted the side of the hotel.

Leaving the rifle on the concrete floor, Otis removed the pair of medical grade latex gloves he had worn, climbed in his midsize Kia and drove down to the ground floor, to leave the car park and head north through the city to pick up the M4, destination London. To have watched as Gibson dropped down from a window, followed seconds later by the detective, Barnes, had been a pleasant surprise, making the hit a walk in the park that came to pass a lot sooner than he had thought it would.

It was over an hour later when Otis stopped at the Welcome Break

eastbound services at Membury. He needed to take a piss, order

coffee and a hot snack, and then make a phone call.

Matt waited several seconds, in case the shooter was still in position, planning to take another shot. He was positive that Gibson was dead, but shouted up to Errol and told him to call for an ambulance, and also to let the local police know that there was a shooter in the area.

The headshot had rendered Carl instantly unconscious, not only concussing him but also compromising his brain. Matt went to him, keeping low and moving fast, to grasp the injured man by the ankles and drag him back to the deep night shadow against the wall of the hotel. He was surprised to find Gibson still had a pulse, although the copious bleeding from his scalp confirmed that his heart was still beating, because the dead do not bleed.

Carl drifted up from an inky blackness, and a part of his brain imagined that he was in the depths of an ice-cold ocean, slowly rising up through lightening shades of grey until he reached the surface.

Matt watched as Gibson's eyes snapped open, full of confusion, to face him through a mask of blood.

"W…What happened?" Carl drawled as he looked up into Matt's eyes. "Did you shoot me?"

"No," Matt said. "But somebody did. Just keep still, an ambulance is on the way."

"Am I dying?"

"I'm no doctor, but I think you could be. You're bleeding like a stuck pig; the bullet ploughed through the top of your skull, probably entering the top of your brain."

Matt felt no measure of empathy for the man who he was positive was the killer he sought. To an extent, the dark side of him savoured the fact that Gibson was seriously wounded but had regained awareness and was able to feel fear and suffer pain.

"I don't want to die," Carl said.

"Sometimes you reap what you sow, Gibson. None of your victims will have wanted to die, but you played God, robbed them of a future and shot them dead in cold blood."

Carl said nothing. He felt a deepening coldness overwhelm him, and darkness seemed to engulf his mind as dizziness sucked him into unconsciousness again.

After retrieving Gibson's pistol from the roof, Matt looked up to where Errol was still framed in the window. "Arrange for a ladder," he said. "The paramedics will need one when they arrive, and I don't plan on staying up here a second longer than I have to."

"Is he dead?" Errol said.

"Not quite, but he's working at it. He's out like a light, his breathing is shallow and his pulse is thready."

The sound of distant sirens drew louder as Errol went down to the reception and asked the owner if he had any ladders long enough to reach the flat roof of the next-door building.

"What do you need ladders for?" Dermot said.

"Because there is a casualty up there, and the crew of the ambulance that is about to arrive will need to get to him."

"Oh, right," Dermot said, and shouted, "Mick get out here, now."

Mick came through from the back with his mouth full of food. Waste not want not he'd thought as he had tucked in to the fish and chips which he was sure the guy in number fourteen would not now be needing.

"Go and get the ladders from the shed, son, and put them up against the rear wall of the furniture store."

An ambulance and several police cars arrived as Matt descended the ladder to join Errol and the other team members, who'd gathered around, eager to know what had gone down.

Getting Gibson off the roof and in to an ambulance was a work of art carried out by the paramedics.

Marci and Pete followed the ambulance to the Bristol Royal Infirmary on Upper Maudlin Street, where they stayed as Gibson was rushed to an operating theatre, still alive but in what they believed to be a critical condition.

CHAPTER FORTY-EIGHT

JERRY Parker was with his wife and four close friends at the Bella Luna Italian restaurant in Oxshott when his smartphone trilled. He accepted the call, to be told that his order had been dispatched. He already had the details of an offshore account to send the balance of the fee to, and so thanked the caller and disconnected. He didn't need the specifics over the phone; the pro hitman he had hired to deal with Carl Gibson was a contract killer he had done business with eight times over the previous decade, who was totally dependable, having never failed to eliminate whoever he had been paid to.

Six days after the shooting in Bristol, Carl was recovering from the head wound he had suffered, but although not having been charged with any crime as yet, he was now in a private room under constant police watch, fearing that any second of every passing day the cop, Barnes, would arrive to charge him with several counts of murder, to then arrange for him to be transferred to a London hospital, where he would no doubt be handcuffed to a bed until he was deemed fit enough to be moved to a police cell and be interviewed at length. His prior belief that no evidence would be discovered to link him to the crimes was in tatters. Barnes had told him that a forensic team would search the Cortina for fibres, and his paranoia led him to believe that they would no doubt find some from clothing he had worn, which would be more than enough to formally charge him. Then what? Would they guess that he had dumped the gun and other stuff in the brook at the rear of his house, to have police divers meticulously search the bottom of it? He also thought that Jerry Parker had hired whoever had taken a pot-shot at him on the roof of the building next to the hotel, but having gunned down two of the men Parker had sent to abduct him previously, he was in no position to mention it to the police. The jam he was in seemed to be escalating. Would the shooter endeavour to finish what he had obviously been contracted to do? The answer was probably yes. From believing that his identity would never be known, he was now in deep shit with no feasible way to crawl out of it. It would definitely have been better if the bullet which struck him so high in the forehead had been lower and blown his brains out. If and when he was convicted of murder and sent down, then he would end his own life, because freedom was paramount, and a prolonged existence without it was not something he could even begin to contemplate.

The day after the attempted hit, Otis Crawford had seen the news and was utterly dismayed to know that an unnamed man had been shot in Bristol and seriously injured, but was now in a stable condition and expected to make a full recovery. This was the only time in his twenty-five years as a hitman he had failed to fulfil a contract. The first thing he did was contact Jerry Parker on a cheap prepaid burner phone.

"Yes," Jerry said, having expected a call from Crawford, now that he knew Gibson was still alive.

"Is your line secure?" Otis said.

"Of course."

"As you will no doubt know, I botched the job, which is very embarrassing. I apologise for my failure. If your contact can find out the mark's current location I'll finish what I thought was a job done, and will also waive the remainder of the fee."

"I appreciate that the best laid plans can go pear-shaped, my friend. Give me a number and I'll get back to you."

In one way, Jerry was pleased. He had initially wanted to personally torture and kill Gibson, but this would work out just fine. His daughter's killer had been seriously wounded, survived, but was still in the line of fire, and would know it and be fearful for his life, suffering not only from the gunshot wound but also in the knowledge that he had been targeted, now fully aware that the police were the least of his problems.

Randy Grant made the call to the cop on the take.

"Yeah?" DS Noel Edwards said, too inquisitive to ignore the call, even though there was no caller ID.

"I'm an associate of Larry's," Randy said. "We need an update as to the current location of the person that you gave us details of."

"Why didn't Larry call?"

"He's out of town taking care of other business."

"Give me a number and your name. I'll see what I can find out and get back to you. It could take a while."

Noel smiled as he disconnected. Whoever had attempted to take Carl Gibson out had failed, and he already knew that Gibson was in what they called protective custody in a Bristol hospital, in case the shooter was dumb enough to make a further attempt on his life. Noel also knew what the plan was; when Gibson was deemed fit enough to be moved, he would be transferred to a private north London clinic where, if and when they had enough evidence to charge him with a lot more than having been in possession of an unlicenced handgun, he would, when medically discharged, be relocated to a police cell.

Ninety-six hours after receiving the call from a guy who had said that his name was Randy, Noel used a public phone to contact the number he had been given.

Three rings and the call was accepted, but no one spoke.

"Are you there, Randy?" Noel said.

"Yeah. You took your time getting back to me."

"It wasn't easy finding out what I've got for you."

"I'm listening."

"How much will I get for this information?"

"How much do you want?"

"Ten grand."

"That's too rich. I'll go to five. Don't forget we have enough on you to ensure you'd lose your job, pension, and face charges. You need to remember that we own you."

"Five will be just fine, then," Noel said. "Gibson is due to be driven from Bristol to London tomorrow evening, and will be lodged at the Willow Bank Clinic in South Hampstead."

"In a private room?"

"Yes. Probably but not definitely in number twenty-six on the third floor, which is an en suite room we've used a few times. It's at the end of a corridor. He'll be there until adjudged to be fit enough to be discharged, at which point he will be wholly in police custody."

"Nice work, Noel. I'll get back to you if what you've told me pans out."

Randy walked across to the house from the office above the garage block, to tell Jerry what the cop had told him.

"Sounds as if we have a window of opportunity," Jerry said. "I'll contact the shooter and have him take care of Gibson asap. Worst case scenario is that if he fails again, then I'll have to wait until he's on remand in Belmarsh and arrange for an inmate to use a shiv to carve both of his eyes out."

CHAPTER FORTY-NINE

IT was late evening when Carl was driven to the clinic in London, to be admitted under the name of Jonathan Swift. Escorted to a room with en suite bathroom on the third floor, he was informed by one of the four detectives who had accompanied him that for his own continued safety he would be confined to the room, with an armed officer sitting outside it.

"Are you saying that I'm under arrest?" Carl said to DS Marci Clark.

"Not at the present time. But someone out there will no doubt want to finish what he started," Marci said. "Just think of us as your guardian angels."

"Where's Barnes? How come he isn't here?"

"Off duty, perhaps enjoying a little R and R. Or maybe he's checking with forensics to see if they've found anything to link you to the murders we know you committed."

"You've got no fucking proof that I've done anything. I want to contact my lawyer."

"You haven't been charged with anything, yet, Mr Gibson. If, or should I say *when* you are, then you'll get to make a phone call. And an innocent man doesn't do a runner. For the time being I suggest that you chill out and think good thoughts."

"Fuck you."

Marci grinned and said, "No chance, Gibson, you're not my type."

Matt was at home, mentally sweating as he waited impatiently for the Forensic Science department to come up with some hard evidence that would give him enough to charge Gibson with murder. If they didn't, then knowing beyond any reasonable doubt that he was the killer would not be enough to put him in front of a judge and jury at the Central Criminal Court, affectionately known for centuries as the Old Bailey. Ballistics had checked the handgun which Gibson had been in possession of, but it was not a match to the weapon used to carry out the shootings, or had any history of being used in other crimes.

"You told me that there is always an exchange of trace evidence between perpetrators and victims at crime scenes," Beth said as they shared the chore of washing and drying the dishes from the evening meal of spaghetti Bolognese, which they had cooked together.

"Perhaps *nearly* always would be more accurate," Matt said. "Some crimes never get solved. This one hopefully will be."

"Where is your suspect now?"

"In a north London clinic, supposedly being guarded from a possible follow up attack on him by whoever shot him in Bristol."

"What's his current condition?"

"He's on the mend. They operated on him and put a metal plate in his skull. I daresay he has a severe headache and has been prescribed strong pain killers."

"Wine or Scotch?" Beth said. "And then we should relax and watch a movie."

"Scotch for me," Matt said.

Once settled in the lounge with drinks to hand, they put aside all problems and became immersed in watching Jurassic World Dominion, which was a movie neither of them had seen.

It was almost one a.m. when they called it a night and went to bed, both a little tipsy from at least one drink too many.

Matt entered the squad room at eight thirty a.m. to be met by Pete, who was grinning as broadly as the Cheshire Cat.

"What have I missed?" Matt said.

"I got a call ten minutes ago from Martin Frost, head of FSS, forensic science section."

"I know who he is, Pete. What has he got for us?"

"Results. Fibres found in the Ford Cortina which Gibson kept in the lockup and drove to Bristol in are a positive match to those recovered from two of the murder scenes. That gives us what we need to get warrants to enter and search his house, factory and the Jag he owns, plus enough for us to charge him initially with the murders of Brenda Cummings and Melanie Parker."

"Have you told Julia the good news?"

"Not yet. You can have that pleasure while I acquire the warrants and arrange for a CSI team to search Gibson's properties."

It was just before five p.m. when the tall black man wearing gold-rimmed spectacles, a dark grey pinstripe suit and a crimson necktie entered the Willow Bank Clinic. He was carrying a bouquet of cut flowers and walked purposefully through the bustling reception, unnoticed by a uniformed guy with his back to him, whom he judged to be security, to follow a long corridor leading past treatment rooms until he came to a stairwell and climbed up to the third floor, where he opened the landing door a few inches to check out the lie of the land in the corridor beyond.

Eileen Galanis had been a kitchen worker at the clinic for nine years, and was, as per usual at this time of day, up on the third floor delivering meals to the private rooms. One of the large food trolley's wheels squeaked as she pushed it, and she made a mental note to get the janitor to give it a spray of WD40 as soon as she had finished up. Eileen was also thinking about the weekend ahead. She and her hubby, Stav, were flying out to Athens for a week, to stay with his parents in their villa in the port city of Piraeus, just a few kilometres southwest of the capital.

On reaching number twenty-six, Eileen paused while the copper in civvies got up from his chair, removed a key from a side pocket of his jacket and faced the door to unlock and open it. She had no idea who the patient inside the room was, and didn't want to. It was none of her business, and life always ran smoother if you minded your own.

Neither Eileen nor the MIT officer, DC Dale Clayton, heard the soft hiss of the landing door close, or were aware that a man was walking briskly towards them, no longer holding a bunch of flowers, which had been replaced with a nine millimetre handgun fitted with a silencer.

CHAPTER FIFTY

WITH the car parked in a space at the side of the Clinic, Matt and Pete made their way to the main entrance at the front of the building, entered the large reception area and identified themselves to the uniformed security guard at the desk, informing him that they were there to visit the patient in number twenty-six on the third floor.

"You'd think it was a bank," Pete said as they headed towards the two lifts. "Seems to be a security presence everywhere these days."

"It's the way of the world, now," Matt said. "Nowhere can be regarded as being wholly safe anymore. There seems to be a growing number of homicidal maniacs and terrorists out there, all with some unfathomable belief that killing strangers to them is in some way justifiable, to their warped way of thinking."

Stepping out of the lift, they walked along a corridor which had framed prints of mainly floral scenes on one wall and windows facing the city on the other. Up ahead of them was a junction with signs displaying the relevant room numbers on them. Before they reached the turn, two soft pops rang out, which could have possibly been something innocuous, but to both of them was far more likely to be the sound of suppressed gunshots. Drawing their pistols, they ran towards where the sounds had come from.

DC Dale Clayton entered the room with Eileen directly behind him. She had removed a food tray from the heated trolley, which she inadvertently upturned onto Dale's back as someone pushed her forward into him. Knocked down to the floor, turning as he landed, with Eileen on top of him, legs either side of his waist, Dale reached for his gun as he saw a man enter the door holding a firearm in a two-handed grip, pointing it at his head. Even as his hand curled around the butt of the police issue Glock pistol, he knew that he was about to die. Mercifully for Dale, he felt nothing as a bullet hit him in the right temple, to pass through his brain and exit the other side of his skull.

The bed was empty, and even as Otis turned towards the only other door in the room, which he rightly assumed to be a bathroom, Carl

Gibson charged out of it with his arms out straight, to strike Otis hard in the chest, knocking him down over the fallen woman, even as he pulled the trigger to send a slug harmlessly into the ceiling.

Carl ran out of the room, gripped the handle of the food trolley and swung it lengthwise, for it to half enter the open doorway. He only had one thought in his mind, to evade the hitman and survive the attack. His head roared with pain, due to the initial gunshot he had suffered, and he felt dizzy and nauseous as he made it to a stairwell door and opened it.

Otis gave no thought to the dazed and moaning woman. He scrambled to his feet, pushed the trolley back out into the corridor and fired another shot as he saw the door closing on his mark.

The bullet passed through the door, missing Carl by a hairsbreadth as it blew splinters of wood out, some of which penetrated Carl's cheek and neck. He raced down the stairs two at a time, and on the landing of the second floor he left the stairwell and ran along a corridor, to collide with a gurney being pushed by a porter, causing him to fall, roll sideways and crash into a wall.

Matt and Pete heard another shot as they rounded the junction just in time to see a tall black guy holding a gun, who was about to enter a stairwell door.

"Armed police," Matt shouted. "Drop the weapon, now."

Otis took a shot in the direction of the two detectives before continuing his pursuit of Gibson. He looked down over the waist-high railing just in time to see the door on the landing below him close.

"Check the room, call for backup, and have the clinic and surrounding area cordoned off," Matt said to Pete as he opened the landing door and went through it, ready to shoot the hitman on sight. He knew that the guy had not had time to travel far, and was sure that in all probability he had made his way out onto the second floor of the clinic.

Pete entered the room to find two people, a man and a woman laid on the floor. The woman was moving, attempting to push herself up into a sitting position.

"Police," Pete said to her. "Are you okay?"

Eileen nodded, but her marble white face, unnaturally wide open eyes and shaking hands told another story. She was in shock and had not yet assimilated what had happened, although was full of underlying relief at having survived the ordeal.

Pete only needed to glance at the DC's face and the pool of blood that his head was laying in to know that he was dead. Taking out his phone, Pete made calls, and then told the woman that she was safe, before leaving the room and running to the door which the shooter and Matt had vanished through, hoping to find them before anything happened to his close colleague, whom he also regarded as being his best friend.

The force with which Carl had ran headlong into the gurney had injured his right leg. He pushed up off the floor and limped along the corridor, only to stop frozen in place as a loud, deep, penetrating voice from not far behind him shouted his name and ordered him to stop.

There was no way that he was going to just stay where he was and be executed. Shambling along as fast as he could, he reached a nurses' station and hobbled behind it, telling the three staff members present that someone was attempting to kill him, as he dropped to his knees and crawled into the space under the large crescent-shaped desk, to sit in the shadows with his arms clasped around his knees and his eyelids tightly shut, as if the danger he could not see would be unable to harm him.

Reaching the desk, Otis grasped one of the nurses by an arm and swung her backwards into the wall, away from the only place in which Gibson had been able to seek sanctuary, under the desk.

"You just ran out of luck, bigtime," Otis said as he crouched down to see his quarry sitting in deep shadow.

"No, please, don't kill me," Carl pleaded in a whiny voice as he put both hands up in front of his face.

Otis smiled as he shot the mark three times, for the bullets to pass through his hands; the first to enter his left cheek, the second between his nose and top lip, shattering teeth, and the third dead centre between his tightly closed eyes.

Matt approached the nurses' station with his gun raised, to see the tall black man stand up from behind the desk and put his left arm around one of the female nurse's neck and hold the silencer-fitted barrel of his pistol against her right temple.

"You know that it's over," Matt shouted. "There's nowhere for you to go. If you want to leave here alive, drop the gun, let her go and get down on the floor with your hands clasped behind your head."

"Fuck you," Otis said, keeping low behind the shaking, gasping woman. "That isn't going to happen. I'm going to take my chances, and if you don't want to see this bitch's brains plastered on the wall, drop the gun and let me leave."

"Looks as if we have a stand-off, then, because I have no intention of letting you go anywhere."

Pete walked up to near where Matt was standing, to position himself several feet to his left, his weapon drawn and pointing at the hitman.

"The officer who was guarding Gibson is dead," Pete said to Matt. "What do you plan on doing?"

Matt took a deep breath, exhaled slowly and did the only practical thing he considered would save anyone else – bar the shooter – from being injured or killed.

Otis Crawford had finally run out of luck. Holding the nurse as a hostage was no protection against the man in front of him.

Matt could only see the right side of the man's face, but trusted in his expertise with the semiautomatic pistol. The time for words was over.

Otis did not have time to react as a single bullet almost shaved the nurse's cheek before obliterating his right eye as it passed through it. He was driven back into the wall behind him, to leave a swathe of bright red blood as he slithered down to the floor and toppled over onto his side, clinically dead as the gun he had held slipped from his limp hand.

"That seems to have resolved the situation," Pete said as he and Matt approached the desk to confirm that the assassin was dead.

"Are you okay?" Matt said to the nurse, who was being attended to by her colleagues.

"Y…Yes, I'm fine," nurse Carrie Higgins said. "Thank you."

"You're welcome," Matt said as Pete kicked the handgun away from the corpse, even though it was obvious that the as yet unknown perpetrator was no longer a threat to anyone.

Matt ducked down under the large desk, and was not surprised to find that Carl Gibson was in the same lifeless state as the man who had shot him.

CHAPTER FIFTY-ONE

IT was normal procedure for any shooting carried out by a police officer to be rigorously investigated. The rules were fixed; the primary intention of the police, when discharging a firearm, is to prevent an immediate threat to life by shooting to stop the subject from carrying out their intended or threatened course of action. In most circumstances this is achieved by aiming to strike the central body mass (the torso) and is known as a 'conventional shot'. However, if – for example – only the head of the subject is visible and a shot must immediately be discharged in order to prevent an immediate threat to life, then the authorised firearms officer (AFO) will have no option but to employ a 'critical shot' by aiming at and firing at the only part of the subject which is visible, namely the head, which is what Matt had done, as witnessed by a fellow officer. The risk to the nurse's life *had* necessitated the subject being incapacitated by a shot to the head.

"You get to catch up on paperwork for a few days while the powers that be dot the I's and cross the t's before giving you a clean sheet," Julia said as she settled in Matt's office with a cup of Earl Grey she had brought down from her office on the floor above.

Matt hiked his shoulders in an exaggerated shrug. "We closed the case, saved the taxpayers a few quid and did the legal beagles out of big fees, so I guess it's a result," he said. "As you know, a forensic team found more incriminating fibres at Gibson's house, and also a small trademark photocopy of a clown's head in a plastic packet, which was wedged in the side of his desk drawer; the icing on the cake, damning proof confirming that he was the Killer Clown. The only downside is that we couldn't bring Gibson or the hitman who shot him in alive. We may have been able to come up with some sweetener for the shooter and hopefully been given the name of his contractor, whose identity I already believe I know."

"You know?"

"Yeah. Jerry Parker most likely hired him. He wanted retribution for his daughter's murder. He'll be feeling a certain level of closure now that Gibson is dead."

"But we have no way of proving it, do we?"

"No, but I'll drop by his place, just to have the pleasure of letting him know that we have him in our sights."

"Don't piss him off too much, Matt," Julia said. "If he *did* arrange for Gibson to be killed, he could always hire another hitman."

"He isn't the type of lowlife gangster who would have anyone that just badmouthed him taken out. He's very protective of his bogus 'law-abiding citizen' image," Matt said, but took what Julia had just said to him on board. Provoking Parker could feasibly put Beth or one of his team in harm's way. This was one of those times when he knew it would be best to let sleeping dogs lie.

"Shame that we have no idea how Parker knew Gibson's exact location," Julia said.

Matt nodded. "It had to be some MIT detective on the take," he said. "DCI John Stott needs to take a very close look at each and every member of the team who dealt with the case and had the pertinent details."

"Have you arranged a celebratory squad piss up for closing another serial killer case?" Julia said.

Matt shook his head. "Not personally. I've told Pete to go ahead and arrange one if he wants to carry on the tradition. He probably will when he gets around to it, because he doesn't pass up any chance of a boozy night out. He's been busy arranging for the protection to be lifted on the young woman, Jasmin Walker, Jaz, who gave us the description of Gibson. She and her mother have now returned to their respective homes, Jaz plans on going back to flipping burgers at her local McDonald's, and the families of Gibson's victims have all been contacted and informed of his death. It's another case closed. The annoying part is that we'll never know his motive for murdering complete strangers to him."

"Doesn't matter," Julia said. "He was a psycho killer, and now he's dead. End of story."

"True," Matt said. "And now I'm going to find Pete and let him take me for a pint. I need some liquid fortitude to help me face all the paperwork on my desk."

It was on the last Friday of September when, dressed in their best bib and tucker, Matt and Beth walked into the Old Marylebone Town Hall, to be led to The Paddington Room accompanied only by Beth's parents, Robert and Maddie. After discussing it on and off for weeks, they had decided not to make a fuss by inviting a crowd. They had taken time off work to get hitched at the registry office, and booked a ten day break in a suite at the all-inclusive Azia Resort on the west coast of Cyprus.

Matt needed to kick back with Beth; just relax and enjoy a hiatus from the murder and mayhem, which was all part and parcel of the profession he had chosen to follow; a job that was a love-hate relationship in which he was driven to run down serial killers and stop them from carrying out their heinous crimes against others.

About The Author

I write the type of original, action-packed, violent crime thrillers that I know I would enjoy reading if they were written by such authors as: Lee Child, David Baldacci, Simon Kernick, Harlan Coben, Michael Billingham and their ilk.
Over twenty years in the Prison Service proved great research into the minds of criminals, and especially into the dark world that serial killers - of who I have met quite a few - frequent.

I live in a cottage a mile from the nearest main road in the Yorkshire Wolds, enjoy photography, the wildlife, and of course creating new characters to place in dilemmas that my mind dreams up.

What makes a good read? Believable protagonists that you care about, set in a story that stirs all of your emotions.

If you like your crime fiction fast-paced, then I believe that the books I have already uploaded on Amazon/Kindle will keep you turning the pages.

Connect With Michael Kerr and discover other great titles.

Web

www.michaelkerr.org
Michael Kerr's official site

Facebook

https://www.facebook.com/MichaelKerrAuthor

Kindle Store

http://www.michaelkerr.org/amazon

Also By Michael Kerr

Printed in Great Britain
by Amazon

39195284R00148